UNDER A SPANISH SKY

T. A. WILLIAMS

Boldwood

First published in 2017 as *Chasing Shadows*. This edition published in Great Britain in 2025 by Boldwood Books Ltd.

Cover Design by JD Smith Design Ltd

Cover Images: Shutterstock

A CIP catalogue record for this book is available from the British Library.

Paperback ISBN 978-1-80625-138-4

Large Print ISBN 978-1-80625-139-1

Hardback ISBN 978-1-80625-137-7

Trade Paperback ISBN 978-1-80635-353-8

Ebook ISBN 978-1-80625-140-7

Kindle ISBN 978-1-80625-141-4

Audio CD ISBN 978-1-80625-132-2

MP3 CD ISBN 978-1-80625-133-9

Digital audio download ISBN 978-1-80625-135-3

This book is printed on certified sustainable paper. Boldwood Books is dedicated to putting sustainability at the heart of our business. For more information please visit https://www.boldwoodbooks.com/about-us/sustainability/

Boldwood Books Ltd, 23 Bowerdean Street, London, SW6 3TN

www.boldwoodbooks.com

To Mariangela with love

Love looks not with the eyes, but with the mind.

— SHAKESPEARE, A MIDSUMMER NIGHT'S DREAM

1

FRENCH PYRENEES, APRIL 2016

'Ouch.'

Amy squealed as her knee made painful contact with the bedside table. Feeling for the edge of the bed with her hand, she sat down to rub the bruised area, muttering to herself under her breath. Bruises caused by bumping into things are a fact of life when you're blind, but that still doesn't stop them hurting. Luke had given her his usual tour of her room before leaving her on her own. She now knew the location of the bathroom, how to operate the shower, and the fact that the towels were hidden away at shoulder level in the corner of the room, above the radiator. He had warned her of the slight step at the door and the television placed dangerously at head-height on a bracket attached to the end wall. He hadn't thought to warn her about the sharp corners of the bedside table, but she didn't hold it against him.

After a few moments the pain diminished and she stood up again, felt cautiously for the offending bedside table and, avoiding it, headed for the window rather more carefully this time. The heating was full on and the room was boiling hot. Three paces and she reached the curtains. The window was old traditional French, with an oval metal handle set in the middle. She located it and gave it a hefty twist. With a screech of protest, the sashes swung back towards her and a breath of cold mountain air swept in.

Along with it came the sound of an owl, out there somewhere in the hotel grounds. She stood there for a few moments, breathing in the night air and reflecting on the events of the past few weeks. There was no doubt in her mind, her decision to follow the pilgrimage route to Compostela had been the best she had made for years. She could genuinely say that, for the first time since the accident, there had been a smile on her face every single day of this amazing trip.

She returned to the bed and sat down again. Reaching into her bag, she located her laptop and switched it on. The disembodied voice she had come to know and love greeted her and asked her what she wanted to do. She directed it to her favourite website dealing with the Pilgrims' Way and had just started to hear about tomorrow's stage of the journey when her phone rang.

'Hi, Amy, it's me.'

'Hi, Jude.' They rang each other most evenings for a rundown of the day's events. 'Good to hear your voice. All well?'

'They're saying it's the coldest April in London for a hundred years. Otherwise I'm fine. How're things with you?'

Amy lay back against the pillow. 'We've reached the mountains and we've checked into a hotel just on the French side of the Pyrenees.' She went on to tell Judie about their day driving through rural France, stopping here and there to visit places that took their fancy. And for two medievalists, this part of the world held any number of historical sites. It had been a lot of fun and some of her enthusiasm must have reached across the Channel. 'To be honest, I'm having a whale of a time.'

'That's great. You certainly sound pretty bubbly tonight. Is it the mountain air, or your hunky guide?'

'I couldn't possibly say, Jude.' She had introduced Luke to Judie a month ago, when they were making the first arrangements for the trip, and had made sure she got a full and frank appraisal of him. No unsightly blemishes, the correct number of ears, eyes and fingers, and a face that wouldn't scare little children. She might not be able to see him, but other people would. 'After all,' she had told Judie, 'a girl's got her reputation to think of.' Now she found herself smiling as she replied.

'We're getting along just fine. He knows all about the history of the pilgrimage and he's very good at descriptions of the places we're going through. Mind you, he's rubbish at names of things like cheeses and desserts. He can just about recognise crème caramel, but that's it.'

'So, have you found out all about him?'

'Well, I know he's done his History PhD and he's spent some time living in Africa. Mind you, Father Tim told me that way back. But, more than that, I don't really know. He doesn't like talking about himself at all.'

'So no mention of a wife or a girlfriend? I mean, you need to know what you're up against, don't you?'

'No, I don't, Jude. His personal life's of no interest to me at all.' She surreptitiously touched her nose to check that it hadn't grown longer as a result of her last comment. Although she had done an MA in Medieval History, she was honest enough to admit to herself, if not to Judie, that it wasn't just the journey that was proving to be so great. Reassured, she decided to change the subject. 'Anyway, tomorrow promises to be good. We're planning to go up to the high mountains to look for an old pilgrim hospice.' They had started in France and tomorrow they would climb over the Pyrenees, and then travel onwards on the Camino to Santiago de Compostela in north-west Spain.

'Is the hospice in France or in Spain?'

'Just over the frontier inside Spain. We're not very far from the border here, but there's a whole heap of snow forecast for tomorrow.'

'Well, make sure he drives safely in the mountains.' Judie hesitated. 'You going to be all right with that?' Judie had been Amy's friend since primary school and she knew her very well, probably as well as anybody, since the death of her parents and her sister. She had been one of the first people Amy had called after the accident five years earlier. Their car had plunged off a snowy road in the Italian Alps and this would be Amy's first time back to any mountains since then.

'I'm fine. I'm in good hands.' Amy felt and sounded relaxed.

Judie kept the tone light. 'And just which parts of you are in his hands?'

'Just behave yourself, Jude.' But Judie didn't give up.

'That's what I should be saying to you.'

'Listen, you. This is a business arrangement. He's employed to act as my guide. Nothing more than that. Get it?'

'Whatever you say, sweetie. Anyway, you take care.'

'Bye.'

Amy dropped the phone back into her bag. Standing up, she reached for the sides of her jumper and pulled it off over her head. Before taking any more off, she went over to the door, checked it was locked and located the light switch. As usual Luke had left it on. She flicked the switch into the off position. She didn't want to provide a free show to anybody outside. Reassured, she stripped and made her way into the bathroom.

As she stood in the bathtub, holding the shower hose as it coughed and spluttered cold water, she allowed herself a few moments' reflection. Yes, it was a business relationship and he was being very well paid for his time. Mind you, she thought to herself, he seemed to be enjoying it too. After a particularly loud cough, the water coming out of the shower head began to warm. As she started to wash herself, she realised that she was humming a little tune. She couldn't remember doing that for a very long time.

By the time she emerged from the bathroom, the stuffy heat in the room had been replaced by the chill of the evening air. Although it was April, it had been a cold winter and the close proximity of the snow-covered mountains meant that the outside temperature was already approaching zero. She closed the window before discarding the towel and searching for underwear in her suitcase. She pulled her jeans back on again but, this time, she felt for a different top. Her hands landed on the unmistakable feel of mohair. Her fingers confirmed that it was one of her old favourites with a roll neck. She knew it to be pale blue. She had bought it just before that last family holiday. She had chosen it because it perfectly matched the colour of her eyes. Only a few weeks later her eyes had still been the same colour, but the jumper and everything else in her life had turned a uniform grey.

Snap out of it, you idiot. She gave herself a good talking-to. She was alive, she was finally doing something she had wanted to do since she was ten, and she was going to have dinner in a French restaurant with Luke. And Judie had said he was very good-looking. With that thought in mind, she brushed her hair, slipped on her shoes and reclaimed her watch from the bedside table, ready for his knock on the door.

She pressed the side of her brand-new Snoopy watch and heard Charlie

Brown's voice telling her that it was seven o'clock. This, as usual, was followed by a woof. With a contented smile, she settled back on the bed, but almost immediately there was a soft knock at the door and she got up to open it.

'Hi, Amy. Feeling hungry?' He smelt of that same deodorant she had grown to rather like. She would recognise it anywhere.

Her smile broadened. 'After visiting two castles, a pope's grave and goodness knows how many churches today, I'm definitely ready for something to eat. And I'm sure I don't need to ask you.'

They strolled across the gravel to the restaurant, her hand, as usual, resting lightly on his arm. The accommodation block was a short walk from the main building. A tree-lined avenue, studded with lamps, led up to the front of a fine white four-storey building and Luke did his best to describe it to her.

'It's sort of nineteenth-century mock-château style, with mansard windows peeping out of the steeply sloping slate roof. The deep green shutters at each window give a geometric precision. It could almost be Tyrolean, but still definitely French though, if you can imagine what I mean. It's the shutters in particular that give it away. But it's unusually tidy and clean-looking.' As he was all too aware, his verbal description of her surroundings had to be as accurate and evocative as he could manage.

They went into the small hall and were greeted with a courteous, *'Bonsoir monsieur dame,'* by the lady behind the counter. They returned the greeting and walked on down the corridor towards the door marked 'Restaurant'. As they walked, she guessed.

'Late fifties, maybe early sixties, twin set, pearls, gold-rimmed glasses on a string and a Pekinese at her side?' She enjoyed this game and they had played it quite a bit on the way down through France. She gave his arm a squeeze. 'Well, was I right? Tell me what she's really like.'

'You got the age right and, miraculously, the glasses on a chain, but she's wearing jeans like yours and if there's a Pekinese, he's inside the Pyrenean mountain dog.' His hand was already on the restaurant door, but she stopped dead.

'Did you say a Pyrenean mountain dog? Where? I love those big fluffy giants.'

'See if you can find him.' The dog was stretched out on his side at the far end of the hall, just behind the door, and he enjoyed teasing her.

Amy turned back in that direction, pricked up her ears and set off confidently, straight down towards the sleeping dog. As she approached, the heavy white tail began to whack lazily on the ground. She followed the sound and then bent down to make a fuss of the big animal. The rhythm of the wagging increased and she was rewarded with a very slobbery lick. As Luke slowly walked back down the hall towards her, he watched her stroke the thick, curly coat. At the same time he saw her feeling the length of the dog's back, ears, tail and legs, as well as gently running her hand over the outline of the head and face. This was her way of seeing things. He never ceased to be amazed at how accurately she could formulate a clear idea of an object just by touch.

The effort of wagging its tail clearly tired the dog to the extent that it let its head fall back onto the floor with a thud and a deep sigh. Mission accomplished, Amy stood up and turned to take Luke's arm again. The lady behind the desk smiled as they went back down the corridor and Luke hesitated as they reached the restaurant door.

'There's a door here with *Dames* on it, if you want to wash the dog off your hands.'

'Probably a very good idea.' Leaving him in the corridor, she slipped through the door. While he waited, he peered into the restaurant.

The room boasted no more than about ten tables and only three of these were occupied. The wooden floor was spotlessly clean, the walls and ceiling freshly painted. A bunch of wild flowers in a little pot stood on every table and the scent of violets was in the air. Along with this were good kitchen smells that reminded him just how hungry he was. When Amy reappeared, they were guided to a table by a girl who looked fourteen, and surely wasn't a day over sixteen.

They chatted for a few minutes until the waitress arrived to take their order. The menu was verbal and they both listened carefully to get the various choices. Although his French was more fluent than hers, she did quite well and had a pretty broad vocabulary. They both chose salad with goat's cheese as a starter and *confit de canard* for the main course. When the girl returned with the bread and a carafe of water, he started to give a thumbnail sketch of the occupants of the other tables, just as he had been doing every night since starting from Dover over two weeks ago.

'On the far side there's an old couple. They look as if they're in their eighties, if not more. Her face is so gaunt you can see the outline of every bone. He's drinking water and she's drinking red wine. Next to them there are two ladies. One about ninety; red-faced and stout. She doesn't seem to be touching the food on her plate. Her companion's probably about twenty years younger. Could even be her daughter. Unnatural-looking red hair and she's eating everything in sight.'

'So that makes us relative youngsters.' Amy was just thirty and he had told her he was thirty-six.

'That's right, but don't get too complacent. Our waitress is about half my age, maybe even half yours.'

The salad and the pâté arrived, along with a bottle of dark red wine. Luke filled their glasses and they both tried it, pronouncing it good. Then she set the glass down and he noticed yet again how organised she was. Whenever they ate, she always kept a space clear just to the right of her plate for her glass. If she had more than one glass in use, the larger one would always be on the outside so she knew automatically which was where. She was the same with everything. Blind people can't allow them-selves the luxury of disorder. Being with her had even made him a bit tidier.

He gave her a brief tour of her plate of salad. 'Looks lovely. Four slices of toasted cheese on bits of bread. About three or four different types of lettuce as far as I can see; some sort of dandelion leaf shaped, some red and some frizzy green stuff.'

Amy raised her head towards him. 'A voyage of discovery.' She smiled to herself and remembered what she had told Judie. Describing food really wasn't his strong suit. Sensing his incomprehension, she elaborated. 'A simple plate of salad turns into a plunge into the unknown with you as my guide. "Frizzy green stuff" doesn't often appear on menus.'

He adopted what he thought was an apologetic tone, but she sensed that he was smiling and she smiled back as she listened to what he had to say. 'Yes, I'm afraid you could have chosen a better guide, at least as far as descriptions of food are concerned. And it's not just salads, is it? I'm not that great at names of cheeses either. You just can't find the staff these days, can you?'

'Still, you do have redeeming features. Considering I've got my very own medieval specialist driving me around, I can't really complain.' His PhD had been on the main pilgrimages of the Middle Ages and the Compostela pilgrimage had been of special interest to him. She lapsed into a reflective silence for a few minutes, concentrating on her salad. 'So remind me how many times you've done the pilgrimage to Compostela?'

'This'll be my third. Although, to my shame, I've only walked about half of it.' She was only partway through her salad while he had almost finished his plate by now but, he told himself, they had only had a sandwich for lunch. He picked up the last slice of baguette and toasted cheese and forced himself to nibble it slowly as he watched her formulate an answer. As he did so, he couldn't miss the way her lovely jumper so perfectly matched her eyes in that perfect face. Yet again he reflected how bitterly ironic it was that such a beautiful girl should have lost the power of sight.

'I wish I could walk it.' There was a plaintive note to her voice that was quite unlike her. By now, he had got used to the way she resolutely did her best not to let her handicap get in the way of doing things. He swallowed the bread and took a mouthful of wine to wash it down.

'I don't see why you couldn't. I tell you what, as long as it doesn't snow too much tomorrow, let's try walking a stretch of it.'

She nodded as she chewed a mouthful of salad. 'That would be great. So, for people on foot, how long would it take to get from here to Compostela?'

Luke did a quick calculation. 'I suppose a bit over a month, depending upon how far and how fast you walk. I think the average is twenty to thirty kilometres a day.'

'What's that in old money? Fifteen miles a day?'

'Bit more, bit less. It also depends on the terrain. Tomorrow we're going to climb to over fifteen hundred metres. In our big comfortable car, that'll be easy, but just imagine doing it on foot. And, remember, back in the Middle Ages, there would have been all sorts of other obstacles, like bandits for example.'

A few minutes later, the waitress came to remove their empty plates. As she carried them off, Luke glanced across at Amy again. He still felt uncomfortable doing so, when he knew she couldn't see him in return, but he was gradually getting used to it. They had been on the road now for two weeks, zig-zagging their way down through France, en route to Spain, and he was getting very familiar with her and her mannerisms. Now, it didn't need the slight furrowing of her brow for him to know that she was thinking hard. She paused for a moment, took a mouthful of wine and then, clearly, made her mind up. 'Luke, I've been thinking, and I wonder if we could do something.' She sounded unusually hesitant, which was not her normal way. He hastened to help her.

'Whatever you like.'

'All right, then, I've got a suggestion for you. Tell me, are you any good at telling stories?'

'Erm, you've lost me there. Stories?' He picked up the bottle and topped up their glasses. She murmured a quiet thank you and then carried on.

'As a child, did you and your brothers tell each other stories? My sister and I used to do it all the time.'

He cast his mind back. 'As I remember, most of the stories I told were to explain why I hadn't done my homework.'

'That'll do. It shows you've got a good imagination. Anyway, I'll tell you what I'd really like. How would you feel if we were to try to come up with a story?'

He smiled at the thought. 'Us make up a story? I'm not sure I'd be much good at that. But I'm prepared to give it a go. About what?'

'About people doing what we're doing, but years ago.' As she said it, she realised that this was something she really did want to do. *Why not?* she thought to herself. *Maybe we could even turn it into a book.* Blindness makes it impossible to do a lot of things but nowadays, with her computer, she knew that writing wasn't one of them. This might just, she thought, with a rising sense of anticipation, be the answer to the question of what to do with her life now that she had finished studying. She raised her face towards him. 'People just like us, doing this.'

'Driving around in a brand-new Range Rover and eating too much foie gras?' He saw her smile and shake her head.

'No, following the pilgrimage route, of course.'

'And when you say years ago, just how many years ago?'

'Oh, lots... centuries. Before cars and planes and phones and things.' He could hear the animation in her voice and he could understand why. Making up a story would be a way of heightening the experience for her. Unable to see the magnificent scenery or the succession of outstanding historical monuments, she needed something extra. He owed it to her to help, so he didn't hesitate.

'All right, then, I'll give it a go. And as for the when, it's got to be the Middle Ages, surely? We're both medievalists after all. Sound good?'

The expression on her face showed that the idea pleased her. He could see that she was thinking hard. After a few moments she spoke out loud. 'So when in the Middle Ages? Early? High? Late? That period lasted a good long time.'

He gave it some thought. 'The pilgrimage route's been operating for over a thousand years. It was your idea, you take your pick.'

She was smiling now and he felt a wave of affection for her. The prickly persona she had exhibited the first time they met had disappeared without trace. As they had got to know each other, she had definitely mellowed. There was no question that this trip was doing her a power of good and, if he was honest, he felt it doing him good, too. He couldn't remember feeling this relaxed for a long time. Just then, the waitress returned with the duck. As usual, he launched into tour-guide mode.

'The confit looks wonderful. The skin's crispy, so you should be able to eat the lot. Hang on a minute.' He prodded the meat on his plate. 'It just falls apart. You'll hardly need your knife. There's a whole heap of chips and a little bundle of asparagus, tied up like a sheaf of corn. It all looks very, very hot, so be warned.' By now, it was second nature to him to give these descriptions.

She made no attempt to start eating, her mind evidently still on this story idea. After a few more moments, she raised her head towards him, the pale blue eyes looking disconcertingly straight through him. 'Right, off you go, then.' There was a smile on her face 'You start.'

With a martyred sigh he put his fork down. 'All right, if I must, I must. Let's see. Once upon a time there was a man...'

'...who was big and strong.' She finished the sentence for him and he sighed even more theatrically.

'Why does he have to be big and strong? Maybe he was a little chap.'

She shook her head. 'Definitely big and strong. Remember, he's our hero and he's got to fight off the bad guys.'

'What bad guys?' He was smiling and she could hear it in his voice.

'I haven't got that far. But he was definitely fighting off the bad guys.'

'Whoever they might be...' He paused for thought. 'All right, then, once upon a time there was a man who was big and strong, but he had a problem. A serious one; not just hitting thirty-six and the onset of middle-age spread.'

'You haven't got middle-age spread yet.'

'What have I got to do with it?' Luke affected surprise. 'This is our fictitious hero we're talking about, not me.' He paused as he had a thought. 'Besides, how do you know my waist measurement?'

'Um, I guessed. I know you're tall and strong and fit, so it seemed logical.' She realised she was at risk of digging herself into a hole here. His next question confirmed her dilemma.

'Hang on a minute. How do you know that I'm big and strong and fit? I haven't bent any iron bars or lifted any weights in your presence.' Maybe, he thought idly to himself, Father Tim had been letting his tongue get the better of him again. Amy's answer cleared the priest.

'You go running most days, so you must be fit and, anyway, the receptionist in that lovely hotel at Chantilly last week told me about you.' This sounded fairly safe. She decided to leave Judie out of the equation, at least for now. Even though she couldn't see the expression on his face, she guessed. 'Don't look at me like a stranded whale. We girls tend to chat a bit, you know, and she asked me if you were a rugby player. I know enough about that particular sport to know that it's not normally for the small and frail. Then...' now it was her turn to look just a little embarrassed '...I got her to describe you to me.'

'Ah, I see.' He took a big mouthful of wine. A ready response didn't occur to him, so he decided to steer the conversation back to their fictitious hero. 'Setting aside our man's physique for the moment, let's have a think about what he's doing. Isn't he maybe just a pilgrim, doing what hundreds of thousands of others did every year?'

Amy shook her head. 'Weren't you listening? I said he was escaping from the bad guys.'

'So we're back to that again. Wait a minute, maybe the bad guys were really the good guys. Could it be he's a villain, rather than a hero?'

She explored the concept. 'That's a thought. Maybe he's killed somebody and is escaping from justice. And he has to get out of the country quick, otherwise he'll end up in jail...' her voice dropped to a melodramatic growl '...or worse.'

He saw the animation on her face and knew that the story was going to be a lot of fun for her, and probably for him too. But, he thought to himself, in spite of having made the suggestion, he had better sort out the main character before things went any further. 'No, let's leave him as a good guy. I have no idea what he might have done, but I'm sure he's not the type to murder somebody in cold blood. No, let's not make him a villain. Okay? If he's running from the law, maybe the authorities have got him confused with somebody else and are really after the wrong man.'

Amy nodded her agreement. 'All right, he's a goodie. So, what's his problem? I wonder where he is at the moment.'

'Walking, like the thousands of other pilgrims on the way to Compostela.'

'I hope he's got good boots.'

2

FRENCH PYRENEES, APRIL 1314

'Boots and Shoes. Boots and Shoes. Get your boots here. Last chance to buy your boots before the mountains.'

The shoemaker bellowed his wares jovially from the shelter of his shop, while the pilgrims splashed through the mud of the main street. Uncharitably, the suspicion crossed Luc's mind that the particularly deep and unwholesome mud right outside the shoemaker's might not be a coincidence.

'If the boots are half as strong as that man's lungs, they'll last all the way to Compostela.' He glanced round at the pilgrims in the group and saw a few faces smile, among them Friar Laurent, their leader.

A coarse voice cut in. 'That's if we get through the mountains in the first place.' The stonemason from Beauvais was as pessimistic as ever. 'They say the snow's the thickest it's ever been over the pass. The bandits are murdering, robbing and raping everybody who dares to cross. Yes.' He stared back belligerently at the raised eyebrows of the people around him. 'They say the bandits up there are devil-worshippers, sodomites and perverts. Nobody's safe!'

Luc groaned inwardly. He had heard it all before; in fact they all had. The stonemason appeared to do nothing but complain and drink red wine, which only made him complain all the more. Luc had joined Friar Laurent's

group a few days earlier in an attempt to gain some extra cover when travelling through the busy city of Bordeaux, but Laurent and the others had had
to put up with the moaning ever since leaving Vézelay almost a month
before. The man was one of the most morose individuals that Luc had ever
encountered and he had been wondering to himself exactly what or who
might have pushed the mason to undertake the pilgrimage. He certainly
wasn't enjoying it. That was quite clear.

The others weren't so bad, though. Luc glanced to his left. The friar was a
jovial man who had welcomed him into the group with open arms. The fact
that this might have been in view of his size and strength didn't matter. He
was now a member of the group and, as such, far less conspicuous than a
man alone. Laurent caught his eye.

'Are you worried about bandits, Luc?'

Luc gave him a wry smile in return. 'I'm more worried by the height of
those peaks. And the snow. I'll take my chances with the murderers and
perverts. They must be pretty cold if they've been up there all winter.' Nevertheless, if the stonemason was right, they might have to fight their way over
the Pyrenees and the others, Laurent included, were likely to be of little help
if they did meet bandits. Luc squared his shoulders. This was something he
would have to deal with if it happened. There was no point worrying unduly
right now.

They had formed a nucleus of about a dozen pilgrims. There was the
mason, the baker, accompanied by his wife and daughter, and a handful of
nuns from a convent near Cluny. Along with them was an assortment of
peasants from the Champagne area, who had quite obviously been sent on
this pilgrimage for some collective misconduct. All in all, it was a pretty
average collection of people.

'How far is it from here to Compostela?' The baker was still staring at the
boots.

'A long way.' Brother monks who had already made the pilgrimage to
Santiago de Compostela had briefed Laurent as best they could. 'We're not
in Spain yet. First we've got to cross the Pyrenees. Once we're in Spain, Santiago's still way over in the far north-west. It's going to take at least a month,
maybe two. It all depends on the weather in the mountains.'

'But, once we get over the Pyrenees, it'll be flatter and warmer, surely?' The baker's wife wasn't looking forward to the climb ahead.

'I'm afraid not; at least not flatter. From what I've heard, there are mountain passes over there that are as high as the Pyrenees.' The friar glanced across at Luc, but he refused to respond. His contacts in Paris had briefed him very carefully on every single stage of the route and Luc had done his best to memorise everything. But there was no reason for him to give away that fact, so he stayed silent and shook his head.

They were aiming for the Somport pass in preference to the lower and more usual route through the mountains above St-Jean-Pied-de-Port. Friar Laurent had chosen this route on the advice of his abbot and that suited Luc perfectly. As he looked up at the huge bulk of the mountains ahead, he had only one place on his mind: the mountain hospice of Santa Cristina. That was where he had been ordered to go, and it lay in the high mountains close by the Somport pass. Snow or no snow, bandits or no bandits, he knew he had to get there, but it wasn't going to be easy.

A few hours later, it suddenly got a whole lot more difficult.

It was a chance conversation with an old man coming down the road towards them that set off warning bells in Luc's head. Apparently there was a roadblock ahead and troops were searching every vehicle and checking the identity of everybody who came by. Luc slowed down and let the group of pilgrims overtake him until he could slip, unobserved, into the stables at the rear of what looked like an abbey or priory. He squeezed into the shelter of a big pile of firewood against the courtyard wall and took stock, his mind turning over the possibility that word of his mission might already have got out.

As he was still considering his options, he heard horses' hooves approaching up the road from the town, accompanied by the unmistakable creaking of carriage springs. He shrank back into hiding and watched the entrance to the courtyard. As the first riders appeared, he froze. They were soldiers. For a moment he wondered if they had come for him, but was relieved to see that their swords were sheathed. They were obviously not expecting trouble. They clattered to a halt just in front of him and let their mounts stretch down and drink from a water trough. Behind them came a carriage driven by more soldiers and followed by another four on horseback; far too many guards for an ordinary cargo, that much was clear. He studied the men and the vehicles closely, trying to work out what they contained, and if they posed any threat to him.

The curtained door of the carriage opened and the occupant stepped down. Luc shrank back even further into the shadows. The man was without doubt a cleric, and from the expensive cloth of his cloak, and the deference with which he was treated by the soldiers, Luc deduced that he was of high rank. He watched the priest disappear through the archway towards the main part of the monastery while the soldiers dismounted and clustered together on the stone benches over on the other side of the courtyard, enjoying the last of the late afternoon sunshine. They made no move to unsaddle their horses, so it looked clear that their visit was to be a short one. The carriage door hung open invitingly and Luc suddenly realised that he might indeed get a lift after all. Casting a cautious glance across at the soldiers, he emerged from the pile of wood and slipped across to the carriage.

He glanced in and was immediately heartened to see that it was empty. With another swift glance over his shoulder, he climbed in, trying to tread as lightly as possible. These carriages, set on massive springs, had a tendency to sway wildly at the slightest touch. Inside there were two bench seats facing each other, and above them a luggage rack. It was this that attracted Luc's attention.

Although it was only the width of the carriage it went back quite a long way above the heads of the passengers and, importantly, it looked solid enough to take his not inconsiderable weight. Hastily, in case the priest were to return, he pulled himself up and found to his satisfaction that he could lie fairly comfortably with his knees bent. And he was sufficiently far back to be invisible to any but the most inquisitive of fellow travellers.

He settled down to wait. But in fact it was only a matter of minutes before he heard footsteps and felt the carriage shake as a passenger climbed aboard. A voice, which sounded perilously close to him, shouted a command and they lurched into motion. Luc braced himself by wedging his feet and shoulders against the sides and hoped the priest would not decide to investigate the luggage rack. He closed his eyes and was beginning to drift into a sort of waking dream, when he was shaken back to full consciousness by a voice.

'How long do you think it'll take to get there?'

The voice was so close that, for a moment, he was sure that he had been discovered, and this some form of mockery. He tensed, readying himself for action, although he was under no illusions that his cramped conditions made him near helpless. Before he could make any move, however, he was stopped in his tracks by the sound of another voice.

'If we keep up this pace we should arrive at Santa Cristina before dawn. Let's hope we can get some sleep, Your Grace. It's not the best road in France, and I'm sorry to say that this is certainly not the best carriage in the land.'

Luc's spirits lifted as he heard their destination. As long as he remained undiscovered, this was a perfect solution to his problem. However, 'Your Grace' could mean only one thing. He was travelling with a very senior cleric, maybe even an archbishop.

'Do you think he's still in the country, or has he made it across the frontier?'

Luc shrank back as far into the shadows as he could, fascinated by the conversation below him.

'He's still here, Your Grace. I've had the whole valley under surveillance since his sighting at Oloron. There's no way he could have got past. My guess is that he's gone to ground, in the hope that we drop our guard. Don't forget who we're dealing with here. This isn't just anyone, this is Luc de Charny. He's a veteran, an experienced warrior, with years of active service behind him. He's successfully avoided capture now for the best part of seven years, so he knows what he's doing. Believe me, he's still around.'

Luc listened in awe. The speaker seemed to know a lot about him. How was it that down here they could be so well informed? Around the king and around Paris it was logical that there would be people who knew the full picture. But who would know about him down here?

'I've been following him since he left Paris, and he's no fool. All the way he's been one step ahead of us, mainly because he chose to take a highly unusual route. If he hadn't been spotted in Bordeaux we might indeed have lost him.'

If the priest had travelled from Paris, it was logical that he was closely linked to either the king or the inquisitors. Either way, Luc knew he was in very hot water indeed. He had no doubt he could kill these two men without difficulty, but the remaining guards would be a different matter. A sharp dagger was no match for half a dozen broadswords. He settled down and forced himself to stay awake, even when he heard the snoring of at least one of his travelling companions. He couldn't risk even the slightest noise.

For seemingly endless hours they continued along the winding road up the valley. In spite of the springs, the carriage lurched drunkenly on the potholes. More than once, he found himself in imminent danger of being thrown out of the luggage rack onto the laps of the men below. In the background, to remind him of the precarious situation in which he now found himself, he could hear the hooves of the armed escort. From time to time, he heard them shouting to each other as they picked their way through the darkness.

Then the carriage began to lean heavily backwards. The serious climb to the top had begun.

3

FRENCH PYRENEES, APRIL 2016

The next morning Luke had to scrape ice off the windscreen of the car. It was a dry day with a hazy sun, but dark clouds on the horizon threatened snow later on. As they set off towards the mountains, he thanked the instinct that had made him choose a vehicle with four-wheel drive. If the weather forecast was to be believed, the snow was going to be heavy.

They stopped a few times as they made their way up the valley towards the pass and Spain. The relatively gentle hills had now been replaced by rocky outcrops and scree slopes. Ahead of them, brightly lit by the spring sunshine, was the seemingly impenetrable barrier of snow-covered peaks that stood out clearly against the pale blue of the sky.

'It's going to be a hard climb from here to the pass.' He cast another searching look upwards at the sky. 'And if the snow sets in, we might not see anything. It would be so good to get the view from the top down into Spain, just like millions of pilgrims over the centuries.'

'Like our mystery man.' Amy sounded very definite about this and Luke smiled. The previous evening they had made a start on their story and had decided that, seeing as they were going that way, their hero would also be making for the former pilgrims' hospice of Santa Cristina, high in the mountains, near the Somport pass. They had had quite a discussion about just who the main protagonist of their tale might be, as well as exactly when it might have been, but without coming to any conclusions. Without admitting it to each other, or maybe not even to themselves, both of them now had a mental picture of a medieval character who looked suspiciously like Luke himself. So far there wasn't an Amy character, but he, at least, felt pretty sure she would put in an appearance before too long. Meanwhile, modern-day Amy was trying to remember exactly where the abbey had been positioned. 'And Santa Cristina's right at the top?'

'Just the other side, but it's no more than a ruin these days. Quite possibly it's hidden under a few feet of snow at the moment, but we can always hope.'

Amy nodded. 'Such a pity, considering how important it used to be.'

'Third only to the Great St Bernard and Jerusalem itself.' Amy nodded. She hadn't heard of Santa Cristina before, but half an hour on the Internet after dinner the previous night had made her realise its significance in the medieval world.

As they began to climb, the road got progressively more tortuous, and the valley sides tightened towards them more and more. The road was now squeezed alongside the banks of the fast-flowing river. Luke glanced across to the passenger seat. Although Amy looked happy enough, it was difficult to know what she was getting out of this part of the journey, spectacular as it was to a sighted person. He gave her a quick description of their surroundings, finishing with the words, 'I wouldn't want to fall into that river.'

She half turned towards him. 'Dirty or cold?'

'We'll take a closer look.' He braked, pulled off the road, bumped down a steep track and drew up with a crunch of gravel beside the river.

'Come on, let's see what you think of a real mountain stream.'

As they opened the doors, both felt the noticeably colder air.

'That's straight off the snowy mountains.' Amy had correctly worked out the direction of the wind and was reaching for a jacket. He leant over to the back seat and handed her a down-filled body warmer. As she stepped out of the car and pulled it on, he took her arm and led her to the edge of the water, helping her across the bank of pebbles. Hearing the water, she crouched down and dipped her hand in.

'I see what you mean. It's freezing.'

The word *see* had caused him all sorts of embarrassment when he first met her. It kept leaping uninvited into his mouth in expressions like *Let's see* or *Come and see*. This had caused him acute discomfort each time as he'd felt he had made some dreadful gaffe in the face of her blindness. If he had, she never gave any sign of it. Gradually, he'd started to notice that she herself used the verb as often and as naturally as he did. Relieved, he had reverted to his normal figures of speech.

She hastily withdrew her hand from the water and replaced it lightly on his arm. Although she told herself this was just as a precaution as they were near the water's edge, she did admit to herself that it was also because she found she increasingly enjoyed physical contact with him. Even through his jacket, she could feel the strength of his arm muscles that flexed as he stretched. She did her best not to let anything show on her face and took refuge in a safe topic, the weather. 'Brr! Of course, at this time of year, and with sun on the mountains, I suppose the winter snows are melting fast. I imagine it's really clear, clean water. The pilgrims would have been able to drink it with impunity, wouldn't they?'

'No question. I'm sure it's as pure as pure.' He was acutely aware of her hand on his arm, the warmth reaching through the sleeve of his jacket, and the sensation, while pleasant, was disturbing. He made sure he kept the conversation of historical matters. 'Who knows? Hundreds, if not thousands, of medieval pilgrims may have come to this selfsame spot to fill their water bottles.'

'Were they really bottles?' She missed nothing. 'Surely glass was horrifically expensive in those times. Is that what they really used?' She gave his arm a squeeze, which he had come to recognise as the sign that she wanted something. The question was not difficult to answer.

'If we're talking about the Middle Ages, you're absolutely right. Glass was a real luxury until centuries later. As far as water bottles were concerned, the usual container in those days was unquestionably a gourd or a sheep's stomach, sometimes soaked in pitch. Personally I'd favour the gourd to the dead sheep, but each to his own.'

She giggled and he smiled with her. She really was a very good travelling companion, not at all the cold, aloof woman he had encountered in London. He thought back to when they had first met. It seemed so very long ago now. In reality it was barely a month and that meeting, he now knew, hadn't been easy for either of them. Her home was a wonderful, elegant house in High-gate. He'd wondered idly to himself as he'd walked up the steps to the front door just how much the three-storey Georgian mansion might be worth in this part of London, where an apartment could sell for millions. Father Tim who had persuaded him to go for the interview, had told him virtually nothing about Amy, apart from the accident that had robbed her of her parents, and her blindness of course. In particular, Tim had totally omitted to mention that Amy Hardy was, without question, one of the most star-tlingly beautiful girls Luke had ever seen. However, beautiful or not, her atti-tude that first day had been far from welcoming; decidedly cool in fact. Why had she been so prickly? No time like the present, so he asked her.

'Why were you so grumpy when we first met?'

A look of surprise crossed her face, closely followed by one of remorse. He had to wait a while for her reply.

'I know, Luke, and I'm so sorry. I think, more than anything, it was fear. Fear that you might take one look at me and decide you didn't want the responsibility of taking a blind girl halfway across Europe. You see, it took me five years to make up my mind to get up and start doing something with my life and, while I was waiting for you to come to the house that day, I was suddenly terrified it might not work out, and I'd be stuck there all on my own once again. It came across as grumpiness, but it was fear of rejection. Rebuilding a life isn't easy.' It was said with stiff finality. She was still holding onto his arm, but her face was towards the rushing water.

He followed the direction of her eyes and found himself watching a bird's nest swept downstream over the rapids. A back eddy caught it, held it uncer-tainly for a few moments, before a fresh wave collected it once more and whirled it away downstream. He was conscious of the inner turmoil in her voice as she continued.

'The accident's still ever-present in my head. At least, it has been up to these last couple of weeks. In the space of a few seconds my life changed completely and forever. One moment I was a privileged, or rather over-privi-leged, member of the 1 per cent of the 1 per cent. Then the next moment, my whole world, my family and my future were smashed to smithereens. In the morning I was skiing back over from Zermatt. In the evening I was in a hospital trying to come to terms with losing my family and my eyesight.'

There were tears in the corners of her eyes, but she refused to let them run. Angrily she rubbed her forearm across her face.

'They said my father had a heart attack as we were going down just about the steepest part of the road. I didn't even realise. Suddenly we were off the road and falling. I don't remember what happened after that until I woke up in the hospital...' Her grip on his arm, which had been getting tighter and tighter, suddenly relaxed. 'It hasn't been easy. I'm afraid the net result has been to make me grumpy. At least, I was then.' She released her hold and sat down on the cold pebbles. She took a deep breath and did her best to smile. 'But I'm much less grumpy now, honest.' She picked up a handful of pebbles and started to throw them into the river, one by one.

After a moment's hesitation he sat down as well, choosing a place close beside her, but not touching her. His whole body cried out to him to offer the comfort that she so patently lacked. He would have put his arm round her and hugged her, but for his sense of propriety. Apart from anything else, he was, after all, employed as her guide.

The enormity of what she had lost was only too obvious. He wondered, not for the first time, how he would have coped in similar circumstances. Certainly the torment he had endured in his own life, which had seemed so overwhelming over the last few years, was put into stark perspective. She settled back, one pebble remaining in her hand. He saw her fingers gently feel it and he started to speak, compassionately and cautiously but, as he saw her response, increasingly freely.

'Thanks for telling me that, Amy. I take that as a great compliment. From what you've just said, I imagine you don't often have conversations like this.' He cleared his throat. 'For what it's worth, I was just thinking that I couldn't wish for a better travelling companion. No grumpiness at all and I certainly don't know many others as knowledgeable on medieval matters as you.'

Her expression softened.

'You've lost a lot; a lot that's irreplaceable, but in return you've got some things I haven't. You can see that pebble you've got in your hand more fully than I can. I just rely on the one main sense, while you're seeing it in more ways than I can. You feel things and hear things so much more intensely than I can. For all I know you can probably hear the car even though the engine's switched off.'

She raised her head and replied in a brighter tone.

'That's easy. I can smell it from here and, for that matter, I actually can hear it. I bet you can too. Listen, can't you?' Her arm pointed straight at the car. He pricked up his ears obediently. She was quite right. The big engine ticked and crackled as it gradually cooled down in the mountain air.

'QED.' He smiled at her and she picked it up from his voice and smiled back. Then, in more serious vein, he added quietly, 'And never convince yourself that your problems are insurmountable. I can tell you from very painful personal experience that everybody has problems, some physical and visible, others, the worst kind, invisible inside the mind.' In response to something he read in her face, he made a promise. 'I'll tell you all about it one of these days.'

Her eyes crinkled into a little smile as she heard that he had correctly interpreted her unspoken question. She had always known he was secretive about his past, but this was the first time he had hinted that he, too, might be suffering some hidden trauma. She turned back towards the river, glad she had said what she had said, feeling ever more comfortable with him and wondering what had happened to him that he wasn't saying. Raising her arm, she lobbed the last stone into the freezing water. Then she took a deep breath and turned her head back towards him.

'Thanks, Luke. It's good to talk.' She dried her hands against the sides of her jeans and reached for his arm, her expression relaxed once more. 'So, onwards and upwards?'

They were soon back on the road, heading up towards the mountains. Luke watched the massive snow-covered barrier in front of them coming ever closer and wondered just how daunting it must have appeared to a medieval pilgrim on foot. Beside him, Amy was thinking along the same lines. Her voice broke into his thoughts.

'So our man must have come up this selfsame road?'

'No alternative. If you're a pilgrim going to Santiago de Compostela, you need to get over the Pyrenees. And there's only one pass at the end of this valley.'

'What about the road? Would that have been there in those days?' She sounded pensive, and he realised how important their invented story was becoming for her, although there was still a lot of detail missing. About all they knew was that they had a big strong hero who was trying to get away from somebody, but they still hadn't decided who he was or just when the story was taking place.

'I'm sure there would have been a road, but it certainly wouldn't have been smooth tarmac. But, whatever the road surface, if he's trying to escape from the authorities, he wouldn't have been able to use it, at least during daylight hours. He would never have dared run the risk of being seen. Remember his dark secret!' Although at this stage they still had to establish exactly what the dark secret might be, she replied totally seriously.

'But how on earth can he get up the valley if he can't use the road? Surely they would have set up roadblocks and so on.'

'Absolutely. No, he must have either disguised himself or concealed himself to escape detection. I'll tell you what, I bet he hid in a cart or carriage belonging to the authorities themselves.'

'Sort of like Robin Hood hiding underneath the Sheriff of Nottingham's carriage.'

The road ahead was empty so he risked glancing across at her again. Her eyes were half closed as she tried to imagine the scene. He read the concentration on her face.

'Mmh...' he let his mind roam '...I'm not so sure about the Sheriff of Nottingham thing.' He had her full attention now. 'A ride up this valley, clinging to the outside of a carriage in the dark, wouldn't have been that easy, especially at this time of year. And it would have had to be by night for fear of being seen. The area would have been crawling with soldiers on the lookout for him. Even at this time of year, the temperature drops to zero or below on a clear night. Remember the trouble I had this morning scraping the windscreen? Our chap would run the serious risk of getting hypothermia or worse. No, I reckon he would have been in the back of some sort of cart, maybe under a heap of straw or inside a carriage, either disguised or hiding amongst the luggage. But, who's after him? We haven't sorted that out yet, have we?'

He glanced at her face. She had obviously been thinking carefully about this. Her forehead furrowed with concentration. She started speaking slowly, as the ideas took shape.

'If he really isn't just a common criminal, then the only other authorities who could be after him in those days would have to be the church authorities. Maybe he was wanted for some terrible irreligious act?' He could clearly hear the question mark. She paused for his reply.

'I've been wondering about that too. But, to be honest, I'm not sure that I see him as a heretic or a blasphemer. Who knows? Whatever the reason, I'm sure you're right. In medieval days the Catholic Church was every bit as much a temporal state as the national governments. After all, excommunication was a powerful arm to brandish at people. Don't forget, the Middle Ages were a time when religious faith wasn't an option, but a natural fact of life. God existed, there was no question.'

'Not like these days.'

He hesitated before answering, choosing his words carefully. They had briefly touched on religion in their talks so far and had established that neither of them was particularly religious, in spite of both having a Catholic priest as a close friend. 'Not among most of the people I know, at least, although religion's still a hot topic elsewhere. Look at all the awful things happening in the world at the moment, supposedly in the name of religion. Anyway, I'm sure our man's clever enough to get himself a lift up to Santa Cristina without being seen and without catching his death of cold. By the way, I imagine you know that in the Middle Ages they referred to it as a hospital, but it was to all intents and purposes what we would call a hospice for weary pilgrims. But what happens to him when he gets there? Is he going there for a reason, or is he just passing through on his way to the Spanish border?'

'I reckon he was heading for Santa Cristina for a specific reason.' He could hear how hard she was concentrating and he knew the story was having the desired effect of involving her all the more in the trip. He listened as she went on. 'He had to meet somebody there or find something there, don't you think?'

He thought about it for a few moments as he accelerated past a truck and trailer laden with timber. 'You could be right. The question is who or what?'

'So, come on. You're the PhD after all. Think about it. Just who was he expecting to meet at the pilgrim hospice?'

'I'm working on it.'

It was unusually quiet in the car from then on as both of them spent the rest of the morning turning the problem over in their heads. At just before noon, they stopped for a cup of coffee in Etsaut, just about the last bit of relative civilisation before the final climb to the pass. The café was warm and smelt of freshly baked bread. From where they were sitting Luke could see into the bleak square of dour stone houses. Behind them were the mountains. He described the view to Amy and then their conversation returned, naturally, to their story.

'We're agreed that our medieval friend's travelling through the mountains at this time of year. Right?' He saw her nod and continued. 'So, if we work on the basis that he's trying to cross the mountains this same day of the year, albeit a good few centuries ago, he's going to be in trouble. It's still only April, after all, and the mountains are seriously high around here. The snow's still up there on the pass, although it's pretty much melted away down on the plains. I would say that the pilgrimage season, at least in the days before snowploughs and four-wheel drive, wouldn't even have started. If that's the case, then the person he's going to see must've spent the winter in the abbey.'

She nodded again pensively and suggested, 'So who, then? A monk? Could he be going up there to meet a monk?'

'Yes, that could be it, although the question of why has to be answered.'

'For help of course. Our man's fleeing justice, either temporal or spiritual or both, and he hopes to be able to hide at Santa Cristina.' It sounded a very plausible explanation, but neither of them was totally happy with it. It was a bit too simple somehow. He saw the concentration on her face and strove to give it serious consideration. He was sceptical.

'Not that it would be that easy to do. A mountain hospice in the winter must have been a bit like a ship in the middle of the ocean. Everybody would have known everybody else, through and through, right down to the ship's cat and a few of the rats. A new face would stick out like a sore thumb. In a month's time it would be a different story. By then there would be hundreds of pilgrims coming and going every day, but not yet.'

He watched the expression on her face as she concentrated, desperately trying to find a solution. He did his best to help.

'So rather than why, let's think about who. Who is our man? And, for that matter, when is this all happening? The Middle Ages lasted an awfully long time. After all, the pilgrimages to Compostela have been big business since before the first millennium.' He sipped his coffee and racked his brains for a solution.

Her voice interrupted his reflections. 'I'll tell you when.' She sounded really excited. 'I'll tell you. I'll tell you precisely, Mr PhD History Professor.' Her voice was triumphant and her expression rapt. 'This was all happening in exactly the year...' There was a pause, while she did a rapid calculation. 'It happened in exactly 1314. Yes, April 1314 it definitely was, and I even know why he was escaping up the valley and why they were after him.' She gave him a challenging look and sat back to finish her coffee while he struggled to find the answer.

In fact it wasn't that hard. Here in France, if not the whole of Christendom, the first years of the fourteenth century were dominated by one main event: the fall from grace of the Knights Templar. Few people could have been unaware of the reputation of these warrior knights who had battled in the Holy Land for two hundred years. Their war cry of *Beaucéant* had struck fear into enemy hearts since the early twelfth century.

Luke made a suggestion that was far less tentative than it sounded. 'So you're saying our man is a Templar escaping from the clutches of the Inquisition? Could that be right?'

Amy's face shone with the sort of expression normally reserved for winners of Crufts in the presence of their victorious pets. She slapped the tabletop hard enough to rattle the teaspoons and leant towards him. 'Okay so far, but why April?' There was a distinct challenge in her voice.

'How far is it from Paris to here?' Now it was his turn for the mental arithmetic. 'Say about seven hundred kilometres. At an average of, say, twenty, maybe even thirty kilometres a day, how many days would it have taken a man on foot to get here from Paris? I never was much good at that sort of problem at school.'

'Twenty into seven hundred goes about thirty-five times.' She was happy to supply the answer as he worked it all out in his head. 'If my memory serves me right, although the Order of the Temple was officially suppressed in 1312, nobody much outside France paid a lot of attention until the Grand Master of the Templars, Jacques de Molay, was executed in mid March 1314.

He was burnt to death over a slow fire on an island in the Seine along with the Preceptor of Normandy, Geoffroi de Charny.' She was showing off a bit.

'Quite so.' He decided he might show off a bit as well. 'And I presume you know the significance of the slow fire. That way, they really burnt to death, with all the agony you can imagine. Normally on a big bonfire, most people actually died of asphyxiation, when the fire consumed all the oxygen, before the pain of the flames really bit.'

Her cocky air left her and she looked bleak. He didn't notice, as he was still caught up with his calculations.

'Anyway that was the moment the whole of Christendom realised that the Templars' time was finally up. The last few still at liberty would have made for safety elsewhere.' He did another calculation and realised it really did fit. 'So four or five weeks from the middle of March brings us pretty close to where we are now in April.' There was amazement in his voice. 'So that's what it's all about.'

'But why was he heading south, and who was he going to see?'

'Remember that the kings of Spain and Portugal took scant notice of the order to arrest the Templars. They owed a great deal to the Templars, who'd helped them over the years to rid the Iberian peninsula of the Moors. Escape through the Pyrenees wasn't such a bad idea.'

'All right, then, he was a Templar escaping from Philippe le Bel.' She didn't sound totally convinced. 'But who was he going to see at Santa Cristina?'

She leant forward on her elbows towards him. His eyes fell upon the open neck of her shirt, presenting him with an unsettling glimpse of white lace and shadowy curves. He cleared his throat guiltily, swilled the remains of his coffee, and did his best to drag his thoughts back to who on earth could have been waiting for a fleeing Templar in a mountain hospice.

4

ABBEY OF SANTA CRISTINA, SPANISH PYRENEES, APRIL 1314

The carriage pulled into the arched courtyard of the Abbey and Hospital of Santa Cristina just after first light. Sleepy monks came out and took charge of the exhausted horses and the equally tired escort of soldiers. The noise of their arrival attracted the attention of virtually everybody. Above all, it announced the fact that the road was now well and truly open. Their period of hibernation was over. The younger monks welcomed the arrival of fresh people with new tales to tell, while many of the older men regretted the fact that their peaceful winter routine was once again to be disturbed.

For Aimée, it brought mixed feelings. On the one hand it meant renewed contact with reality, with all the problems and troubles that could bring. On the other hand, this break in the regular routine of the abbey was welcome. She had very soon worked out that she was not the stuff that nuns were made of. A changeless daily ritual did not give her the solace that it gave others. She badly needed the stimulus of contact with the outside world, however frightening the thought of this might be.

She rubbed her eyes. It was a habitual, if futile gesture. She knew she would never see again, and she had even ceased to hope any more. Instead, in her own characteristic forceful way, she was pushing herself to learn to see with her other senses, just as quickly as she could. She already knew her way around the hospice without the need for any more than the most cursory of touches. Her nose told her whether the kitchen doors were open, her ears whether there were monks in the church. The skin of her cheeks could sense whether it was day or night, freezing or thawing. She had learned a lot in three months.

Aimée listened to the noises from the courtyard. The sounds were funnelled upwards by the sheer stone walls to the window where she was standing. She counted at least six horses, maybe eight. She felt the air on her face and knew that dawn had broken and the temperature was already above freezing. The snow must have melted off the road that led from the Somport pass. If it was possible for this carriage to get through, then, before long, pilgrims would again be streaming across. Memories of what she had come to think of as her previous life crowded uninvited into her mind. She shook her head angrily to chase them away, but still they came pouring back in unstoppable waves.

There had been six of them in the group: three men, two women and a little girl. All of them, for various reasons, had been desperate to get across the pass, despite the arrival of heavy winter snows. She had known little or nothing about any of them apart, of course, from Bertrand; Bertrand her husband and the secret mission that had cost him his life.

Even now, two full months later, she found it hard to think of Bertrand without breaking down. They had been married for so long, and through so much in the last few years, that she still could hardly believe that he was gone. But he was. Of that there could be no doubt. She had watched him die in a vain attempt to save her after the other four, even including the little girl, had been butchered by the bandits who had been waiting at the top of the pass. If her eyes had seen anything after that moment, her mind had mercifully blotted it from her memory forever. After his death there had been only the horror, the defilement and the pain.

She wiped her eyes again and found her hand wet with tears. The irony was that the attack had come from ordinary bandits, rather than the massed forces of the King of France. And Bertrand and she had been so close to their goal. Angrily, she rubbed her face with her sleeve and tried to break the train of thought. There had been times during the first weeks in the hospice when she had come very close indeed to taking her own life. It was only the knowledge that she had a mission, Bertrand's mission, to accomplish that stopped her. Deep in her heart she felt sure that, when she had finally done what he had sworn to do, she wouldn't hesitate to leave this lonely life and join him. But first she had to carry out the mission. And there was no doubt that her blindness complicated things a thousandfold.

She leant back against the carved stone window surround and took deep breaths of ice-cold air.

'Ah, there you are, Aimée.'

She started. It was the abbot. She had been so preoccupied with her thoughts that she hadn't heard him approach.

'I thought I saw you up here. I came to warn you that the soldiers have told us there's a desperate, dangerous man coming our way. It would be best if you stayed inside for the time being, until they've apprehended him.' His tone became drier. 'The information comes from a distinguished source. Amazingly, it appears we've been visited by His Grace the Archbishop of Sens.' Aimée jumped as if she had been stung. If the abbot noticed, he gave no hint of it in his voice. 'I just thought you might be interested to know.' With that, he carried on down the long corridor, leaving her in disarray.

The Archbishop of Sens; Aimée knew his name so well. He was none other than Philippe de Marigny himself, the brother of the Royal Chamberlain. He was the man responsible for the terrible deaths of so many Templars, often as a result of inhuman torture. And now he was here in the high Pyrenees in person. What would a senior church dignitary be doing in pursuit of a dangerous criminal, unless...?

There could be no other explanation: they knew about Bertrand's mission. And they would soon know, if they didn't already, of her survival. She had no illusions as to the treatment she would receive from them when they apprehended her and she shuddered. Her alternatives had suddenly become brutally simple. She had to get away, or she had to take her own life. Either way, there was no time to lose.

She racked her brains as to what to do. There was no way she would be able to get far without assistance. To make matters worse, even if she managed to get out of the abbey unchallenged, the thought that the same gang of bandits might still be in the neighbourhood was terrifying. She clenched her teeth and forced herself to consider her options logically and rationally. Of the monks in the hospital there were few, if any, to whom she could turn for help.

That left nobody apart from, she thought with a surge of excitement, apart from the man they were expecting to come up the valley towards them. Her pulse quickened. Of course, if such a high-ranking figure as the Archbishop of Sens was here in person, there could be no doubt about it. The dangerous, desperate man who was expected had to be one like Bertrand. And there was only one man to equal him that she knew, at least still at liberty. Could it be Luc? There was nobody better and he, when he arrived there, would prove to be her salvation. Her spirits soared for the first time in months. She turned and hurried back to her cell to collect her few belongings. She needed to be ready to leave as soon as she made contact with him.

5

HIGH PYRENEES, APRIL 2016

'So this is the top, is it?'

Amy's breath was clearly visible in the cold mountain air and both of them could feel the keen wind that blew down from the peaks on either side of them. Luke had parked the car on what would no doubt become a picnic area in summer. As it was, the car crunched off the road onto at least a foot of frozen snow, the tyres gripping sure-footedly as the weight of the big vehicle cut deep tracks into the icy surface. He switched off the engine and turned towards her. 'As I feared, the idea of walking a stretch of the Pilgrims' Way will have to be put on hold. The snow's so deep, there's no trace of a path. In fact, the only markings on the snow are a few ski tracks crisscrossing the open area leading to the summit.'

'Is that where we're going? Is it a long way to the top?'

'Not too far. We'll give it a try. It all depends how deep the snow is.'

They dressed in their warm clothes and he led her up through the snow. It took them some time as they kept stumbling in the deeper drifts, but they finally made it to the highest part of the pass. She was hanging onto him with both of her hands for most of the way and on a couple of occasions he had to encircle her with his arm and support her. Feeling the strength of his arm was really rather good and she could feel a smile on her face. At last they reached the top and he stopped, their breath forming clouds in the frozen air.

'Is this it?' She, too, was panting after their exertions.

'Yup, this is it. Turn towards me a bit. That's right. Now tell me which way you're headed.' He glanced in her direction and saw her take a deep breath and run her tongue across her lips. He noticed, not for the first time, how really beautiful she looked in profile. He did his best to keep his mind on historical matters, but it wasn't easy. Unaware of his eyes upon her, she was trying to work out the right answer.

'We must be looking due south. I can feel the sun just a bit off to the right and it must be about...' She felt for the watch on her wrist. Charlie Brown's voice obligingly told her it was 3.27. 'About half past three, as I thought.' She sounded pleased with her estimation. 'I reckon we must be looking straight down into Spain. Maybe straight down onto the ruins of the abbey hospice of Santa Cristina?' Her tone was interrogative.

'Dead right on both counts.' He was equally pleased for her. 'But you aren't missing a view of either of them. The ruins of the abbey are virtually invisible under normal circumstances, but with a couple of metres of snow on top, I doubt if we'll even be able to locate what little's left. And as far as seeing down into Spain's concerned, there's a huge great mountain in the way. Mind you, that looks pretty nice with a load of people skiing down towards us on the north-facing slope. There's still a good snow covering on that side.' For a moment he wondered whether the mention of skiing would bring back uncomfortable memories for her, but her face showed no sign of anything untoward.

'Brr.' In spite of her thermal jacket she was cold. 'Just imagine what it must have been like up here for pilgrims in leaky boots, or even bare feet.' She stamped her feet in the snow and pressed closer to him. 'Did they have woolly jumpers in those days?'

'Oh yes.' Although he tried not to think about the feel of her against him, he didn't succeed. 'They also had furs, mostly rabbit, but a few fox or even wolf, and above all they had their cloak. Every pilgrim had a waterproof cape that would protect them from the worst weather.'

'And a sturdy staff to protect them from dogs, wolves and other pilgrims.'

She sounded relaxed and happy. There was no doubt about it, her

warmth against him was definitely pleasant. More than pleasant, he thought
with a guilty start and he did his best to sound matter-of-fact.

'Come on, then, before we freeze, we'd better make a move. Stay out in
this wind for long and we'll both soon start losing body heat.' They started to
make their way back to the car. Avoiding the tracks they had made on the
way up, he cut straight across the virgin snow. The sensation of breaking a
new trail was exhilarating, but hard work, as their boots sank into the snow
to the ankles.

'This is nice.' Her voice sounded happy. She reached over so that she was
gripping his arm with both hands again. They walked on in silence for a
while, until a large rock loomed ahead of them. The snow had melted off it
completely in the spring sunshine, and its bulk formed an effective wind-
break. He guided her towards it.

'Fancy a rest in the sunshine?'

'It'll be nice to get out of that bitter wind.'

They took up positions side by side, the sun warming their faces. She
could feel the warmth of his body beside her. It felt very reassuring. *More
than reassuring,* she thought to herself. *This feels right.* She breathed deeply
but said nothing. He cleared his throat in that way she had come to recognise. It meant he was embarrassed. She heard him launch into tour-guide
mode.

'We're facing west now and are in the lee of the rock. That's why that cold
wind's stopped. You can see the tracks we've made in the snow quite clearly.
We're the first humans to come across here since the last snowstorm. Mind
you, from the mass of other tracks, it must be a real wildlife show when we're
not around. Those are deer, I would think, and there are lots of rabbits or
hares. There are bigger tracks over there, but I suppose they might have
been made by a dog. No wolves left now, though the area was crawling with
them in the Middle Ages.'

He rattled on, conscious that he was overdoing it. Deep inside he was
afraid that if he didn't, the conversation might take a more intimate turn. His
emotions, held in check now for so many years, were still so uncertain and,
as ever, he did his best to suppress them. Anyway, he reminded himself, he
was here as her guide. It would be all too easy to abuse the trust placed in
him. 'Bears, too, of course. There are still supposed to be ten or twenty

brown bears in this area nowadays, but it's very unusual to come across one. Mind you, in—'

'In the Middle Ages, the area must have been crawling with them.' She finished the sentence for him, a gently mocking note in her voice, but she let him off the hook by asking, 'What's this place like where we're sitting? Is it just a big rock or what?'

'It's certainly a big rock.' He answered gratefully, glad of the change of subject. 'I'm not sure what the name of this stone is, but it is a deep red colour, probably loaded with all kinds of minerals. It's more or less in the middle of the open area. It would have made a good lookout post for bandits on the prowl. It flattens off above us and a person could lie stretched out quite easily there.' As he said the last words her expression changed to one of apprehension, no longer carefree as a moment before.

'What's wrong?' He was concerned.

'Help me up, would you?' She scrambled to her feet and had pretty well found her way to the top of the rock by herself before he was able to reach her with a guiding hand. She dropped to her knees, her hands running lightly over the smooth rock surface, her expression ever more concerned.

'So what is it?' He sounded puzzled, unable to explain her behaviour.

She turned towards him as he climbed up in his turn. He saw fear and another emotion, maybe pity, on her face. She reached out for him and he took both her hands in his. This time his concern for her removed any feeling of disquiet. She was trembling as she spoke.

'This is a really bad place. It's an evil place. I don't know what happened here, but something truly terrible took place right here, up here where we are standing. Can't you feel it? There's something awful about this rock.' Her voice tailed off and he saw her eyelids flutter. Before she could faint, he caught her in his arms. This caused him to overbalance and he jumped off the rock down onto the snow. Their combined weight took them through the top crust of ice and he almost fell. With a great effort he managed to keep his feet and struggle out of the hole he had made. He stumbled off across the field towards the car with Amy in his arms and his breath was getting laboured by the time he reached the road. He opened the passenger door, slipped her onto the seat, then made his way slowly round the back of the car and climbed in the driver's side.

As he regained his breath and his pulse began to return to normal, he studied the face of the girl beside him. Her eyes were tightly shut and her fists were clenched so hard that her knuckles were white. She was breathing rapidly in and out, for all the world as if it had been she who had just run across a field. He wondered whether to say something but opted to give her time to compose herself. A flash of inspiration struck him and he reached to the back seat. The bottle of thirty-year-old brandy should do the trick. Amy had insisted on buying it for him several days earlier in Cognac, when they had stopped off to visit the cellars. He tore open the box and broke the seal, twisting out the cork before holding the bottle under her nose.

'Here. Take a drop of this.'

The combination of his voice and the smell of the spirit had the desired effect. She reached out absently and took a mouthful. By the time she had finished coughing, she was back in the land of the living. He retrieved the bottle and breathed in the heady aroma before deciding he could risk a sip, even though he was driving. The taste was every bit as good as he had hoped and he felt the warmth spreading pleasantly around his body. After a brief hesitation he regretfully replaced the cork and returned the bottle to its place on the back seat.

He looked across at her. 'Want to talk about it?' He was relieved to see her half turn towards him, no longer with the agonised expression on her face. She pulled out a tissue and blew her nose while searching for the right words.

'I had an overwhelming feeling of evil. A sensation, no, more than a sensation. I just suddenly felt the absolute conviction that something really bad happened in that spot. I don't know how to describe the feeling. Totally overpowering. One moment I was as happy as I have been for months... years, and then smack, this awful feeling of dread. It was as if somebody just walked over my grave. You don't think I could be turning into a witch, do you?' She paused for a few seconds while she collected herself. 'I very nearly fainted.'

'You certainly did.' He said it with feeling. 'In fact, I would say that having to be physically carried qualifies as the next best thing to a dead faint.' He flexed the muscles of his shoulders and groaned theatrically. 'You weigh a ton in all that thick winter clothing.'

She turned towards him with a smile and reached up to his face with her hands. Before he could stop her, she pulled herself upwards and planted a soft kiss on his cheek. This was the first time ever her lips had touched him and the effect upon him was stunning. Suddenly all his fears and uncertainties returned with a rush. Memories came rushing, unwanted, into his head and he had to struggle hard to maintain his equilibrium. Meanwhile, apparently unaware of his discomfort, she settled back in her seat and switched to a pretty convincing Zsa Zsa Gabor voice.

'But, darlink, maybe I did it just so that I could fall into your so schtrong arms!' She smiled to herself while he did his unsuccessful best to banish the mass of memories pulsing through him and reply in a normal tone.

'Have a heart. I'm not used to all this excitement.' He thought for a moment about another nip from the cognac bottle, but prudence prevailed. 'If you're going to insist upon being carried around much more often, I'd better go into training again.'

'Which reminds me.' She was getting back to normal. 'What's all this about you not being used to excitement? Why's that? When do I get to hear your story? About you, that is.'

She heard him clear his throat. 'What do you want to know?'

'Oh... just everything.'

'Surely Father Tim told you all about me.'

'Father Tim told me next to nothing about you. You've got a PhD. You're a jolly good chap and you're a close friend of his. I don't even know what you did before going back to university. For all I know, you might have been in jail.' She was smiling now. 'Is that it? Did you murder somebody?'

Luke found himself smiling back at her. 'So, if you think I might be a murderer, why on earth did you agree to come away with me like this?' He allowed his voice to deepen with menace. 'Why, I might be about to tear your head off at this very moment.'

'I notice you didn't answer the question. That's pretty damn incriminating, I'd say.'

'Well, let me set your mind at rest on that score. I'm not a jailbird or a murderer.' His voice became more serious. 'But I've been going through some pretty difficult stuff and I'm still trying to sort my head out.' He paused, doing his best to drum up the courage to try to talk about everything that had happened to him, but knowing in his bones that he still wasn't ready. 'I'll tell you that much, and I promise I'll tell you more very soon. Just be patient and bear with me. Please.'

She reached over, located his hand and gave it a gentle squeeze. 'Take your time. It's all right. Tell me more when you feel ready. In the meantime, I'm very happy to take you as you are.'

For a few seconds, a wave of emotion swept over him and he came very, very close to kissing her, before deciding to return to safer ground.

'Thanks, Amy.' He found he had to clear his throat before continuing. 'It's a promise. Now, tell me something, my witch friend, do you think the opposite could also apply?' In response to the puzzled look on her face, he explained. 'If you can have such a strong reaction when you sense that something evil has taken place, do you think you could have a reaction of equal intensity if you found yourself in a place where something good has happened?'

'You don't find so many of them, I'm afraid.' Her light tone belied the sad truth behind her words. 'At least, not so strong. Boy meets girl, girl marries boy, boy and girl live happily ever after doesn't hit the headlines of history. The place where hundreds of thousands of people were murdered for no good reason, now that sticks in the historian's mind, whether we're talking about Auschwitz or the Somme. Maybe I picked up a force that intense suffering can leave in a place. One warm happy moment, however intense, doesn't seem to have the power to linger on and influence me.'

He thought for a moment before asking his next question.

'So have you any idea when and how thousands of people may have been made to suffer up here? None of the history books mentions a battle of any kind in this part of the High Pyrenees. Indeed, the terrain's so inhospitable and the access so difficult that I just can't imagine two armies making it up here in a fit state to start a monumental battle.' Receiving no reply from her, he started again.

'Or do you think this could be the site of some deeply painful and bitter experience for a smaller group? After all, it was only at that precise spot on the red rock that you felt it. Could the intensity of the feeling of a few be comparable with the lesser suffering of the many? Could there have been a particularly painful cry that still echoes down to this day?' He looked hard at her face and saw the concentration. It was a while before she replied.

'Yes, I suppose it's possible. I know what you mean about the armies or any other mass confrontation here. I just can't imagine it either. Unless, of course...'

He was with her. 'Unless of course the memory was of an event of special poignancy and significance to you personally. Maybe it was not so much somebody walking over your grave, but rather that you just walked over somebody's grave.'

'I just walked over somebody's grave...' She explored the concept. Her sightless eyes were trained on some distant object and didn't waver. He didn't ask any more for fear that the snow and the mountains had revived the deep trauma of her parents' accident in her. Her first return to the mountains would mean that her subconscious must still be full of it. He decided to introduce a more positive note into the conversation.

'Anyway, think about this for a moment, Amy. I can give you one place where the opposite has happened, time and again through history. You haven't visited Santiago de Compostela yet.' She shook her head. 'When we do, we'll walk into the cathedral together. Then you can tell me whether your sixth or seventh sense works only in places of evil. The accumulated joy of millions of people, I'm sure you'll feel it. You don't need to be religious to feel it. So many people, who've walked for hundreds and hundreds of miles to get there, they must have left a mark. I've been there twice in my life and, although I wouldn't describe myself as a religious man, I felt it both times.' He glanced at her. 'And I'm certainly not a witch.'

'Can you get male witches?'

'I'm not even sure you can get female ones, present company excepted.' He decided it was time to move on, both as far as the conversation was concerned and in practical terms. 'Anyway, it's getting late. We'd better start thinking about finding a hotel for the night.'

She ran her hands through her hair and sat up, looking more relaxed. 'Sounds like a good idea.'

'Dig in the door pocket. There should be a booklet about this part of northern Spain. It's not very thick.' Obligingly she reached down and retrieved a handful of Spanish Tourist Board brochures. He took them from her and selected the one dealing with Jaca and its immediate area.

'Looks like there is no shortage of accommodation in Jaca. Shall we head for there?'

She nodded in agreement, so he started the engine. His head was still spinning from the after-effects of that simple little kiss. He knew he would have to find the strength to start speaking to her about his past. She needed to know and maybe, just maybe, it might help him to start talking about it in all its horror.

6

ABBEY OF SANTA CRISTINA, APRIL 1314

Aimée picked her way carefully down the stairs to the courtyard. It was freezing cold and she had recovered her thick travelling cloak from the place it had been lying for the last three months and she clutched it tight around her shoulders. When she reached the cobbled yard, she stood quietly for a few moments, trying to work out if anybody might still be around. Hearing nothing, she stepped forward cautiously until her outstretched hands felt the side of the carriage. Feeling her way to the door, she climbed up into the velvet-clad interior and was stopped dead by a voice.

'Is it you?' The voice was less than a foot from her ear. 'Aimée, is it truly you?'

She started, casting around for the source of the voice, recognising it, but unwilling to believe her ears. It was as if she had drifted back in time, and none of the horrors of the past months had happened.

'Luc? It *is* you, Luc, isn't it?' Instinctively she kept her voice to a hoarse whisper. Indeed, she could hardly remember a time when she had been able to address him in any but hushed tones.

'It's me, Aimée. It's really me.' His voice was as charged with emotion as hers. 'I'm up here, in the baggage rack. Can you see me?'

See him? The overwhelming tragedy of her circumstances struck her like a mallet. In the space of a few seconds, she totally lost the precarious control she had gradually been able to establish over her emotions. A wave of misery washed up and over her, drowning rational thought and reducing her to a sobbing wreck. The carriage creaked and then she felt herself enveloped in a bear hug. There was no mistaking the broad shoulders and powerful arms. It was truly Luc. She abandoned herself to her sorrow and wept uncontrollably.

She felt him tighten his grip on her as he was overcome in his turn. There was nothing either of them could or needed to say. They stayed like that for an age, while she sobbed out her desperation. Finally she came to her senses. She shook herself back to the dangerous reality of their present situation.

'Luc, Luc, listen, listen to me.'

She hissed violently into his ear until he relaxed his grip. She reached up to his face with her hands. There were tears on his cheeks. Maybe they were hers. She fought hard to keep control of her emotions.

'Listen to me, Luc. Listen. Can you hear me, Luc? Luc?' Her insistent tone finally got through and she knew that she had his attention.

'Bertrand's dead, Luc. Do you hear me? He's dead. He was killed this winter and I was the only survivor. Do you hear me? Do you?'

She felt, rather than saw, his eyes studying her from close range. A sharp intake of breath told her he had realised.

'That's right, Luc. I'm blind. I'm blind, but it doesn't matter. Do you understand? It doesn't matter. We're going to get out of here and carry out Bertrand's mission, your mission, our mission. Do you understand? Do you...? Speak to me, Luc...' Her voice tailed off despairingly, but he was back with her now.

'Oh, dear sweet Jesus. Oh, dear Lord God Almighty. Is there no end to it?' His voice was bitterly saddened, but rational once more. 'Tell me about it.'

So she told him. She told him more than she had told anybody up till then. She told him about the laughter, the taunts, the obscenities and the searing pain of it all. She told him about the deep sensation of disgust and defilement that had made her, and still often made her, want to end her life, in the hope of a cleaner, purer future. She told him about the cuts, the bruises and the blows that had finally brought blessed oblivion. And from oblivion she had awoken into a colourless world of loneliness. She told him all this without once breaking down. It was as if another were recounting her experiences, and she a mere spectator. When she finally came to a halt, she felt his hand against her cheek and heard his voice, little more than a whisper.

'I'm here now, Aimée. I'll take care of you. I promise.'

7

SPANISH PYRENEES, APRIL 2016

They were barely aware of crossing from France into Spain. A dilapidated customs post was the only sign, but it clearly hadn't been manned for many years now. Snow had been banked up on both sides of the road by the regular passage of snowploughs, and the road surface itself was running with water, although it would probably be May before the thick covering of snow on the fields disappeared. As they began their descent, the sun disappeared behind the clouds and the standing water started to freeze again.

'So this is Spain now?' Amy sounded her usual self again and Luke felt relieved that her mood of despair appeared to have left her. He too was back to normal, apart from a certain residual stiffness in his shoulders, and a lingering concern that his feelings for her might be straying from the strictly professional. Back in London just a few days before they had started out, Father Tim had raised that very point.

'She's an attractive woman, Luke. Do you think you can cope?'

In all honesty he had replied that he wasn't worried. And he hadn't been, then. Keeping a tight rein on his emotions had become second nature after everything that had happened to him. He'd felt sure he would have no problem. Anyway, her prickly nature, although less and less in evidence as the days went by, had made its presence felt often enough initially for him to be very wary. The practical concerns relating to the logistics of the journey, from buying the car, to booking ferry tickets and obtaining detailed maps, took up most of his waking moments. He really hadn't given any serious thought to the fact that she was a woman, and he a man. And also, if he was totally honest to himself, her handicap instantly put her into a different category.

There was the matter of physical contact, for example. It had quickly become second nature to him to give her his arm when leading her somewhere new. There was no secret electricity in the touch, no unexpected charge of excitement. It very soon became what it quite simply was: a means to an end. Without his guiding hand she would be lost, and he would not be fulfilling his responsibilities. Then the fact that he found himself describing things to her and doing all the preparatory paperwork further reinforced the guide/client relationship. And finally, he had to admit there was the reluctance on his part to do more than flick his eyes across her face or body. Somehow it felt improper for him to gaze on her, while she was unable to do the same in return.

'I can cope, Tim. We'll keep it professional. Don't you worry.'

Now, after that simple peck on the cheek from her, he felt totally at sea emotionally. He turned towards her and allowed himself to study her face properly for a few seconds. She really looked amazing. The long golden hair was tied back in a businesslike ponytail but was still very feminine. The fine lines around the aquamarine eyes added character to an otherwise perfect complexion. There was no doubt about it, she would most certainly have been fighting the boys off in her earlier years. Now, just thirty, without her handicap, she would doubtless still have had the pick of the eligible bachelors. Just then she turned towards him and her voice interrupted his reflections.

'I suppose there's no chance of a cup of coffee around here, is there?'

The idea of a beer also had considerable appeal to him. They were driving through a scruffy little village with no shops but, this being Spain, there was a bar. 'As luck would have it, there's a place right here.' He pulled up outside a sad-looking building. 'Bar Somport. Not the most inspired of names, but welcome nonetheless.' He switched off the engine and stepped out onto the slippery tarmac. He went round the back and met her as she climbed down onto the slush at the side of the road. She took his arm and they made their way inside.

They were probably no more than a couple of kilometres from the French border, and less than thirty or forty kilometres from the French café where they had had coffee earlier that day. The scenery outside was the same, the snow and the cold were the same, but the atmosphere inside was totally different. The television was tuned to a football match. The volume was high enough to set the bottles behind the bar humming whenever the ball was anywhere near either net. Somebody had clearly just done something significant because the commentator sounded as if he was in the throes of a hysterical fit that caused him to howl like a wolf. They were unmistakably in Spain.

In one corner of the bar there was a table of men, quite clearly just finishing their lunch. Luke glanced at his watch and saw that it was almost five o'clock. Yes, that would definitely make it lunch. With a shudder he realised that here in Spain the earliest they would be able to expect dinner that evening would probably be gone nine o'clock. He steered her to a table as far as possible away from the television, and started his description of the surroundings.

'Welcome to Spain.' She peeled off her thermal jacket and hung it over the back of her chair. She was wearing a denim cowboy shirt underneath and the top three buttons were undone. As much for his own peace of mind as for anybody else's sake, he thought he should give her a warning. 'You'd better do up a few buttons in here. There's not another woman to be seen in the place and you have, at least temporarily, replaced the Big Match as the main point of interest. Can you feel the eyes on you?'

He still had not fully come to terms with the effect her appearance seemed to have on men of all ages. Today she was dressed very casually and she wore no jewellery, but still looked stunning.

She ran a hand casually up the front of her shirt, checking just how many buttons were undone. Reassured, she returned her hand to the tabletop.

'Let me guess. One of them's got a stomach that makes him look about eight months gone, and between them they have enough facial hair to house a family of squirrels.' She laughed happily. He realised that being the centre of male attraction for her was an experience that took her back to happier times.

As if aware of his embarrassment, she repeated her question, so as to give him something to talk about. 'Well, was I right about these characters?'

'Not bad at all. There are at least three fat stomachs and one of the moustaches looks the size and shape of a badger. In fact I'm sure I saw it move.' She giggled. 'There are pennants belonging to just about every football club in Spain on the wall behind the bar and a whole shelf of bottles of Spanish brandy. There's even a photo of a bullfighter. Looks a bit old and yellow. Who knows? Maybe it's El Cordobes. No sign of anybody behind the bar. No, wait a minute. Mine host is approaching now. He's one of the stomachs from the corner table. What are we having?'

'I'll have an espresso, and I'm prepared to wager you could murder a beer.'

'You know me so well, but I'll make it a little one as I'm driving.'

As the landlord went off to fetch their drinks, Luke looked out of the window. Heavier clouds had bubbled up and blanked out the sun. It was already quite dark and very grey outside. When the waiter returned, Luke picked up his glass and took a mouthful of cold beer gratefully. He glanced across at her. She was looking quite happy now, sipping her coffee and leaning forward, elbows on the table. As if sensing his eyes on her, she raised her head.

'How's your beer?'

'Just what I needed after carrying somebody across a snowfield.'

Her hand felt across the tabletop until it touched his. 'Thank you, Luke. I don't think I said thank you. I wouldn't want you to think I make a habit of fainting and needing to be carried.'

'At your service.' He let his eyes rest on her face, the pale blue eyes as mesmerising as ever. 'Mind you, that was quite some reaction to a lump of rock. Has it ever happened to you before?'

She shook her head. 'Never.' She squeezed his hand and then released it. 'You know what I was thinking? You know we were talking about my blindness enhancing my other senses? Well, maybe it's enhanced the sixth sense as well.'

'I'm not sure we have a sixth sense, are you?'

'I don't know. There's so much that goes on inside our brains that the experts can't explain. Maybe there really is a sixth sense; something that picks up on vibrations that the other senses miss.'

'But the problem we've got with that big rock back there is to work out why it sparked a chord with you.' He let his mind roam. 'This is going to sound pretty silly, but I've been wondering over the last few days whether this story we've invented isn't maybe a bit too close for comfort. Maybe we would have done better if the main character hadn't been so much like me and not following this selfsame route.'

A smile spread across her face. 'So you've been feeling it too? I thought it was just me.' She sat upright. 'Who knows? Maybe it really happened.'

'Maybe it did.'

'There's something else I've been thinking, Luke. You know earlier on when you asked me why I was grumpy the first time we met and I said it was fear?' He grunted and she carried on. 'There's something else, to be totally honest. You see, it's my immune system.'

'Your what?' He started, surprised at her words, but she carried on.

'I'm not sure that's the right way of describing it.' She paused, searching for the right words, knowing that she was talking about things she had never revealed to anybody else, not even their mutual friend Father Tim. Somehow, here with Luke, it felt right to air these things. 'We all have a mechanism inside our bodies that fights off attack from outside. Something that protects us from harm; and I'm talking about mental as well as physical. I used to think that I had that side of things sewn up. I was pretty confident that I was totally in control of my life. And the same went for people. Especially men.' There was a moment's hesitation before she continued. 'Then there was the accident.'

Luke wondered if he should intervene, say something, but she hadn't finished. 'I used to be quite good-looking.' Her voice was tense, but in control, so he made no comment. 'There were always men around my sister and me. Whether for Daddy's money or for us was difficult to tell, but when you're young, it's easy to convince yourself that it is you they're after.'

He stared compassionately at the pale face with the disconcerting light blue eyes and wondered whether to speak. But she hadn't finished.

'After the accident, various friends tried to comfort me.' He heard the note of bitterness in her voice. 'With some of the men, one in particular, I thought I'd found what I'd lost, but I soon discovered I was mistaken. It's a bit like being in a pit and somebody throws you a rope. You start to climb up the rope, but then, before you reach the top, they let go. You end up still in the hole and, what's more, you're bruised. So that's what I am, I'm bruised and that's why I wasn't as hospitable as I could have been. And with each passing year my metaphorical immune system, that's my internal self-defence system, struggles desperately to repair the damage and, in the meantime, I keep on getting grumpier. I'm afraid it's been a losing battle up to now.' She lapsed into silence.

'Apart from that first day, I haven't seen you grumpy at all.' He tried to lighten the tone. 'Not even when you dropped your earring in the toilet. Anyway, you said it yourself, when you used the words, "up to now". So surely that's got to mean things are improving?' Politically correct or not, he reached across the table and took hold of her hand in his. She raised her face towards him and managed a nod of the head and a little smile.

'Definitely. After all, I've got my very own Sir Galahad to carry me away from danger. I bet you'd fight for my honour if you had to.'

'I promise that if anybody challenges me, I'll slap him with my glove and set about the knave.' He saw a smile appear on her face. 'See, not grumpy at all.'

'Well, if I'm not, it's down to you. Thank you once more.'

They sat in silence for a few more minutes, each immersed in their own thoughts. Finally he glanced out of the window again. 'The sun's disappeared behind the mountains.' He drained the remains of the beer. 'We'd better get moving, otherwise we won't stand a chance of seeing the ruins of Santa Cristina, assuming, of course, that there's anything left to see.' Obediently Amy finished her coffee and stood up. He paid the landlord and they returned to the car.

The road was a fine modern highway. Unsurprisingly, a sign announced that it had been built with money from the European Union. He slowed right down, searching desperately for any trace of Santa Cristina. They stopped in a couple of places and ventured out into the ever colder air in search of any clues, but without success. He saw nothing. The snow was too deep. At last, the light fading fast, he had to admit defeat. It was sad to think that such a significant construction should have just disappeared off the face of the earth.

He led Amy back to the car just as the first big powdery snowflakes started to fall. By the time they had climbed back into the car and removed their jackets, the snow had already obscured the windscreen. Luke set off down the hill with his windscreen wipers struggling to clear the weight of snow, and within ten minutes the road was white, the visibility deteriorating by the minute. To make matters worse, his screen washers froze up. On their departure from Britain in fine spring weather it had not occurred to him to put anti-freeze in the screen wash. In consequence, even with the air conditioning blowing hard against the glass, he was now restricted to an area the size of a dinner plate in the middle of the screen in front of him through which to find his way down the hill.

They travelled down the slope, albeit at little more than a crawl, for almost half an hour before they met another vehicle. The snowstorm was obviously excessively heavy even by Pyrenean standards and people had wisely opted to stay at home. However, in spite of the conditions, they were gradually dropping down from the heights of the Somport towards the flatter lands of Spain. A sign loomed out of the gloom, showing Jaca as being twenty-nine kilometres ahead. It wouldn't be too long now, he thought grimly, his eyes already tired with the effort of concentration.

'Are you tired?' She could sense it. She was tired as well, and she hadn't had to drive through the snow. She had always hated doing that. Snow on the ski slopes was one thing, snow on the roads was another. Her mind flicked back, as it so often did, to the years before the accident. Looking back on them now, they seemed idyllic, although she could remember times when she had been miserable or in despair, mostly as a result of problems with boys. Looking back on those episodes now, she wished she could go back to her younger self and tell her to love and enjoy every minute of what had been a wonderful life. *Carpe diem* was something you so often only appreciated when it was too late. She gave a little internal sigh. 'Luke, you should take a break if you're feeling tired.'

'I'm beginning to feel a bit weary, but I'm okay for the moment. There was a sign back there which said it's only twenty-odd kilometres to Jaca so it shouldn't be much longer. What about you? Ready for a Spanish meal?'

'Mmmh. Any kind of meal.'

He cast a glance across at her and the childlike vulnerability of her pose, curled up with her knees under her chin and her arms wrapped around her ankles. He guided the big vehicle round a corner, the tyres crunching through the foot or so of fresh snow. She turned her face towards him.

'We're lucky to be in a nice warm car. It must be absolutely horrific outside. My thanks to the driver.' A more tender note entered her voice. 'It's nice being with you.'

She sounded warm and happy. He wondered if this was the time to open up about his own problems. Maybe some of her happiness might rub off on him. For a moment he was on the point of embarking upon the whole story, but the enormity of the task defeated him. Maybe if they had been sitting together in a café or over the dinner table. But here, while he was having to concentrate hard on staying on the twisty mountain road, he didn't know how to begin.

He was still trying to find the right words to explain some of what had happened to him and what was going through his head, when he saw a flashing yellow light coming towards him in the middle of the road. He flicked the gear lever into manual and dropped into first gear, the chunky tyres gripping reassuringly and slowing them to a walking pace. He pulled over to the right-hand side, bumping off the road onto the verge, and watched as the snowplough came majestically by, a bow wave of snow shooting out from the blade on the front. He received a lazy wave from the driver, which he acknowledged cheerfully.

'Snowplough?' She wasn't really asking the question. The clanking of the chains and the scrape of the plough were unmistakable. Not surprisingly it was followed by a procession of cars, all with headlights blazing. Luke pushed the gear lever into park, stretched his legs and switched on the radio. Jacques Brel's 'Le Plat Pays' filled the car. As it finished and a French disc jockey cut in, Luke lowered the volume a bit and turned towards her.

'Yes, it's a snowplough. Followed by half of Spain by the look of it and, yes, I think it's really nice being with you, too.' He hesitated. 'More than nice. I really can't think of anybody I would rather be with here, now. Honestly, I can't...' He would have said more, but he still didn't have the confidence. She sensed that he was finding it difficult to talk so she made no comment and they sat in silence, listening to the music.

At last, the stream of lights coming up the hill ended. Luke nosed the car back out onto the road and into the clear swathe cut by the plough. He accelerated up to a decent speed and delicately tried the brakes. The car slowed obediently, and he gave a sigh of relief.

'So what about our story, then?' Amy turned towards him, determined to cheer him up.

In fact, Luke was feeling more relaxed now, pleased that the snow was on the decrease. Their invented story was a welcome break from the seriousness of his own personal past and his spirits rose. 'The authorities are on their heels and they've come perilously close. They have to get out of Santa Cristina before daybreak, or they'll be captured. But, hang on a minute, why am I talking in the plural? Why *them* and not just *him*? Surely he's on his own... isn't he?' He hesitated and she leapt in.

'He met somebody at Santa Cristina. Somebody he was expecting to meet. But who? Was it something to do with his mission, whatever it was that he had to do?' Her voice was insistent.

'His mission...' He thought hard. 'We're talking about the months immediately following the final suppression of the Templars in France. The other countries took their time about imposing any sanctions upon the Templars. Maybe he had no special mission other than that of getting out of the clutches of the king's men. Maybe he was just trying to escape with his life.'

'Not him.' Her voice was scornful. 'This is a man who fought his way through the Holy Land and saw hundreds of his companions die around him. He's after more than just a way of escape. He had to go to Santa Cristina to get something and he ends up with a travelling companion. But who?' She was thinking hard.

His reply came automatically, without his having to think about it.

'His travelling companion is without doubt an intelligent, beautiful, self-opinionated girl who also happens to be blind. Of that I have no doubt.' He edged the car back across into the deep snow as the lights of another vehicle came slowly uphill towards them and then past.

'Did you say beautiful?' Her tone was light, but she didn't fool him.

'Definitely beautiful.' He answered mischievously, feeling more relaxed in her presence now. 'In fact she had long golden hair and the lightest blue eyes. But remember that I did say she was self-opinionated. That's a polite way of saying that she could be a bit difficult when she wanted.' A car came up the road towards them and he concentrated on cutting gently back through the thick snow to let it pass before returning to the cleared track on the other side of the road.

'And what's his relationship with her?' She beat time to the music with her fingers, while he tried to find a way out of the hole he had just dug for himself. It came to him in a flash, just as a sign appeared announcing that Jaca was now only twenty kilometres ahead.

'Who knows? Maybe she's the wife of a friend of his who's been marooned at the abbey since before the winter, and he's helping her get away.'

It sounded a diplomatic way out. She was silent for a while before asking: 'What happened to the friend, then? Where is he? In Spain or what?'

'Goodness knows. Maybe he was killed, or captured, or maybe he's waiting for her somewhere else in Spain. Maybe our man's taking her to him.' He noted with pleasure that both sides of the road were clear down here and the thick white wall of falling snow in front was finally waning. For the first time that evening he was able to flick the headlights onto full beam without dazzling himself. 'Not long to go now.'

'I've got an idea.' Amy was concentrating on the story more than he was. 'Maybe she'll lead him to someone who has secret information for him. But isn't it going to be tricky for one man to lead a blind woman all the way to Compostela?'

'You're telling me!'

He managed to avoid the first punch, but the second caught him on the shoulder.

8

ABBEY OF SANTA CRISTINA, APRIL 1314

There wasn't a sound to be heard in the abbey, although it wouldn't be long before Matins would be called and the sleepy monks would file out of their dormitories into the abbey church. For now, all was still and Luc and Aimée had no trouble getting out of the carriage and making it across the courtyard unobserved. It had started snowing again and their feet left clear tracks in the snow, but Luc could see it wouldn't be long before these were concealed again. Around them, nothing and nobody stirred. Or so it seemed.

There was an unexpected movement from their right. A figure detached itself slowly and deliberately from the shadows and stepped towards them. With a swift movement, Luc caught Aimée and pulled her round behind him while at the same time drawing the dagger he kept concealed in his sleeve. The other man spoke in little more than a whisper.

'I should like to come towards you and shake you by the hand, my son. I would not wish you to misinterpret my movements. That is why I'm announcing my intentions to you in advance. May I approach? I wish you no harm.'

Aimée was amazed to recognise the voice. She tugged at Luc's sleeve. 'Luc, it's the abbot.'

Luc weighed up the abbot's intentions and the potential risk. Then he replied equally quietly.

'Approach me by all means, Father, but keep your hands where I can see them.'

The old man nodded and crossed the few feet that separated them. He extended both hands in greeting and clasped Luc's left hand warmly, fully aware that the right hand held the weapon. Then he stepped back a pace and spoke, mainly to Luc, but deliberately loud enough for all three to hear.

'I believe I know who you are, but your name shall remain unspoken. I've been waiting for you. I waited for your colleague two months ago, but I waited in vain. Tragically, he was killed before I could offer him assistance.' A look of astonishment appeared on Aimée's face and the abbot spoke directly to her before she could utter a word. 'That's the truth, Aimée. I regret the death of your husband more than you can imagine. There have been many occasions when I would have spoken to you about this, except that natural caution always stopped me.'

She was speechless. So he had known who she was all along. She was still trying to take this information in as he returned his attention to Luc.

'Do I assume that you weren't told who your contact at Santa Cristina would be?' He noted Luc's almost imperceptible nod and went on. 'I imagine you were told merely that you would be contacted. No names. That's how we've always done these things. Each link of the chain only needs to know so much. In this way there's more chance of the whole chain remaining intact. We both know about the methods which can be used to obtain information, from even the most courageous of men... or women.' His voice stopped for a moment, his tone bitterly sad. After a brief pause, he turned and raised his eyes towards Luc once more. 'I have information for you that you will need. I can also confirm what you doubtless already know; namely that you're in very grave danger. Indeed, if you stay here, you'll be in custody by midday, I'm sure.'

In answer to the question on all of their lips, he continued. 'I believe I can be of material assistance to you in making good your escape, at least this time. Be mindful, however, that they won't cease until they've caught you or killed you. The frontier means nothing to them. They'll follow you through Spain as they've followed you through France. Be constantly on your guard, and may the protection of the Almighty be with you.'

Luc straightened up and relaxed. With a smooth movement he slid the dagger back into its sheath and breathed deeply. He spoke quietly.

'I was told to come here to Santa Cristina. That is what Bertrand was trying to do in January. They told me I was to receive something here, something of inestimable value, and take it safely along the Pilgrims' Way to Compostela.' His voice betrayed his frustration. 'I wasn't told what it is, nor where I am to deliver it.'

The old man laid his hand on Luc's forearm. 'Links on a chain, Luc. I told you.'

The snow was still falling relentlessly and the silence remained absolute. Now, however, the atmosphere was less menacing and Luc felt the stirrings of hope. A slight movement at his side made him reach out and lay a comforting hand on the girl's shoulder. He cast a look towards the abbot and asked quietly, 'Should we both leave, or is there anything you can do for Aimée?' He felt her body tense, but the expression on the abbot's face offered no hope.

'Alas, you must both leave, my son. The order went out from the archbishop.' His tone when saying the word was acid. 'The archbishop ordered that his men were to search the abbey for a man and a woman. No, I'm afraid that there's no safety for either of you here.'

Aimée reached up and gripped Luc's hand tightly. Her expression was one of relief. Luc realised, if he had needed to, that his destiny and hers were now inextricably linked. He nodded before continuing.

'Time is of the essence. What help can you offer us, Reverend Father? Where is this precious object, and how do we make good our escape?' He eyed the snow falling ever more heavily. He knew there was little chance of escape on horseback. And on foot through the snowdrifts would be next to impossible.

'There's a secret way out. It's a narrow passage that runs right under the abbey. Its existence has been passed on from abbot to abbot since the abbey was founded. I feel confident that its existence is unknown to all here, Luc. When you emerge from the passage, your means of escape should be immediately apparent.'

Aimée's hand gripped Luc tighter, and he leant towards her, his voice still low. 'Aimée, are you sure you're coming with me?' The question was rhetorical, the answer inevitable. 'It'll be dangerous.' Again her response was written on her face.

'And if I stay here, Luc? How would you rate my chances of survival?' Her voice was strong and determined. Deep inside, Aimée knew there was no choice, and she wouldn't have it any other way. Only a few hours earlier, she had been close to taking her own life. Now she had hope and she had Luc. She had known him for years now, since the early days of her marriage to Bertrand, and during the long years of hiding he had been one of the few trusted faces she had seen. He had always occupied a special place in her heart, a very special place. 'I'm coming with you, Luc. If you'll have me.' She pressed herself more tightly against him to reinforce her decision.

'But you have nothing...' His voice tailed off helplessly. 'Clothes, boots, women's things...'

'Oh, ye of little faith.' She replied in a lighter tone. 'What do you think's in here?' She held up her shoulder bag. 'With all these soldiers about, it seemed prudent to plan for immediate departure.'

In spite of the gravity of the situation Luc was able to smile. 'So be it.' He returned his attention to the abbot.

'I can't thank you enough, Father. We owe our lives to you, of that there is no doubt.'

Before responding, the abbot reached up to his throat. He released the clasp that held his heavy cloak fastened and slipped it off his shoulders. He held it out to Luc. 'Could I ask one thing of you? Could I persuade you to exchange cloaks with me? This one I wear belonged to the Master of the Temple of Ponferrada, far away on the road to Compostela. Would you do me the favour of wearing it for the rest of your journey, please? I promised him I would return it to him. It's a good cloak, if not brand new, and from what I can see of the one you're wearing I would say that this will be warmer and stronger. Would you promise me you'll do that as a favour?'

Luc took the heavy leather cloak from him, knowing full well that it was many times better than his old one. He felt touched at both his generosity and his tactful approach. He had little doubt in his mind that, if he ever reached Ponferrada, and if the Templar Order were still present there, the Master of the castle would have never seen it before. He shrugged off his own cloak and held it out to the old man, the cold air biting into his unprotected shoulders. He lost no time in pulling on the leather one, relishing the warmth it provided.

Seemingly impervious to the freezing temperature, the abbot made no move to put on Luc's cloak. Instead, he continued more urgently.

'Now listen carefully, Luc. What I tell you is of the utmost importance. Concentrate hard and commit everything I say to your memory.'

Luc bent forward.

'The first thing you must know is that the object that cannot be named will be revealed to you further along your journey. I can't tell you anything about it.'

'You can't?' Luc could hardly believe his ears. 'But I was told to come here to collect it.'

A more authoritative note entered the old abbot's voice. 'Luc, do you remember what I told you about security and links on a chain?' Luc nodded blankly, feeling like a schoolboy in front of the headmaster. 'The less information we all carry, the better and the safer for everybody. Just believe me when I say you'll learn about it at the right time.'

Luc dropped his head obediently and gave no response.

'Your orders are to follow the directions I am going to give you and take it to safety in Portugal.'

'Portugal?' Luc had only the vaguest notion as to where this might be.

'As soon as you can, rejoin the pilgrimage route to Santiago de Compostela. Many, many pilgrims follow the way of Saint James every year. There should be safety in numbers for you and, of course, Aimée. Compostela is many weeks away from here in north-west Spain. When you reach that most wonderful of cities, you turn south. Portugal extends from there to the Mediterranean Sea. Now, listen carefully while I tell exactly how you should be able to get away from the abbey without being seen.'

9

'God be with you both.' The abbot's hand was raised in blessing and they both crossed themselves. 'May Our Lord Jesus Christ be with you always.' He caught Luc's eye and spoke with feeling. 'May you succeed, Luc. You carry a heavy burden of responsibility. Carry it well.' Then he stepped back as Luc manhandled the heavy stone-clad door back into place, leaving him and Aimée alone in the damp, dark tunnel. Luc took her hand and gave it an encouraging squeeze.

She responded by reaching up and kissing him on the cheek. 'Just tell me there are no spiders down here.'

He raised the burning torch and sliced a swathe through a curtain of cobwebs before replying with as much sincerity as he could muster.

'Spiders? No, too cold for them, I expect. None around here.'

She clutched his arm and whispered, 'Liar.'

'But make sure you keep your hood up and your head down so you don't bang your head.' A spider the size of a small bird materialised in front of him as he spoke and he banished it with a sweep of the flaming torch. Conscious that the torch would not burn for long, he crouched down to protect his head and started to creep along the passage, the torch held as high as possible, silently counting his steps so as to have an idea of distance. The tunnel sloped gently downwards and after almost a hundred steps he noticed water running out of a rounded hole set in the side wall and into a channel down the middle. He looked across at Aimée.

'Water coming out here. Could it be from the kitchen or the latrines?'

She paused for breath and gently straightened up until she was able to stand fully upright. He, on the other hand, still had to crouch. She, too, had been counting. 'I've taken a hundred and twenty fairly hesitant steps, say a foot or so each, so yes, I suppose it could be from the kitchen. It's not the latrines. The smell of them's unmistakable. If it's the kitchen, then we've passed right underneath the abbey church and are just about at the outer wall of the hospice.' She sounded tense but in control, and he was relieved at how well she was coping.

'All right, then. Let's keep going. Try to keep your feet out of the channel down the middle of the tunnel where the water's running.'

They moved off down the passage into the current of air, which got steadily stronger and colder. Luc's counting had reached two hundred and fifty when the narrow tunnel suddenly finished and they had to scramble with great difficulty down a slippery, part-frozen waterfall into a natural cave. Here, at least, it was possible to stand normally and he stretched his back gratefully.

'What's this? A cave, a bigger bit of tunnel or a building?' Aimée could tell without seeing that the tunnel had finished. She cast about keenly, using her senses to work out where they might be. 'The way out is to the left of us. I'm sure of it.' She held out a pointing finger and, unhesitatingly, he led her in that direction. After a few twists and turns the tunnel divided but, again, she knew without question which way to go. The floor of the cave sloped more steeply and she clung to him with both hands as he picked his way down. Then a flurry of snow carried by the swirling wind told them both that they had reached the outside. The abbot had told them that they were supposed to travel the next part of their journey by sledge and Aimée was deeply suspicious.

'The abbot wants us to use a sledge?' There was incredulity and horror in her voice. 'Where's it supposed to be, this... thing?' Her tone made quite clear what she thought of the idea.

'He said it's in the coal store. Apparently there's a shed round here some-where for storing coal. They bring the coal up here in the summer on a big flat sledge, which is dragged by a team of horses. The good news is that there is a fairly well-marked track for us to follow, always assuming that we can find the shed and the sledge in the first place.' At that moment the torch flickered weakly and expired, leaving them in a featureless world of dark-ness, broken only by flurries of snow borne down on them by the gusty wind. He could see nothing, but to her it didn't matter.

'Did you say coal?' She tugged at his sleeve and he bent towards her to hear better above the constant battering of the wind. 'I think I can smell coal over here. I might be wrong but I'm sure I... yes, there it is again. There's defi-nitely coal over this way.' With that, she took his hand and led him out of the cave mouth and down through the snow. In places it was waist deep and the treacherous ice underneath made it almost impossible to move. He hoped fervently that she had got it right or their mission, not to mention their lives, would stall right here.

'Can you see the coal shed?' She was shouting to make herself heard. 'It's definitely here somewhere close by.'

As she spoke he imagined more than saw a solid square building to one side of them and pulled her to it. They slumped against the stone wall, temporarily sheltered from the wind, and rested. He pulled her head towards him and shouted joyfully in her ear: 'You're a wonder. I'd never have found this place without you.'

The door was mercifully unlocked and inside there was a strong smell of coal, although little of it appeared to be left after the long winter months, and, along with it, he found the promised sledge. Now that his eyes were no longer dazzled by the flaming torch he was beginning to see a bit more clearly. The carpet of snow outside the door was distinctly lighter than the shadows of the coal store so he heaved the heavy wooden sledge out of the doors and was able to take a clearer look at it.

'What's it like?' Her voice was deeply suspicious. He looked across at her and saw that she was shivering. There was no time to lose. He turned back to the sledge and worked out that there were wooden posts, for all the world like oars, protruding from the rear. He lifted the heavy construction onto its side and saw that these would act as brakes and even a primitive form of steering if pressure was applied to them by the people on the sledge. He was very dubious about their efficiency and the ability of one man to make them work properly, but the die was now cast. Straight in front of them was a faint V shape in the snowy slope, which he assumed to be the track to follow. He took a deep breath.

'Here, climb on and hang onto this for dear life. I can see what looks like the track dead ahead and I think I've worked out how to steer.' He helped her into the bottom of the sledge, near the front, wedging her between its raised sides. He crammed his bag in alongside her, murmured a heartfelt prayer and then pushed off. The hill sloped quite sharply and the sledge started to run so quickly that he almost missed his footing while scrambling on.

'Here we go,' he shouted as he reached for the wooden brakes. At first he only succeeded in making the sledge weave dangerously, but quite quickly he got the idea and was gratified to feel them slow as the brakes dug in. The track twisted and turned from side to side as it dropped down the hillside and somehow he managed to keep them on course. The further down the hillside they travelled, the better the visibility became as the wind dropped and the snowfall moderated. Still they followed the track as they came down into the first trees. The snow-covered track was simpler to see and follow through the dark backdrop of trees and his spirits rose. He shouted encouragement to the little figure huddled at the front, but was unable to hear if she responded.

In fact, as she crouched down low, hanging on for dear life, Aimée was lost in her thoughts. All her married life she had had eyes for no other man than Bertrand and she had loved him dearly. She had so badly wanted to bear him children, but fate had decreed otherwise. She had met many of his fellow Templar knights, but none had appealed to her as much as this big, generous, brave man with her now. She remembered tales told by Bertrand of their exploits in battle together, of feats of bravery about which he never boasted. She could remember Luc's appearance with complete clarity, his broad shoulders, his unruly mop of hair and his deep green eyes that could be warm and friendly with her, but then hard and ruthless in the face of danger. Now, Bertrand was gone and she found herself tied to Luc as closely

– well, she admitted to herself, almost as closely – as she had been tied to Bertrand. Her life and Luc's, she now realised, were inextricably bound together. Only death would part them, or, at least, that was the way she felt. As the sledge bumped and swayed down the hill, she murmured prayers for the soul of her dead husband, for herself and now also for this wonderful man who had come to save her.

They slipped on down the hill, in and out of the trees, crossing open fields, before plunging back into the dark of the forest again. Finally, unspectacularly, their ride came to an end as the track, after crossing a frozen stream in a gully, for the first time started to go uphill and they slid to a gentle stop.

The first impression was one of relief that they had somehow managed to do it. The second was one of silence down here where the wind had disappeared so completely that it required a conscious effort to remember that it was blowing ferociously just a short distance above them. The third was a strong smell of woodsmoke.

'Can you smell it?' His voice sounded disbelieving.

Aimée was gradually uncurling herself, equally relieved and not a little surprised to have got off the mountain in one piece. She got to her feet and Luc steadied her with his hand. He thought for a moment and then slid the sledge to the side of the track and over the edge into the dark forest below. Hopefully, this would conceal their escape at least for a while.

'But does the smoke come from a friendly fire?' He thought aloud. As he did so, he looked down at her pale face reflecting against the snow. Although he was still sweating from his exertions, she was shivering, so he clutched her to him, wrapping her into his arms. He spared a grateful thought for the abbot, who had insisted upon his taking the heavy leather cloak. Aimée snuggled against him but still shivered uncontrollably, and Luc realised they had to find warmth and shelter very quickly now. Under these circumstances it was really fairly academic whether the fire they could smell had been lit by friends or enemies. If they were friends they would survive. If they were enemies they would die. But they would just as surely die here if they didn't get shelter very soon.

'Let's go and find out.' He tried to sound as cheery as he could and shouldered his bag. She took his arm and they walked up over the side of the gully, the snow no more than ankle deep on the track. Rounding a corner, they were greeted by a wonderful sight.

'God be praised.' He hugged her to him. 'There's a whole village here with an inn. Come on, there really is an inn.' He started off down the road at a jog and she hurried along with him, part carried by him as his speed increased. It was too dark to see the name of the inn, but the smell of stale wine was clear enough proof of its existence. He pushed the front door, which, unsurprisingly at that time of night, was bolted, so he knocked hard on the carved wood until a light showed under the door and a voice shouted something in a language he had never heard before. He shouted back in French, hoping that the innkeeper's multilingual clientele would have stirred some linguistic talent in him.

'We're pilgrims from Compostela on our way back to Toulouse. Can we stay here for the night? We'll never get over the pass at this time of night.'

There was a silence when he feared they would be turned away, and then a jingling of keys and the door was thrown open by a sleepy-looking man with bushy whiskers, a bald head and the sort of beer gut that only dedicated publicans can achieve.

'What in the name of God are you doing on the road at this time of night, at this time of year, and in this weather?' His French was good even though his tone quite clearly indicated his conviction that they were totally mad.

'We've been hiding in a cave until now so as to escape a bunch of bandits.' The explanation came fairly easily to Luc's lips, but he didn't reckon on the amount of interest the innkeeper would show.

'Bandits? Did you say bandits? Describe them to me.' The man sounded aggressive, clearly doubting Luc's story. 'We haven't had bandits around here for months.'

Luc tried desperately to think of the description of a few shady customers he had seen in the past, but the strain on his nerves and body of the last few days had taken its toll and his mind went totally blank.

'Um, they were dangerous-looking men. Sinister and dangerous...' He knew it sounded weak but he was past caring. All he wanted now was a bed for the night.

'Dangerous-looking, you say? That all?' The innkeeper's tone was even nastier. 'We don't like liars round here, do we, Ignacio?' From the shadows behind him a giant of a man emerged, a head taller than Luc with the shoulders of an ox. He, too, had obviously just been roused from sleep and he was clearly not in a good mood. His lips bared and a growl escaped from them. Wearily Luc began to realise that he might not after all get shelter from the cold here. Where else could they go? His thoughts were interrupted by the sound of Aimée's voice.

'Five, no, four men. One a Moor with a curved dagger, one with a patch over his eye, and the leader...' Aimée's voice faltered for a moment. 'The leader had a white horse and wore a leather cloak. Down the side of his face was a long white scar and he carried a studded whip looped onto his wrist. His eyes were black and cruel; you can't imagine how cruel until you've looked into them...' Her voice choked off into a sob.

The effect upon all three men was electric. The innkeeper's aggressive expression was wiped from his face, to be replaced by a pasty look of fear. Behind him the giant edged back towards the shadows, his little eyes wide open and afraid. As for Luc, he was marvelling once again at her presence of mind and courage. The innkeeper stepped back, still with an expression of awe on his face, and beckoned them in. No sooner had they crossed the threshold than he slammed the door shut behind them, bolted it and scuttled off to the bar, to return with a bottle of aguardiente and a handful of clay mugs.

With a shaking hand he filled the mugs and pushed them across the table. Before they had even touched theirs he had upended his and refilled it. Luc handed one to Aimée and they both drank gratefully. The rough spirit burnt as it went down, but the warming glow it spread through them was more than welcome. They both sat down on a long wooden bench, their backs to the smoking embers of the fire. The innkeeper muttered something and the giant obediently set about rekindling it. Within seconds, flames were already licking at the sticks he threw on, the heat along with the drink gradually starting to return them to normal. When the innkeeper began speaking, both of them listened intently.

'The Whip. Oh, dear God, the Whip's back.' His voice was little more than a whisper. 'We thought, we dared to hope that he'd gone forever. Every winter he disappears and every spring he returns. Every winter we live in hope, which is then dashed as soon as the snows begin to melt. God have pity on us.' He snuffled to himself and carried on with what was presumably intended as an apology. 'We get lots of pilgrims who make up lurid stories so as to get sympathy. "Oh, sir, I've lost everything to the bandits. Please give me board and lodging for nothing tonight. It's your Christian duty." Christian duty my foot. I kick them out as soon as they start to try it on. I thought you were like them.' His tone was conciliatory, if not totally apologetic, but nothing could hide the fear in his eyes.

'Have you seen this Whip, as you call him, yourself?' Luc's interest was aroused. 'How is it you know what he looks like?'

This time the fear became even more visible as the publican swallowed hard before speaking. 'Oh yes.' His voice was a croak and he had to cough to clear his throat before continuing. 'We've all seen him. He comes here with his men whenever he's tired of the caves and forests. If I'm lucky he pays for what he eats and drinks.' Absently, he reached for a loaf and half a cheese, which he set before them. As the innkeeper resumed his tale, Luc tore the bread into pieces, slipped out his knife and sliced the cheese. He realised he was starving. 'If I'm unlucky he doesn't pay and if I'm really unlucky he smashes the place up.'

'And his luck?' Luc pressed a piece of bread and cheese into Aimée's hand and raised it gently to her lips. She began to nibble although her attention was fully taken by the innkeeper's tale. Luc wondered what memories were flashing behind her sightless eyes, and a rising wave of anger spread over him. 'When does his luck run out, innkeeper? Is nobody here capable of putting an end to him and his friends? What about the army?'

The fat man laughed scornfully. 'The army? Whose army would that be, sir? The French have soldiers to spare when they aren't using them to kill their own people, but they don't come over this side of the border. As for the King of Aragon, he has his work cut out keeping the Moors out of Saragossa and nobody to spare to help us. No, sir, we're at the mercy of any brigand who chooses to come up here.' He refilled their glasses as well as his own and sipped the liquor sourly. The giant threw another armful of wood onto the fire and withdrew.

'But surely there are enough people here to be able to see off a little gang of four or five men?' Luc remembered battles in the Holy Land when they had been outmanned by twenty or thirty of the enemy to every Templar knight.

'But not just ordinary men. Vicious killers and no mistake. No, sir, it would take a massive force to take them.'

'Or just a few with the stomach for a fight.' Luc's eyes couldn't help alighting on the innkeeper's belly. 'You can't turn the other cheek all your life.' For a moment he longed to set a trap and stamp out once and for all the scum who had committed so many atrocities, most particularly to Aimée and Bertrand. He tightened his grip around her shoulders and dragged himself back to reality. They had no time for any such heroics, satisfying as they might be. They had to put as much distance between themselves and the pursuing soldiers as possible before the fresh snow above them melted and the road reopened. But first they both needed a good rest. As soon as he had swallowed enough bread and cheese to take the edge off his hunger, he looked across at the innkeeper.

'It's late. It's best we get some sleep.' The fat man gave no sign of moving, but waved a finger vaguely towards the back of the building and murmured into his drink.

'Down there. The end door. Latrines on the other side of the corridor. Take a candle but for the love of God don't set the place on fire.'

They pulled themselves to their feet and followed his directions. The end room was small and airless, but reasonably warm. Luc dropped his bag behind the door and helped Aimée off with her cloak, noticing to his relief that her hands were warm once more. He took the abbot's thick leather cloak and spread it out on top of the straw-filled mattress. It was only then that he realised that there was only one bed there for the two of them. In spite of his fatigue, a feeling of guilty embarrassment came over him. He cleared his throat awkwardly.

'There's only one bed, Aimée. We can't... we shouldn't... surely...'

Ever practical, she interrupted him. 'I couldn't care whether I have to share with you, the abbot or a dozen strangers. I just want to be warm and to sleep. Go to the latrine if you must and then lie down and enjoy the rest you've most certainly earned.'

Put like that he had little choice in the matter so, after relieving himself, he returned to the room, bolted the door securely, removed his boots and stretched out gratefully on the mattress as far as possible from the little figure under the blankets. He blew out the candle, snuffing it completely with dampened fingers, mindful of the innkeeper's words and the fact that the mattress was filled with straw. He looked across in the pitch dark and whispered, 'Good night.'

There was no reply. She must have gone out like a light.

10

JACA, SPANISH PYRENEES, APRIL 2016

The hotel they found in Jaca turned out to be splendid. Luke and Amy were greeted warmly by a lady who was probably the owner and were accompanied to what looked like a newly refurbished suite of two bedrooms, each with immaculate marble-clad bathrooms. There was a shared dayroom, looking out onto a snowy terrace. On top of this, the price was little more than the cost of a single room in Paris.

As he had done at each hotel since setting off from England, he led Amy into her room and gave her a brief tour, talking her through the facilities, particularly the bathroom. The sensation of disquiet at being with her in these intimate surroundings had diminished, but not disappeared, over the days they had been travelling together. He took a look at his watch.

'Great. It's almost eight, so we should get something to eat before too long.'

'Give me ten minutes to change. I feel decidedly crumpled.'

He looked at her surreptitiously and failed to see even the slightest hint of crumpling, but decided to let her be the judge of that. 'Okay. I'll wait for you in the bar downstairs if you feel happy about meeting me there. Just down one flight of steps and the first door on the left before you reach the reception desk. I could—'

'Murder a beer.' She laughed. 'Go and have your beer and I'll be down shortly.'

He threw his bag onto his bed in the next room, reminded her that the key to the apartment was in the door and made his way downstairs. The hotel had obviously had a serious makeover in the last few months and the bar downstairs was a comfortable cocktail bar. He settled down in a corner seat and ordered a large beer. The barman took him at his word and brought a hefty half-litre mug full of light yellow beer, tears of condensation running down the outside.

He took a long draught of beer and stretched his legs. It had been a long day. He thought back to the snowy wilderness they had crossed. With the Range Rover they at least had been able to get over the pass in comfort. It was sobering to think that millions upon millions of pilgrims had passed that very same way on foot over the last thousand years. The numbers involved were truly awesome. A multitude of people, rich and poor, all heading for Compostela and so many of them seeking the one single most important prize, the remission of sins. As he drained the glass, he reflected that pilgrims had probably been draining glasses in this very same spot for centuries.

'Una mas.' He caught the barman's eye and watched as another glass was poured and brought over. He sipped it appreciatively and looked around the bar. Most of the other clients appeared to be locals, men and women, with a thin scattering of foreign visitors. His thoughts returned, as they did so often, to Amy. Of course it was inevitable that two people, thrown together in close proximity for more than a fortnight, would either grow closer together or begin to get on each other's nerves. There was no doubt that he was drawing closer and closer to her and his sense of impropriety resurfaced. He had been employed to act as her guide, not to take advantage of her vulnerability.

'Are you still on the first one?'

He looked up with a start and saw Amy's face smiling down at him, the proprietor at her shoulder. Luke reached up and took her hand, guiding her onto the bench seat beside him.

The waiter came over and asked what she wanted. 'A glass of Cava, please.' Luke was about to translate when the barman nodded and wandered off. 'So how many beers have you had?'

'I must confess I've already had one beer, but I reckon that drive merits a bit of relaxation. By the way, there's a little bowl of peanuts right in front of your left hand.' He watched her reach out and take a few. He followed suit, then washed them down with some more of the beer.

At that moment the glass of sparkling wine appeared and he pushed it across the table until it rested gently against her hand. She took a sip and licked her lips appreciatively. He did his best not to concentrate on her lips. He took a mouthful of beer and let his eyes rest on her for a moment. The linen shirt looked expensive and almost certainly was. Her hair was newly combed and pinned up rather than tied back, which gave her an air of added sophistication. Her face bore no trace of make-up, but didn't need it. The shirt was just tight enough across her body to reveal the swell of her breasts and he looked away hastily.

'So who or what was he looking for at Santa Cristina? It can't have been anything too heavy as he would have had to carry it. So no cartloads of treasure or anything like that.'

Luke jumped guiltily at the sound of her voice and returned his attention to their story. For a moment he felt like reminding her that this was after all just their invention. There was no logical reason why there should be an explanation. But the idea passed as he saw the concentration on her face. Of course this was heightening the experience for her. Unable to see the mountains, abbeys, villages and countryside, she needed some extra stimulus. He tried to think it through, just as if they were dealing with a real event. *Why not?* he thought to himself. *Who's to say it isn't?*

He tried a few suggestions.

'So not treasure, then?'

He watched her face. An expression of annoyance crossed it and she snorted. He tried again.

'Revenge?'

There was a pause as she thought about it. 'Not this man. Anyway, if it's revenge he's seeking, then surely he'd do better to stay in France. Don't forget, most of the Spanish and Portuguese didn't believe for one moment all the lies that the King of France was putting about. The baddies are back in France, not over here. No, not revenge.'

'Friendship? Loyalty? Love?'

'All of those, but something more. He had a very special mission to accomplish, I'm sure of that.' Her brows were knitted in concentration. 'I know. Maybe the girl he's travelling with can help him. After all, why take her with him otherwise? She would only slow him up.'

'Maybe he liked her. Maybe more.' His old familiar anxiety as to where the conversation might be leading returned, but she went on in a very matter-of-fact way.

'Oh, I'm sure he did like her, maybe even love her, but as a Templar he would have taken an oath of celibacy. So they weren't lovers for sure.' There was an awkward silence, which she finally broke. 'Just because he's a man and she's a woman doesn't automatically mean there's a physical bond between them. They're probably just friends.' The tone of her voice had changed now and both of them heard it. She stopped, unwilling to go any further with the conversation, and Luke decided it would be a very good idea to change the subject.

'I suggest we head for a restaurant. I could eat a horse.' He drained the last of the beer and stood up, gesturing to the waiter that they wanted to pay.

* * *

Luke was awakened by urgent knocking at his bedroom door. He pulled himself up onto one elbow as the handle turned and Amy came rushing in. She was wearing a pair of stripy men's pyjamas, and her hair hung tousled on her shoulders. Her expression was one of considerable excitement.

'Where's the fire?' He watched with amusement as she made straight for the window and felt for the cord to open the roller blind. She pulled it as hard as she could and light flooded into the room. He was still squinting in the sudden brightness when she threw the window open and leant out perilously.

'Hey, no suicide attempts before breakfast.'

He would have run to grab her, but for the sudden realisation that he was naked beneath the blankets. This fact unsettled him more than her apparently lemming-like behaviour. Then she was running back towards him, one arm held out. She bumped into the side of the bed and fell onto him, the outstretched arm catching him across his bare chest. He gave a very un-macho squeal as he realised the outstretched arm was covered in thick, fluffy and extremely cold snowflakes. She gave a guffaw of laughter and rolled off him, a broad smile on her face.

'Not bad for a blind girl who couldn't get her window to open, eh?' She was definitely very proud of herself. 'Go on, then, ask me how I knew it was snowing.' She was kneeling on the floor with her elbows on the bed beside him. 'Go on, ask.'

'How did you know it was snowing, Amy?' He affected an obedient tone.

'I heard it.' She really was very pleased with herself. 'Or rather I didn't hear it. I mean that I didn't hear any of the normal morning noises you'd expect in a town this size. They were strangely muffled and the only thing that could have muffled them at this time of the morning was a thick snow-fall. And it must be really thick. I haven't heard a single car, not even a snow-plough. For a Monday morning that's really unusual, isn't it?' She looked up, disconcertingly straight into his eyes. He felt the same sense of unease that he always felt when the glacier eyes looked through him.

'Yes, pretty unusual. Especially for a place like this that must get loads of snow each year. Tell you what, I'll put the television on. That might tell us a bit more.' He looked around for the remote control and, to his discomfort, discovered it on the floor halfway between the bed and the TV. Gingerly, shyly, he slipped out of the other side of the bed and retrieved it, acutely aware of his nakedness. A quick glance at her face revealed nothing as he slipped back under the protection of the sheets. Not, that was, until she spoke.

'Do you always sleep with no clothes on?'

He dropped the remote control onto the bedcover and very nearly knocked it back onto the floor again. He felt himself blush bright red.

'Um yes, at least, sometimes.' He cleared his throat and tried to affect a tone of normality. 'How... why do you ask?' His voice tailed off and the smile on her face broadened.

'Do you really want to know?' Her voice was full of pure mischief. She was enjoying herself now.

'Um, I'm not sure I should, but yes, how did you know?' He waited anxiously.

'I didn't.' She giggled like a little girl. Her air of mischief increased even more. 'Call it a wild guess, or divine inspiration.'

'At least I see you have better taste in sleeping attire than I have.' He tried to get the conversation back into less troubled waters. Once again there was the schoolgirl giggle.

'This isn't sleeping attire. I don't wear these in bed. These are my clothes for wandering into strange men's bedrooms.'

This time he was determined not to let her have the satisfaction of embarrassing him again. 'Did you say strange? Am I that abnormal?'

'If you're abnormal, who wants normality?'

The expression on her face threw him once more into confusion. He did his best to return to practical matters. 'If it's snowing like there's no tomorrow, what are we going to do? The Range Rover should get through just about anything, but I must admit I'm not that keen on a day of inching my way through thick snow, waiting for some moron to come sliding into the front of us.'

'Besides which,' Amy answered immediately, 'I imagine the snowploughs will concentrate on the main road. They won't get round to the minor roads for a good while.'

He was interested. 'What's the significance of the minor roads? Isn't there just one road out of the mountains from here?' He hadn't looked at the map for a while, but he seemed to remember just the one red road leading down from Jaca.

'Ah, but that's the obvious way. The way they would be expecting him to take. I think his big secret's to be found at the Monastery of San Juan de la Peña.' Once again the note of satisfaction in her voice. She had obviously had their invented story on her mind. He concentrated hard in his turn.

'The Monastery of San Juan would be a hard day's march off the beaten track. Why should the big secret be up there? And what is this secret anyway?'

She settled herself on the floor by the side of the bed, her head on her hands as she started to feel her way through her explanation.

'I couldn't sleep last night, at least it took me a fair while before I finally dropped off. I spent ages thinking about our man, and our woman for that matter, and just what their mission might be. Where are we?' Pretty obviously she wasn't asking about the Hostal Somport in Jaca. 'We're in the spring of the year 1314, aren't we?' She didn't wait for his reply. 'The secret has to be somehow linked to the Templars.' Her voice halted as she thought hard. He did his best to do the same.

'Remember the Templars were supposed to have had close links with the Arabs. Arab culture was streets ahead of Western culture in those days, particularly as far as mathematics and the sciences generally were concerned. Maybe the big secret was the proof that the earth really goes round the sun, two centuries before Galileo, or that the earth wasn't flat after all.' He looked down at her.

'What about the cathedrals?' She nodded slowly as she followed his line of thought. 'It was around then that the broken-arch Gothic style hit Europe. Buildings suddenly started to be taller and taller. To most people it was a mystery the masons kept very close to their chests. There are those who would have the Templars as the source of the information. Yes, that might well be it.' Her voice was more excited. 'Maybe they were going to pick up a document of some kind. A theorem or a calculation. You could be right.'

'Mind you—' he was teasing her now '—it might have been an object. Don't forget that the Middle Ages were the time of holy relics. Bits of saintly bodies were being carted all round Europe. How about a piece of the True Cross, straw from the stable in Bethlehem or a thorn from the crown of thorns?'

She turned her face towards him, her expression puzzled. 'You're right; it could have been anything like that. Wasn't there a nun who bit off the finger of a mummified saint so she could take it back to her abbey? They were deeply into those things then. I wonder...'

He lay back and wondered in his turn, partly about their medieval man and his mission, but more particularly about his own situation. He could smell the scent of her beside him and most probably she could smell him. She was beautiful and very, very desirable. In spite of all his good intentions, he felt a wave of emotion rising up in him. And there was no getting away from the fact that it felt very, very good. She was so close he could have reached out and taken her in his arms. She was silent at his side, happy and content and if she had any worries about being in the same bedroom as a naked man, she was keeping them well hidden. For his part, he wondered what Father Tim would make of this scene. Unsurprisingly, her mind was running along similar tracks.

'I wonder what my guardians would think if they saw us now. It was bad enough getting them to agree to my coming on this trip with you. What on earth was I doing, travelling halfway round Europe with a strange man?' She raised her head. 'I suspect neither of them has ever been any further than Eastbourne. Shock, horror, shame. I was bringing the family name into disrepute, consorting with this ruffian.'

'It's the Irish blood on my mother's side.' He was grinning.

'And now, here I am in his bedroom…'

'I think I might be out of a job.' His voice sounded strained to both of them.

She laughed, but it rang hollow. For an instant, Luke found himself imagining how he would feel if she were suddenly removed from his life. He swallowed hard. There was no doubt he would miss her terribly, even after less than a month together.

He watched her face. It remained expressionless. He found himself wondering if she was aware of his inner turmoil. Maybe this might be the right time to come clean about his background, his doubts and his fears. He cleared his throat, searching for words, but she beat him to it.

'Well, if we're not going anywhere today, I'm off to wash my hair. In fact I might even go out and get it done properly. I have to look my best for this evening after all.' She jumped to her feet and he found himself asking why.

'The date, Dumbo – 25 April. Mean anything to you, does it? It does to Father Tim and he told me.' She stopped at the door and grinned back at him as he realised that it was his birthday. 'I think a night out on the town might well be in order, don't you?'

11

SPANISH PYRENEES, APRIL 1314

Luc yawned and stretched. It was a wonderful feeling to be comfortable and warm, away from the frozen misery of the midnight sledge ride. He lay back on the mattress and savoured the moment. After everything he had been through in the last weeks, without counting the stress of the previous seven years, it was a welcome luxury to be able to relax snug and as safe as could be hoped for. He reached up to move the blankets from his chest and throat and encountered another arm. Still half-asleep, he vaguely registered the fact that another body was draped against, no, clinging to his. He breathed in deeply and the scent of her filled his nostrils. In the wink of an eye he was wide awake.

She was deeply asleep, pressed tight up against him, her arm wrapped over his chest. He felt her warmth through the clothes they were wearing and he felt the softness of her body against his. He froze. The overriding thought going through his head was that, all through the sham trial of the Templars, the Inquisitors had sought to prove that the Order had degenerated into licentiousness, vice and unnatural practices. He had been proud in the knowledge that he, like the vast majority of his fellows, had no such sins on his conscience. And yet here he was in bed with a woman. True to his beliefs and his vows, he had never been in a position of such intimacy with any person since his childhood days with his mother. He would have leapt from the bed to a confessional except for the fact that Aimée was sleeping so deeply.

Opening his eyes, he could just make out her body against him in what little light crept in through the high window. Her hair lay across his chest and her face was buried into his shoulder. She was breathing slowly and deeply and he felt every breath as if it were his own. His heart pounded apprehensively but, underneath his immediate feeling of guilt, there was no doubt that it was a cosy, reassuring position in which to find himself.

As she drew each breath he felt her chest swell and the sensation stirred him. Deep Christian faith, a total commitment to his vows and, if the truth be told, a blinding ignorance of the other sex had kept him firmly celibate like the overwhelming majority of the tens of thousands of monks and clerics living out their lives in the monasteries and abbeys of France. He could truly say that he had felt none of the pangs and temptations that had tarnished and ultimately ruined the careers of a number of his contemporaries.

And now this.

He lay still, lest his agitation should wake her. An illogical fear rose in his chest at what she might think of him if she awoke with them in this position, particularly if she became aware of his unaccustomed state of physical stimulation. Wild ideas flashed through his head, visions of purgatory, devils with vicious forks stoking the raging flames with the obscene, naked corpses of sinners. A series of gargoyles, hideous faces chewing screaming human figures, leapt into his head and he shivered.

As close to panic as he had ever been in his life, he started a gradual and agonising slow-motion manoeuvre to extricate himself without waking her. It took many a long minute as he inched away from her and towards the wall until he finally lost the last contact with her warmth. At that point he stopped and lay limply at her side, his mind whirling as his body relaxed. Had he done anything wrong? Was he doing anything wrong? Did he wish to do anything wrong? The questions did not easily provide answers to one who had so long lived a monastic life. Was this sin? Was he damned?

'A penny for your thoughts.' He jumped so sharply that his elbow hit the wall behind him and caused him to grunt with pain. Luckily, this very same pain saved him as she became immediately solicitous and he was able to marshal his thoughts.

'That's all right. I must have been sleeping very lightly. I was just startled to hear your voice.' His own voice sounded very strange to his ears and he wondered what she would make of it. She made no reaction so he let his mind wander. 'How did you know I was awake?' He was interested to know.

'I just did.' She wasn't trying to be unhelpful. She was as unsure about the reason herself. 'Maybe your breathing or just your position. You didn't feel relaxed.'

Mentally he agreed with her quite fervently. Relaxed was something he had definitely not been. He was however now beginning to feel a bit calmer and he risked an attempt at normal conversation.

'Did you sleep well?' As an opener it was safe, if uninspired. Her reply on the other hand was less safe. She stretched and rolled over towards him until her head was resting on his shoulder, her arm once more on his chest.

'I slept like an angel. I was warm, I was comfortable and I was protected. You can't imagine how reassuring it is for me to find myself cared for and looked after.' Her voice was soft and low and he could hear a break in it that struck him deep inside. While the intellectual, rational and religious part of his brain was telling him that what was happening was wrong and that he should get as far away from her as possible, his emotional side made him reach out and cradle her head tenderly. She purred as she continued to murmur quietly into his shoulder.

'I knew, I just knew. All the time this winter while I shivered in that cold damp abbey I just knew that it couldn't end like that. It would have been too stupid, so senseless somehow. After all we went through to get up to the mountains through the king's guards and the network of spying clerics, it couldn't just finish with a whimper. I wasn't going to spend the rest of my life there. I knew you would come.'

'You knew somebody would come,' he suggested mildly.

'It had to be you. In my dreams it was always you. I knew it would be you.' Her voice was warm. 'Who else could possibly take the place of Bertrand?' The way she said it and the position from which she said it made it hard for him to believe that she was just talking about the mission. 'It had to be one of the best. There was no way they could possibly send anyone less able than Bertrand. And you were the only one who was his equal.'

'Maybe the only one left in liberty,' he added sombrely as he ripped off the blanket that covered him and rolled away from her warmth. He pulled himself to his feet and looked back down at her.

'I'll go and get some hot water for you. Wait till I come back and I'll tell you all the gory details of the latrines.'

'I'll be here.' Aimée lay back and breathed out as she heard the door open and then close behind him. Her pulse was beating fast, her palms were damp, and the reason, she knew, was Luc. Wrapping herself tightly against his body had been comforting, had been reassuring but also, she finally admitted it to herself, it had been stimulating. For the first time in three long, hard months, she had felt like a woman again and a woman alongside the man she loved. No sooner did she admit the depth of her feelings for him than she mentally scolded herself. Of course she couldn't be in love with him, it was surely just the fact that he had come to rescue her from her grim existence and bring her hope. Hope, she told herself firmly, wasn't love. But that didn't slow her racing heart.

As Luc walked down the dark corridor, as always, his right hand was on the handle of the dagger. Years of living on the run had instilled certain habits so firmly that they had become second nature. This time there was no need. The only living being that he encountered was a little child with a thick mane of dark hair who darted past him, no doubt in search of something to eat. He followed the light footsteps.

In the main room a new fire crackled and spat while a group of bleary-eyed travellers clustered around it gratefully. He noticed the bewhiskered face of the publican sleeping peacefully in exactly the same place as he had last seen him. The bottle at his elbow was now empty.

'Good morning, pilgrim.' The words were French and the voice belonged to a pretty girl behind the bar, her jet-black hair tied in a long ponytail. She wore a lacy top that revealed a substantial amount of her substantial figure and her welcoming smile promised breakfast, if not more.

'Good morning.' He was pleased to be able to speak in French. His Spanish was not good enough for conversation that early in the morning. Out of curiosity he opened a wooden shutter and cast a look outside. At first he thought he was looking into a void and stepped back apprehensively until a heavy snowflake landed on the back of his hand and he realised that he was looking out into an impenetrable snowstorm. He was just able to make out a pile of firewood less than a few feet from the window and already so heavily covered with snow as to be almost invisible. Anything beyond the woodpile was invisible.

'We haven't had a blizzard like it so late in the season for years.' The buxom barmaid leant forward and Luc had little doubt that a bored pilgrim would have found ways of passing the time in this hostelry in such conditions. After his recent intimacy he barely blinked at the girl and simply asked for a jug of warm water. With an expression that could have been of disappointment she disappeared into the kitchen. He turned and looked around at his fellow travellers, with whom he would be spending this day at the very least. They were a fairly average bunch consisting predominantly of olive-skinned, jet-black-haired Spaniards with a sprinkling of other nationalities.

'Here's your water.' He turned back and was pleased to see that her smile had returned. Maybe she had reflected upon the fact that, because of the blizzard, he along with all the others would be there for the whole day and the next night. He took the heavy jug and went back to the bedroom. Leaving it with Aimée, who was just stirring, he returned to the bar and ordered breakfast.

Luc had only just started on his big bowl of porridge with warm milk and honey when the front door of the inn was thrown open with a crash that threatened to rip it off its hinges. A flurry of snow came rushing in, together with a group of men. Everybody looked up, but nobody dared to move.

'Barman. Food and drink for my men and make it quick.'

There were four of them, all covered in a thick coating of fresh snow. The biggest was a huge figure of a man with long black hair and a patch over one eye. Immediately behind him was a thin, sallow man who carried a sword unsheathed in his right hand. At his shoulder was a turbaned Moor, his dark skin in distinct contrast to the white robes he wore beneath a fur jerkin.

Luc shrank down as much as possible behind a group of guests, glad that Aimée was still in the bedroom. He did his best to stay inconspicuous while he summed up the situation. He watched as the leader of the group, the man who had shouted, emerged from the shadows into the flickering light of the fire. There was no doubt about it. This was the one.

The scar down the side of his face gave him away. Even without the whip attached to his wrist, Luc recognised him from Aimée's description. The eyes, when the firelight caught them, were soulless, lifeless and without pity. For a moment Luc felt them pass over him, pause and then continue round the room. Slowly and deliberately, Luc reached into his sleeve until his right hand closed reassuringly around the handle of the dagger. His eyes watched every move that the leader and the rest of his group made.

The landlord, woken by the noise, looked up and blanched. He was just dragging himself to his feet when, to Luc's horror, Aimée came out of the passage into the light of the room, the empty water jug in her hand. She stepped into the room and stopped dead, her nostrils flaring, a scream rising in her throat.

'Well, well, well. That's more like it.'

The man with the scar turned towards her, a look of anticipation on his face. His weasel-faced companion beat him to it, racing across to the doorway and grabbing her. His hands tore at her clothing. With a smile on his face, he reached forward for her and died instantaneously, Luc's dagger buried in his throat. The action froze to slow motion as Luc's voice rang out authoritatively.

'Drop to your knees, Aimée. Now. Do it!' The tone of his voice cut through her panic and she obeyed without question. 'Now get back into the bedroom and bolt the door.' As he spoke, he sensed the swish of a missile. He ducked in his turn as the wicked curved sword of the Moor whirled past his head. It crashed against the wall behind him. It was immediately followed by the Moor himself, a dagger in his hand.

Now unarmed, Luc grabbed the heavy jug of hot milk. He threw the contents into the Moor's face, temporarily blinding him. Taking advantage of this momentary respite, he reached forward and smashed the jug straight into the dark face, sending him flying backwards.

He turned and leapt for the Moor's sword on the floor, but found it was wedged under a bench. He glanced up as the one-eyed man threw himself at him, from the top of a neighbouring table. Luc was able to half turn his shoulders to absorb the weight of the charge, but he was knocked back against the granite fireplace. Swarthy hands scrabbled for his throat and he felt himself being pushed back into the fire itself, the flames scorching his breeches. He braced himself against the stone upright and then, suddenly, viciously, he stabbed forward with his knee into his assailant's groin.

There was a satisfying grunt of pain. The pressure on his throat relaxed, as the man clutched despairingly between his legs. His mouth was wide open, sucking in desperately laboured breaths. Luc followed up his advantage with a blow learnt from the Assassins. His stiff fingers slammed into the man's windpipe, just below the chin, and the man dropped like a stone.

Luc ignored him, turning his attention back to the rest of the room. The assembled group of guests sat wide-eyed at the events of the last few seconds. To his relief he saw the scar-faced leader still standing where he had been a moment before.

'Who are you?' The man was staring at him fixedly. There was no fear on his face, just an expression of surprise and rising anger. Luc shook himself violently, angry in his turn. He kicked out at the table in front of him and had the satisfaction of seeing it spin off, to smash spectacularly against the far wall, narrowly missing a group of cowering onlookers.

'You scum!'

There was an intensity of hatred in his voice that everybody in the room could feel. Even the scar-faced man took a half-step backwards at his tone.

'I said, who are you?'

The commanding voice had disappeared, to be replaced by a questioning tone. Luc jabbed his right leg at another table that tipped back out of his way. There was only a bench between the two of them now.

'Tell me, sir. Who are you? How is it that you're such an accomplished fighter? I've never been in the presence of one such as you. Please tell me who you are, and where you've learnt your skills.'

The man's words echoed insincerely around the room. With an instinctive movement, born of years of combat, Luc threw himself to one side just as a heavy iron mace slammed into the bench beside him. He caught the handle, ripping the spiked head out of the wood with a shower of splinters, and whirled round. The Moor was leaning back against the far wall, his face a mask of fresh blood where the jug had cut him, his arms bent back with the effort of throwing the mace. Without hesitation Luc spun the evil

weapon back at him. He was already turning back to the leader as it
smashed into the other man's face with a dull, final thud.

'You were saying?'

He took a pace forward and tried to bring his breathing under control.
There was something about the other man's eyes that screamed caution at
him, while his whole body was crying out for swift, decisive action. His
hands dropped to his belt and reminded him that, without his dagger, he
was totally unarmed, walking towards a heavily armed killer. His brain took
control. The scar-faced man made no movement, his eyes still on the crumpled body of the Moor, his expression neutral. Luc stared at him in disgust
and spoke in a strong, level voice.

'I'll tell you who I am, scum. I'm here with the girl you raped, beat and
blinded on a rock up on the Somport two months ago. You may not
remember what happened, but she does and she always will. Does that
answer your question?'

The other man's expression didn't change. He spat on the floor just in
front of Luc's feet. 'Well, from where I'm standing, I'd say you were an
unarmed fool, about to be chopped into little pieces by me.' There was still
resistance in his voice.

As he spoke, the bandit swept a well-used sword out of its scabbard and
pulled a dagger from his boot. He stepped back lightly, feeling his balance.
Luc realised he was up against an adversary of a decidedly higher calibre
than the other three. He ripped his leather belt from his waist and wrapped
it roughly around his left arm, as a primitive form of defence. His right hand,
however, remained empty. A glance around him brought nothing but the
knowledge that the tables were clear. There was not so much as a mug for
him to grasp. In spite of his predicament, he continued in the same tone.

'The last time I saw an animal like you, I crushed it under my foot.'

The other made no response, remaining impassive. Luc was again
conscious that this was a worthy adversary. He eyed the sword blade warily
and noted the fact that it was rock solid in the other man's hand. There was
no shaking or trembling. The faint light from the only window in the room
reflected off the blue-grey metal straight into Luc's face, without wavering in
the slightest. He looked deep into the other man's eyes and saw uncertainty,
but still no trace of panic. He kept his eyes locked onto the other man's and

continued to walk slowly towards him, regardless of his lack of weapons. The thought of Aimée burnt in his mind, what she had suffered and what she would always suffer.

There was a crash. Both men turned towards the noise. A flying jug of wine smashed onto the tabletop beside the scar face, accompanied by a piercing scream. The scream came from Aimée at the door. Beside her, the innkeeper was reaching for something else to throw. Luc glanced back at the man with the scar. This glance saved his life.

He caught the flash of steel out of the corner of his eye as he looked back. He was just able to turn his chest away from the blade, before it hit him and he gave a roar of pain as the dagger stabbed into his shoulder. He flung himself forward, before the bandit could attack him with the sword. His ankle caught the bench and he tripped, his forehead smashing into the edge of a neighbouring table. As he fell, he was dimly aware of the inn door crashing open. Then he lost consciousness.

12

JACA, SPANISH PYRENEES, APRIL 2016

The restaurant was called El Granc. This, they were informed, meant The Crab in the dialect of Galicia. As Galicia was the province away to the west where Santiago de Compostela was to be found, they took this to be a good sign.

'You look terrific.' He meant it. Amy smiled happily and accepted a glass of champagne.

'I'll take your word for it.' There was no bitterness in her voice. She held her glass up and he clinked his against it. 'A toast to you.' She was looking more serious. 'I'd like to propose a toast to you. I hope you have a wonderful happy birthday and I want to thank you for making these last weeks the best I've had for years. I owe you more than you can imagine.'

Further conversation was interrupted by the arrival of the waiter with the menus. These turned out to be handwritten and quite probably in Galician dialect. Luke wrestled with the strange-sounding words for a while until, mercifully, he spotted a heading that said quite simply *Menu Especial* with a price, no detail. He beckoned the hovering waiter and asked haltingly what this consisted of. The reply was predictably incomprehensible.

'In for a penny, in for a pound,' he said out loud in English and ordered two of these along with a bottle of ten-year-old Rioja Gran Reserva.

'What are we having, then?' Her voice was gently mocking. He admitted the truth that he hadn't the slightest idea, except that it was theoretically going to be special. She giggled and held out her glass for some more champagne. Not for the first time he reflected upon the difference between the girl he was with now, compared to the woman he had first met in that exquisitely furnished but cold, lifeless house in Highgate. It seemed a hundred years ago, but was only about a month.

'Isn't it weird? We've only known each other for a month or so. It's amazing really, I feel I've known you for so much longer.' There was a note of wonder in his voice that was not lost upon her.

'Thirty-three days to be precise, but who's counting?' Her voice was warm. 'I know exactly what you mean.' A cheeky smile spread across her face. 'Of course, it could be we already knew each other in a previous life. Have you had a previous life?' She smiled across at him as the waiter brought a small plate of appetisers for each of them to play with before the first course arrived.

'A couple of enormous orange mussels, probably from New Zealand or somewhere, some huge green olives, a fried onion thing, or at least it looks like onion, some porcini mushrooms in olive oil and a handful of quail's eggs. A delicate end-of-fork or pick-it-up-in-your-fingers job, I would suggest.' The description came quite naturally to him and she nodded gratefully.

'You weren't a Templar, were you? I mean in a previous life. Maybe that's what you were.' She took a small sip of the champagne as he swallowed a mushroom.

'I wouldn't have minded.' The mushroom was excellent and the extra virgin olive oil, if anything, even better. He followed the mushroom with some of the lovely fresh bread before continuing. 'They really were the elite, you know. The Samurai of medieval Europe. I'm sure you know that their holy oath upon becoming a Templar knight prohibited them from surrender to the enemy under almost any circumstances. You either killed a Templar or he killed you. There was no middle way.'

He tried a mussel but found the unexpectedly sour taste didn't match up to its appearance. He swallowed it with difficulty, took another mouthful of champagne and chewed a thick piece of bread to remove the taste. He decided to take a break before eating anything else, so as to allow the mussel to go down, so he picked up the conversation about Templar knights once more.

'It's really no wonder the King of France decided to get rid of them. Just think. Not only was the cream of French knighthood queuing up to join, but the Order's strength and influence had grown exponentially. By the early thirteen hundreds they were far richer than the French monarchy, and quite probably the Spanish and English royal houses too. They had a network of commanderies, castles and farms from Cyprus to the north of England. Oh yes, being a Templar knight wouldn't have been at all bad.'

Amy reached for a mushroom, felt the oil on her fingers and licked them clean before picking up her fork and expertly spearing it. 'Mind you, they got fairly soundly beaten in the Holy Land. Samurai or not, they were no match for Saladin.'

'Don't forget they were outnumbered by about a hundred to one. That would have been too much for a force ten times their size.' He tried the fried onion ring. It was excellent, but the taste of that mussel still lingered on. He reached for a glass of water before continuing.

Unaware of his discomfort, Amy picked up a quail's egg and savoured the delicate taste before laying her fork back on the plate. She intended pacing herself. Her experience of previous Spanish meals told her that she was very unlikely to have room for everything. *Why aren't the Spanish immensely fat?* she wondered to herself.

Luke gulped down some more water. 'But at the height of their power, say around the mid-thirteenth century, it must have been quite something to be a Templar.'

'They were of course monks,' she reminded him. 'With all the restrictions that that brought.' Noticing that they had both stopped eating, the waiter cleared the plates and went off to fetch the first course. 'Having to live according to the monastic clock must have been hard work, what with services in the dead of night and so on, not to mention the fact that they were virtually vegetarian, sworn to poverty and humility and—' her voice held an undercurrent '—don't forget the vow of chastity. I bet the local girls swooned over these big, strong knights. And they must have been big and strong, just to be able to lift the weapons and wear the armour. And what a turn-on, knowing that they were effectively forbidden fruit.'

The first course arrived and he surveyed it dubiously, increasingly troubled by the taste of the mussel that still lingered in his throat. *Oh God,* he thought to himself, *I hope it wasn't off.* He launched desperately into his guide mode.

'Well, my dear, what you have in front of you is a fully grown, freshly boiled red spider crab. Along with the crab you get a pair of nutcrackers, a long hook that would no doubt have been very useful in the days of the Inquisition, and a bowl of water with a slice of lemon floating in it. I wish you luck.'

She forgave him for changing the subject, liked the sound of the 'my dear' and rather dreaded the task of dissecting the crab. She reached down gingerly, locating the claws and checking that it really was dead. She was on the point of bravely picking up the nutcrackers when he touched her hand.

'Hang on a sec.' There then followed a series of muffled blows accompanied by some sharp cracking sounds. A moment later she felt her plate being replaced by his. She touched the crab gently and was relieved to feel the shell and claws broken into pieces. She found it quite easy to pull the meat from one big claw. It was delicious.

The waiter returned with the bottle of Rioja. Luke asked her to taste it for him. It was excellent, rich, woody and aromatic. She nodded in the direction of the waiter and mumbled, *'Muy bien,'* hoping that she had got it right. He filled her glass with wine and she took another sip.

'Here.' Luke's voice was low. 'Take this crabmeat from my plate. It's all ready to eat. I've taken the bits of shell off.' Seeing the surprise on her face, he went on hastily, 'It's all right. I'm not really that keen on crab.' This didn't really accord with her memory, but she made no comment apart from the observation that the Rioja was excellent. She heard him drink and order more water. She was bothered by this unusual behaviour.

'Are you all right? I would have thought you would have drained the bottle and licked the plates by now.' She finished another bit of crabmeat and took another sip of the red wine.

'I'll be all right when we get onto the meat.' He didn't sound convincing, but she let it go and carried on with her meal in silence for a few more minutes. He made no attempt to say anything and she started to get worried.

'Is the thought of your former life affecting your appetite?' She passed the napkin across her lips and waited some moments for his reply.

'I don't think that's it, but I've still got to tell you everything that's happened to me in my life.' His voice sounded terribly subdued. 'And I'm not talking about any time I may have spent as a Templar in some previous existence.' She sat still and listened, spellbound, as he finally managed to make a start.

'I promised you I'd tell you about my past. I owe it to you, and it'll probably do me good to talk about it. I've spent the last few days trying to work up the courage to begin but, believe me, it isn't easy.' He paused to pour himself a glass of water and to top up her glass with the red that he had yet to touch. He took a few deep mouthfuls of air, but was unable to shift the sensation of breathlessness that assailed him. For a moment the thought crossed his mind that he might be having a heart attack. A glance at the virtually untouched crab on his plate, and the immediate sensation of revulsion that followed, confirmed his earlier fear: that blasted mussel.

The waiter appeared, hovered for a moment then pounced, carrying off the offending plate. Luke experienced a keen feeling of relief as the remains of the crab disappeared. He returned his attention to Amy, who looked lovelier than ever. This didn't make the story he had to tell any easier for him.

'The fact is, I didn't start out to study medieval history. I followed a very different route.' He took a few more deep breaths, but there was no getting away from it, he felt terrible. The return of the waiter provided a welcome break. Then he smelt the rich red-wine-based sauce that accompanied the huge slab of meat in front of him and he felt his stomach churn.

'I'm afraid I don't feel so well... the mussel...'

With that, he leapt to his feet and disappeared towards the sign marked *Servicios*.

Amy noticed the rapidity of his departure and waited with concern for his return. She had to wait a considerable time.

13

JACA, SPANISH PYRENEES, APRIL 2016

They stayed at the Hostal Somport for three nights. The first night Luke was sicker than he had ever been in his whole life. Finally, around four o'clock when he had nothing left inside him, he dragged himself to bed. He was feeling very cold at this point; in particular around the stomach and kidneys. He wrapped himself in all the blankets he could find and collapsed onto the bed, feeling as weak as a kitten.

He didn't hear Amy come into his room until her voice whispered in his ear and her hands landed on his shoulder.

'Is there anything I can get you?' He felt so weak, he didn't even jump at the sound of her voice. He tried to reply normally, but the words he produced seemed a million miles away.

'I think I'd better just sleep.' The effort of speaking these few words exhausted him. He lay back, pressing his hands onto his stomach to try to warm it. She felt the movement.

'Are you cold?' He made no response but he obviously was, even to the point of shivering. She went off and stripped the spare bed in her room, returning with a blanket and a quilt. She folded the blanket and laid it over his stomach, pressing it tightly around his waist. Spreading out the quilt on top of him, she tucked him in as best she could. His forehead felt wet with cold sweat so she rubbed it dry with the sleeve of her pyjama jacket and knelt beside him for quite a while, her hand lying lightly against his cheek, until she felt sure he was finally asleep. Only then did she get up and creep quietly back to her room, leaving both his door and hers slightly open in case he might need something.

She lay in bed, unable to sleep, and found herself reviewing the events of the last few months in her mind. The idea of following the pilgrimage route to Santiago de Compostela had been suggested to her by their mutual friend, Father Tim. And he really had been a good friend to her, she thought warmly. She wasn't a regular churchgoer, wasn't even sure if she was a believer, although both her parents had been, but that hadn't mattered to him at all. He, more than anybody else, had helped her through the desperation of the first years of her plunge into darkness. Having lost father, mother and younger sister in the accident, she had been overwhelmed. In a few short hours, she'd found herself having to face the twin shattering blows of being orphaned and blinded. Throughout the grim months that had followed, she had been deeply touched by the care and support she'd received from him.

He had encouraged, helped and sometimes bullied her to do her history MA. When she'd got the result, his had been the very first number she had called. She was very fond of him and he had, in many ways, taken over the role of father in her life. So when he had suggested this practical project, as a first step towards getting her out into the wider world, she had considered it very seriously. Indeed, she thought with a wry smile, she probably listened to him a lot more than she had ever listened to her father. Being a very practical person, she had queried the logistics of the trip. He had been ready with his reply.

'We'll need to get you a travelling companion. No...' He had read the expression on her face correctly. 'No, I don't mean a chaperone like something out of *A Room with a View*. I mean a practical person with a knowledge of the subject who can get you there, and that means driving. You need somebody who can help you get the most out of it.'

Amy had protested that the chances of a chauffeur knowing enough about medieval history were slim to say the least. Then, even without being able to see the smug expression on his face, she had realised that Father Tim had already got somebody in mind.

'All right, I know you well enough by now. Spit it out.'

He had made a half-hearted attempt to appear unaware of what she'd meant, but soon he had capitulated and told her about this friend of his. It had been quite clear from the first that this was not just any friend. This Luke Patterson was clearly a very close friend. So Amy had listened with interest to the sketchy and downright vague description without comment. She had finally agreed to see Luke, as she had known all along she would. However, as the day of the encounter had approached, she had found herself becoming more and more apprehensive and, as a result, prickly.

Fundamentally what had bothered her, she now thought to herself analytically, wasn't just the fear of rejection, as she had told him. It wasn't just the thought that, after she had finally taken the decision to get out of the house and try to restart her life, her efforts might be thwarted before they had even started. The fact was that the only way she would be able to accomplish this journey was by putting herself into another person's hands. She felt the frustration of handicapped people the world over: not being able to just do it, whatever *it* might be, without help. Consequently, his reception by her had been pretty frosty.

And now? She allowed herself a smile at the thought of her tucking him in like a baby and waiting at his bedside until he had fallen asleep. So who was looking after whom now?

It felt good to be able to help someone for a change. And it felt doubly good that Luke was the person being helped. She had grown to know him really well in such a relatively short time. And along with this developing acquaintance had come other emotions, feelings that hadn't stirred in her for years. The accident had happened just over five years previously and the deaths of all her close family had so completely drained her emotions that it was hardly surprising that her few hesitant attempts at forming relationships since then had come to grief.

Now here she was, confronted with a constant companion, every bit as constant as if she were married to him. Almost as constant, she told herself pragmatically, thinking of him lying in the next room, cold and sick, while she lay here comfortable and warm, but alone. She wrapped herself tighter in the thick quilt and tried to think rationally.

Before the accident she had had a series of relationships, some deep, some superficial. Some had given her a lot of pleasure. Since then, her freedom to meet people and enter relationships had been blown out of the water. The accident had robbed her, not only of her sight, but also of her independence.

Her mind strayed to the Welsh nurse. What was her name? Nicky? Jackie? She couldn't remember exactly, but she recalled the occasion. It was when she was sent home from hospital. Or, more precisely, when she was sent back to a near empty house, echoing with the memories of her family who would never again share the house with her. There she found herself alone but for her aunt, who would no doubt have been happier on the Promenade des Anglais, and the new housekeeper, who had only just been engaged. The visiting nurse told her the problems she was encountering with her boyfriend, Wayne or Duane or some such.

Throughout the whole sad story, Amy had listened sympathetically, while deep inside her she would have given a lot for a Wayne or a Duane of her own. But when you're blind – or at least recently blinded – there are very few occasions to meet Waynes and Duanes. And even if you ever did, the chances of them treating you as a normal girl are as good as non-existent. The chance meeting, the casual coffee, the proverbial glance across the crowded room were all things of the past. And as for a casual affair... Being visually handicapped, she had learnt early on, could also mean being physically handicapped in other ways.

So now here she was with a big, strong and mysterious man all to herself. All right, she thought, he was with her because he was being paid to be there. Nevertheless, he was under no obligation to be as nice to her as he had been. And yet she could feel his hesitation. She wouldn't have been a woman if she hadn't felt that. What it was all about was difficult to guess.

Maybe he was just trying to keep things on a professional basis. Maybe he was already involved in a relationship although, if he was, he hadn't so much as hinted at the possibility. Maybe there was some deeper reason. In spite of herself, she wondered if indeed the truth was quite simply that he didn't want to get involved with a handicapped person. Warm and comfortable or not, she shivered at the thought.

Her waking dream was suddenly interrupted by a fit of coughing from the next room. She was out of bed and into his room before he finished. She ran to his bedside and reached out a hand, feeling whether he was still in the bed or not. Had the noise of the coughing in fact been yet another attack of nausea? Her hand reached his shoulder and she felt immediately relieved. Her fingers reached down gently until they touched his face, running lightly up his cheeks and brushing his eyelids. She was pleased to feel a movement and bent closer to him so as to speak quietly into his ear.

'Are you awake? Can you hear me?' She leant closer to him and waited. His reply was unexpectedly clear, if faint.

'Is it my imagination or is it getting warmer?'

She reached for his shoulder under his covers and felt him bathed with sweat. Raising herself to her knees, she stripped a couple of layers off the bed. 'Is that better?'

'Much.' He sounded much more his old self. She felt such a wave of happiness sweep over her that she kissed him on the cheek. This elicited a muffled reaction, but whether of reciprocation or of protest was difficult to tell.

'Is there anything you need?'

He replied quietly, but quite clearly. 'A drink of water would be really good. I think I must be dehydrated.' She easily located the untouched bottle of mineral water on the bedside table and twisted the cap off. With her assistance he raised his head enough to be able to drink from the bottle.

'Small mouthfuls.' She remembered her mother's words from her child-hood days. Obediently, he sipped slowly and, after a few moments, slumped back onto the pillow. She laid the bottle back on the table and touched his forehead once more. This time it felt warm and dry and this cheered her. His hand reached up to her head. Gently, he pulled her down until his lips almost touched her ear. Only then did he murmur so softly that it was all she could do to make out his words.

'Thank you.'

She felt what might have been the lightest of kisses on her ear and then he released her, lay back and breathed out deeply. She sat back upright again, delighted that he seemed to be feeling better now. She also found herself debating whether he had really kissed her, or whether it had been no more than a movement of his lips.

14

SPANISH PYRENEES, APRIL 1314

'How're you feeling?' Aimée felt Luc stir on the mattress beside her and was on her knees beside him in an instant.

For a moment there was no response. Then he yawned deeply and stretched his whole body. When he replied, she was relieved to hear his voice sounding normal again.

'Better. Much better. How long have I been in bed?'

'Most of the day. You woke up a few times, but you've spent most of the time sleeping. Can you remember what happened?'

He raised his hand to his forehead and rubbed the huge blue and red bruise tentatively. 'I remember. Did the bandit leader get away?'

'He disappeared out into the snow just as you slipped and banged your head. You never know, he may have frozen to death by now.' She tried to keep her voice positive and light, delighted his memory appeared unimpaired by the blow to the head. In truth, she had spent the whole day lying here beside him, checking to see that he was comfortable, but all the while struggling to control the overwhelming sense of terror the bandit leader's voice had aroused in her. Hearing Luc once more in control of his faculties brought her a wave of relief. She reached across and laid her hand against his cheek tenderly. 'You can't imagine how happy I am that you're all right.'

'And me, Aimée, and thank you for looking after me. I'm really pleased my head feels almost normal again. At least, the overpowering pain across my forehead's now just about gone. About all I can feel now's a dull ache from my shoulder.'

He pulled himself into a sitting position and swung his arms around cautiously. He was immensely relieved to feel that he still had full movement in both, the knife blade not having severed any major muscle.

'Did they clean the wound?'

His question reminded her of the moment when the burning coal had been pressed onto his shoulder, the cut swamped with aguardiente. She had heard a hiss as the spirit caught fire and a sharp intake of breath from the onlookers. Unable to see what had happened, she had been conscious of the sounds, and then the bitter smell of burning hair and flesh.

'It was well done.' She spared him the details. 'The innkeeper has considerable experience of knife wounds.'

She heard him grunt with satisfaction. The bedclothes rustled as his fingers probed the bandages around his shoulder.

He turned towards her and spoke quietly, his mouth so close to her ear that she felt his warm breath on her. 'Did I tell you we're supposed to be going to a monastery?'

'San Juan de la Peña, yes. And it's all arranged.' She was quick to explain. 'It's all right, I didn't say a thing. It was the innkeeper's idea. He says it's off the normal pilgrimage route and he knows a monk there who'll help us.' She kept her voice as low as his.

'That's perfect. The abbot of Santa Cristina gave me the name of an old monk there who holds the secret. And he'll give us somewhere to rest up and hide until the archbishop's men have gone past. I wonder if it's the same monk.' He reached down and laid the back of his hand against her cheek. 'I owe you my life, Aimée. If you and the innkeeper hadn't joined in, I might well be dead now.' He reached across and took her hand in his. 'Thank you.'

She kissed the palm of his hand. 'There's only one person in this room who's saved a life. And that's you. Without you, Luc, God alone knows what would have happened to me.'

He retrieved his hand from hers. The same sense of impropriety still affected him. She was, after all, a woman, and a beautiful one as well. And he, as a Templar knight, had taken vows of chastity. He cleared his throat nervously and returned his mind to the message the abbot of Santa Cristina had given him.

'San Juan de la Peña, that's it all right. And from there, all the way to Portugal.' He turned back and looked down at her. He flexed his arm muscles and took a few deep breaths. 'I thought that the arrangement was that I was the one who would be looking after you. For the last few days it would seem to have been the other way round.'

15

ABBEY OF SAN JUAN DE LA PEÑA, SPANISH PYRENEES, APRIL 2016

'Are we there yet?' Amy was pretending to be a petulant child.

'I'm delighted to say that, yes, we've almost arrived.' Luke, too, was glad to get there, even though they had only left the Hostal Somport little more than half an hour before. The succession of bends, coupled with the pitted road surface, had started to make him feel decidedly queasy again. 'Mind you, I'm sure it'll be worth it. So—' he adopted a professorial tone '—tell me, Ms Hardy, what do you know about this monastery?'

'I'm glad you asked me that, Dr Patterson.' She pulled herself up straight and affected a serious air. 'The monastery of San Juan de la Peña is unique. It is without doubt one of the oldest monasteries in Europe. It was reputedly founded in the eighth century but, even more than its antiquity, it is the construction itself that impresses.'

'That sounds like it came straight out of a guidebook.' He was laughing, but he had to admire her memory. A sign indicated the monastery was only two kilometres ahead. 'Only two kilometres to go. So, go on, Ms Hardy.'

'It *is* straight out of a guide. While you've been throwing up, Dr Patterson, some of us have been studying on the Internet.' She continued her recitation from memory. 'The whole structure is tucked at the foot of a towering, curved cliff. The cloisters and church are built into the rock face itself.

Arriving on the winding road from Jaca, there seems no sign of it until, at the very last moment, the road drops down a hundred metres through the trees and the monastery suddenly appears.'

'What a memory!' At that moment, the road sloped steeply down. 'Here we go. Trees all around and, yes, there's the monastery.'

He pulled off the road into about a foot of slushy snow, switched off the engine and threw the door open gratefully, gulping in great lungfuls of the cold mountain air. 'Your guide was dead right about the winding road!'

'You having a relapse?' Her voice was studiously light.

'Nothing a bit of fresh air can't cure.' He picked his way round the front of the big vehicle and helped her out. Both of them were wearing boots and jackets, but in no way felt overdressed in the frosty morning air. His stomach and the small of his back still felt cold, and he pulled the jacket tighter around him. However, in spite of his discomfort, he couldn't help but be impressed by the surroundings. He did his best to render it into words for her.

'We've parked right on the corner, directly alongside the monastery. The cliff face sweeps up for a long, long way above us and curves back so that you can't see the top. There's a load of chicken wire spread across much of it, no doubt to lessen the risk of a chunk of rock falling down and killing some unsuspecting pilgrim.'

'Are there any pilgrims here?' Instinctively she reached up to tidy her hair.

'Not a soul. Anyway, there's a high stone wall around the base of the cliff, above which you can just see the tops of the arches and columns of the cloisters. These are built directly into the rock face. The funny thing is that the straight lines and geometric patterns of the buildings seem to be squashed by the rounded shape of the rock above. Sort of like a wave of volcanic lava gradually engulfing it, or rather enfolding it.'

'Sort of like a fat lady sitting on a stool.' She readily understood the mental picture he was drawing. He laughed in agreement.

'Quite so. Back behind us, there are trees on the slope alongside the road. You can see daylight through the branches and I imagine there's a precipice just beyond them that drops clean to the valley floor. It's like being on the Corniche above Monte Carlo.'

'One website I found said that San Juan was supposed to be the home of the Holy Grail. Yes—' she could sense his scepticism '—I know, numerous Holy Grails popped up all over the place in the Middle Ages. But I relay the information anyway. Do you suppose our man...?'

Her question tailed off and he gave it a certain amount of thought. Over the last couple of days since his birthday dinner, the adventures of their medieval hero had been overshadowed by internal physiological considerations. In fairness he hadn't felt at all creative. Now, out here in the fresh air, it seemed a natural topic of conversation. But the idea of the Holy Grail? He protested loudly and with feeling.

'Definitely not another Holy Grail! Chrétien de Troyes, Geoffrey of Monmouth, Richard Wagner and don't forget Indiana Jones. If I had a pound for every time the Grail's been mentioned throughout the last thousand years I'd be a rich man. So let's definitely say that he wasn't here to look for the Holy Grail. Anything but that!'

She laughed at his tone and chided him gently. 'Stop playing the outraged academic. All right, the whole sacred cup thing *is* highly questionable, but not impossible. And what if it wasn't a cup at all? That might well just be the imagination of the medieval writers who weren't sure what they were referring to.'

'Point taken. Not impossible but let's leave it out of our story anyway.' He took her arm and they walked across to the walls of the monastery. Amy was still thinking about their story.

'All right, then, Luke. So if it wasn't the Holy Grail, what was it our folk were looking for here, then? And if they already picked up their precious treasure at Santa Cristina, why bother coming up here?'

'Erm... still trying to work that out.'

The doors of the monastery were firmly bolted, although a sign indicated that it would be open to the public that afternoon. Leaving her for a moment, Luke shinned up one of the surrounding walls and looked down into the shadows of the cloisters. The cliff above shielded it from any sunshine and he could see icicles on the capitals of the pillars. Certainly, he reflected, the monks who wintered here in medieval times must have been a hardy breed. He crouched there in silent contemplation for a few moments before jumping back down and returning to her side.

'Closed.' He saw the disappointment on her face. 'We can either wait here till this afternoon, if that notice is to be trusted, or we'll have to come back in a few weeks' time.'

'Why not?' Her voice was quite serious. 'The rate we are going, we won't get to Santiago de Compostela until some time in May so we could call off here on the way home.' In spite of her confident tone, the thought of this magical journey ending sent a chill through her. Feeling her shiver, he misinterpreted the cause and propelled her out onto the road.

'It's certainly chilly! We've been sitting in the car for too long, not to mention my lying on my back in bed for the last few days, so let's make a move!'

With his hand under her elbow he broke into a trot, pulling her along with him. Together they started to jog along the road away from the monastery and its overhanging cliff face towards the sunshine around the corner of the tortuous road. It took them some minutes until they emerged from the deep shadow and both felt the warmth of the morning sun on their faces. She slowed.

'That feels good enough for me. How about just walking from now on?'

He slowed to a normal walking pace and looked down towards the main valley. The trees at the roadside had given way to bushes. Less than fifty feet below them he saw the undergrowth change to bare rock and then open space. They were quite literally perched just above a precipice. In spite of himself, he felt the shiver of vertigo that he always got in these situations. He led her to a big rock on the side of the road away from the cliff edge and they sat down. Almost immediately, she sensed his interest drawn to something.

'What is it? What've you seen?'

When he replied, his voice was awestruck. 'Eagles. There are five, no six, maybe seven eagles out there. They're amazing.' She could hear the note of pity in his voice that she was unable to appreciate the sight. 'They must be hundreds or probably thousands of feet from the valley floor. The thermal currents here must be just right. The birds have gradually climbed higher and higher. Now they're only a matter of a hundred yards or so out from where we're sitting. Beautiful animals.'

She had no time for pity and she thought this a good time to remind him of it. 'Eagles. I've seen them even closer. In fact, when we were in the Rockies, we almost got our sandwiches taken by one.' He heard the tone and kicked himself.

'Sorry. I was forgetting that you've been everywhere and done everything. I bet you even bought the *I've had my lunch stolen by the eagles* T-shirt.' She punched him in the chest and he caught her fist. They sat like that for a moment without speaking until he spoke quietly. 'I just wish you could see them.'

'So do I, but I can't and that's that.' Her tone was matter-of-fact. It had taken her five years to fully come to terms with what had happened. But, here now, with him beside her, holding her hand, she knew she had finally laid that particular demon to rest. She squeezed his hand. 'I'm pleased for you that you can see them. But I'm really happy just sitting here with you like this.' She snuggled closer to him and let a more flippant note enter her voice. 'Who cares about boring old eagles when we can be here like this in peace and quiet?' A thought struck her. 'Besides, it's not all that silent after all. I reckon I can hear the eagles, even if I can't see them. Anyway, maybe they're vultures, not eagles. That's what it said on the Spanish Tourist Board website.'

He estimated the distance between them and the nearest of the birds. Although they had come a little closer, they were still a good hundred yards out. He concentrated hard and imagined, more than heard, the wind rushing through their feathers. Maybe she really could hear them. He looked down at her affectionately. She was right. It was good to be sitting with her like this. Maybe too good, he thought with a guilty start, conscious that he was coming ever closer to abusing his role as guide. He released her hand and pulled back from her. 'What were we talking about before the eagles or vultures put in their appearance?'

She crammed her hands into the pockets of her jacket, sorry to relinquish her hold on him. She didn't need the power of sight to recognise that he was feeling uneasy. Once again, she found herself wondering just what was going through his head. Her voice when she replied was, however, businesslike. 'Our man, of course. What's he doing up here anyway?'

'Not looking for the Holy Grail.' Luke spoke firmly and then, before she could chip in, he continued. 'And yes, I am trying to think what it might have been. Honestly.'

'He's a Templar. That much we've established.' She was going back over the facts to see whether they could give any help. 'He's obviously a good Templar knight, so that rules out money, spite, treachery and all those negative things. It has to be something positive and good.' She, too, fell silent, so he took up where she had left off.

'Don't forget that he's travelling with the girl. Why is that? If he's as good as you say, then he'll respect his oath of celibacy, so she has to be with him for a reason. Not just love.'

'No, not just love.' Her voice gave nothing away. 'So, if it's not love, then it must be duty or honour.' She sounded as if she was concentrating hard.

'Or maybe he's had to take her with him to protect her from the pursuers. Which reminds me, I wonder what happened to them. Did they give up the chase at Santa Cristina? Maybe thinking that the snow would have got him... I mean them.'

'No chance.' Of this she was quite definite. 'We're not just talking about some minor member of the Order escaping with the bishop's wallet. This is big time. What our man's carrying or looking for has to be of great value. Great value.'

An idea began to form in his mind. 'Maybe he's already found what he's been looking for. What if it really is information, something of vital and earth-shattering importance? What if the information is in the head of his blind companion? Could that be it?'

Amy perked up at the idea. 'That could be it, you know. The girl was being accompanied across the mountains and her companions were ambushed and killed. Miraculously she survived.' Her voice rose. 'Maybe she was blinded in the ambush. Then she had to lie low at Santa Cristina over the winter until our chap appeared to take her away. I wonder what the information could be.' A mischievous grin appeared on her face. 'Maybe it's the whereabouts of the Holy Grail.'

'No.' He jumped to his feet, stamping them to restore the circulation. She followed him up and took his arm.

'Any ideas?'

'Well, actually, yes. I suggest we head off back down to the main valley and look for a restaurant. I haven't eaten properly for almost three days and I'm starving. Come to think of it, I could—'

'No beer till tomorrow. Do as the doctor tells you.' She spoke in her stern she-who-must-be-obeyed tone.

'Yes, Doctor,' he said meekly and led her back to the car.

16

ABBEY OF SAN JUAN DE LA PEÑA, SPANISH
PYRENEES, APRIL 1314

As soon as night fell, Luc slipped out of the undergrowth with Aimée. It was good to get moving after a day spent crouching in the back of the cart that had brought them down here from the inn. They flitted across the track and up to the monastery door. Luc stopped just before the great gate and pulled her into the shadows where a pile of firewood was stacked. He squeezed her into the shelter of the logs and put his mouth by her ear.

'I'll be back in just a few minutes. I want to see if the monk we're supposed to contact is here, if he knows about us and is willing to help, before dragging a woman into a monastery. I'm afraid you'd be rather obvious in there.'

'God be with you, Luc.' She hugged him tight and kissed him on the cheek.

He gave her hand an encouraging squeeze and made for the entrance.

Inside the monastery, there should have been an air of calm devotion, the quiet of meditation and the tranquillity of a hermitage. Instead, as Luc slipped in through the big doors, there was chaos, confusion and noisy bustle. The main entrance hall was teeming with men: soldiers, monks and a number of self-important-looking civilians. Voices were raised and shouts exchanged. The sacred walls reverberated with unaccustomed activity.

For Luc it couldn't have been better. The hood of his leather cloak was pulled down around his face just in case, but the precaution appeared to be quite unnecessary. As he had been instructed, he made his way along a side corridor leading to a series of individual monks' cells. He reached the penultimate door on the right and tapped softly on the rough wood. Without waiting for an answer, he pushed. The door swung open, revealing a bare white cell. It contained little other than a narrow bed, a crucifix and a white-haired monk.

'Brother Michael?'

The old man looked sharply up from his reading and then nodded as Luc recited the words he had memorised.

'My friend told me you could help explain a passage from the Scriptures for me. *Seek and ye shall find* is the passage in question.'

A smile spread across the old man's face. His long straggly beard curled upwards as he grinned.

'May the Lord be praised. I've been waiting all winter long. I expected you months ago, Bertrand.'

Luc shook his head. 'Alas, Bertrand didn't make it. He was attacked and killed as he tried to cross the mountains. I've been sent to take over from him. My name's Luc.'

The old man's eyes fell, as did his tone. 'Another brave man gone? Will it never stop?' Then, after a few moments, he visibly roused himself. 'The Lord be praised for affording *you* his protection, Luc. I feared the worst tonight. At first, when I heard all the commotion and saw the soldiers, I thought they must be on to you. Then I heard the news, and you can imagine my relief. Here, come in, take off your cloak and sit down, my son.'

He pushed aside what looked like a wolf skin and made room for Luc on the bunk. He carefully folded Luc's leather cloak and set it on a low shelf while Luc closed the door behind him and made his way over to the old man. He sat down as bidden. Leaning towards the old man, he kept his voice low.

'What news, Brother Michael? What happened tonight?'

'It's about the bandit, my son. Haven't you heard? The soldiers are the King of Aragon's men. They've just captured the one they call the Whip; one of the most fearsome bandits in this whole area. He's being held prisoner in one of the cellars here, until they take him to Jaca to judge him.'

Luc sat back and stretched his legs, a whistle of surprise escaping his lips. So the evil Whip had finally got his just deserts. No doubt after losing his companions he had become vulnerable and the soldiers had caught up with him. And there was no doubt what his fate would be: death, sooner rather than later. Almost certainly this would be by the most unpleasant means so as to serve as a warning to any other potential bandits. In spite of his hatred of the man for what he had done to Aimée, Luc shivered at the thought of what kind of suffering he would be made to endure.

Shaking his mind back to their own situation, he realised with relief that things were by no means as bad as they had first seemed. He turned to the old man.

'They told me you would give me a very precious object. Do you have it?'

The old man looked at him in surprise. 'But you already have it, my son. Didn't you know?'

Luc couldn't believe his ears. 'I already have it? How can that be? The abbot of Santa Cristina told me you would let me have it...' His voice tailed off helplessly.

'Well, you have it, Luc. I know you have.' The old monk was smiling gently.

Luc shook his head in frustration. 'Brother Michael, we really don't have it. I can assure you of that.' He was almost snorting.

The old monk looked at him in surprise. 'You mean you genuinely don't know?' His voice was astounded. 'Nobody told you?' And then, no sooner had he said it, than he realised. 'Of course, it's better that you shouldn't know. That way you can give less away, in the event that they should capture you.'

'But I tell you I don't have anything. You must believe me.' Luc was close to exploding. 'Do you hear me, Brother Michael? We do not have it.' It was a struggle to keep his voice to a whisper and his hands from grabbing the old man and shaking him.

'Luc.' Brother Michael's voice was stronger now, with a note of authority. Luc looked across and caught his eye. He found himself wondering who this old monk was, what he had been before retreating to the isolation of the mountains. 'Luc, I ask you to believe me. You do, indeed, carry this most precious of things. I know you do! You may not realise now, but you have it. I give you my word on all that I hold holy. You have it.' He crossed himself and Luc followed suit, blankly.

'But, Brother Michael—'

'You have it! Trust me. Now...' The old man shook himself back to the matter in hand. 'You said "we". You have a travelling companion?'

'Yes. Her name's Aimée. She was Bertrand's wife. We were brought here by some friends from up the valley. Unaware that this was my true objective, they gave me the name of one of the brothers here, who would be able to help us.'

The old man cut in sharply.

'I don't need or want to hear his name, Luc. Where's your friend Aimée now?'

'She's waiting outside, hiding by a woodpile.' He decided there was no point in pursuing the question of the precious object for now. 'Can you at least provide us with somewhere to shelter for a few days, until it's safe to resume our journey to Compostela?'

'I believe I can. I know a place where you'll be able to rest safe and undiscovered until the coast is clear. Then you can leave and take your most precious of cargoes with you.' The old monk's eyes were faraway and his expression one of rapture.

'Can I go and fetch Aimée?'

'Yes, of course. The woodpile, you say? Excellent. Just beyond that woodpile, there's a small service door. I'll go and unlock it, if you would like to go and get her. Once you're both inside, I'll show you to your place of safety. A few days lying low and then, if God wills it, you'll be free to join a group of passing pilgrims and finish your journey to Compostela.'

Luc thanked him warmly and slipped out into the long passage once more.

This time, as he passed through the hall, it was empty and he felt much more conspicuous. The main door was half open, the shadows outside deep and sinister. His sixth sense told him there was something wrong. He stopped by the door and searched the darkness, but couldn't see anything out of place. After a brief hesitation, he skirted round the side of the gateway to the woodpile. He called out her name as quietly as he could. There was no reply. He moved a few steps closer and whispered her name once more.

A sudden movement from behind him was followed by a massive shove in the small of his back. As he staggered forward, trying desperately to turn towards his aggressor, a heavy blow caught his shins with a numbing pain. He fell headlong onto the ground. Before he could move a muscle, he felt himself roughly caught by the arms. He was thrown forward onto his face, and he felt the impact of many knees on his back and legs. A silky voice spoke out from the darkness.

'Shackle him. He's as strong as an ox and quite desperate. Get chains and get them quickly.' With a crushing sense of despair, Luc recognised the voice as belonging to the Archbishop of Sens himself, Philippe de Marigny, his erstwhile, unwitting travelling companion.

17

ABBEY OF SAN JUAN DE LA PEÑA, SPANISH PYRENEES, APRIL 1314

The door crashed open and flaming torches flooded the dark storeroom with blinding light. Luc blinked hard and squinted as the little room filled with people. As his eyes gradually became used to the brightness, he saw that the Archbishop of Sens had taken up position directly in front of him, safe in the knowledge that Luc was secured to the wall by heavy metal shackles. For a few moments the two men stared at each other. The young archbishop, only a few years older than Luc himself, had a mocking half-smile on his face.

There was a movement at the door. The archbishop stepped back to allow space to the men who came crowding in. In spite of his resolve, Luc felt his stomach churn. The men carried a heavy trestle table and set it up between him and the archbishop. Then they began to lay out a collection of implements, slowly and carefully, directly in front of him. There were knives, hooks, heavy leather belts and hoods, gags and blindfolds. Alongside these was an assortment of evil whips and goads, screws and tongs, along with a brazier of glowing red coals.

Luc raised his eyes from the table and caught those of the archbishop. 'How will you explain this at your next confession?' He eyed the man clinically and coldly, doing his best to master his fear.

'Explain what, my Templar friend?' The voice was heavy with cruel mockery.

Luc made no reply, but his eyes must have flicked down to the array of instruments of torture before him. The archbishop's smile broadened as Luc played into his hands.

'Oh, this?' He reached down and took his time over selecting a suitable instrument. He finally settled on a cat-o'-nine-tails, tipped with vicious steel barbs. 'I have to admit that it would give me a lot of pleasure to see my men use these on you.' He stretched out his arm, until the whip touched the side of Luc's face, just below the eye. He smiled before continuing.

'But you see, I'm afraid these are not for you, my friend. At least, not yet. I will not need to use a single one upon you, gratifying as it might be.' His expression hardened. He turned sharply to one of the soldiers by the door and spat out a command.

'Bring the woman in.'

Luc's resolve disappeared as if it had never existed. He looked on aghast as the soldier dragged in a dishevelled, bruised Aimée, her clothes torn and her face bloodied. The archbishop stepped up to her. He took her face in his hand, turning it roughly towards Luc.

'None of this display is for you, Templar. It is for my men to amuse themselves with upon this young woman. You know her, I believe.'

The mockery was overpowering, but Luc forced himself to take this chance to communicate with Aimée. He shouted as loud as he could at exactly the same time that she, realising that he was finally near her again, shouted to him in her turn. The result was a confused clamour, incomprehensible to both sides. At a sign from the archbishop, a soldier roughly strapped a leather gag across her face. At the same moment, a hairy hand caught Luc's nose, forcing him to open his mouth in order to breathe. As he did so, a foul-tasting cloth was stuffed into it. They both struggled, but could emit no more than muffled noises.

'Now then.' The cleric was enjoying the power of the moment. 'Prepare her.' Luc strained against his fetters, cutting his wrists as he did so, but to no avail. One of the soldiers produced a knife and reached forward eagerly, ready to slit the front of her dress. He was halted by a cry from the door.

'What in the name of the Almighty is this?'

There was general confusion as the soldiers stepped back and a small, misshapen creature limped into the room. He was wearing a threadbare black Benedictine habit that was barely held together by the numerous darns and mends in it. His one good eye took in the scene in a flash. He pushed past the soldiers and made his laborious way across the room, until he was standing directly opposite the archbishop. His fists clenched and unclenched, and the muscles of his face twitched angrily.

'I asked what you think you are doing here.' Receiving no response from the archbishop, he continued. 'This is a holy place, a place of worship, a place of quiet contemplation. There is no place in my monastery for any who do not come in peace and practise the ways of peace. There is no place here for torturers, rapists and perverts.' His burning stare seared the room and the soldiers shrank back, some crossing themselves. Only the archbishop made any attempt at resistance.

'Reverend Father, forgive me, I beg of you. I didn't have time to visit you formally to appraise you of the situation. This man is a fugitive from justice, a foul devil worshipper and a pederast. He's about to reveal to us information of the utmost importance to the Holy See.'

'And to your master, the King of France.' The little man snapped back with venom. 'You will no doubt continue to do your evil business, but you will not do it here in this holy place. I will not tolerate it!'

The strength and authority of the voice, in spite of the frailty of the frame from which it emanated, were inescapable. Even the archbishop made no further protest as the abbot ordered that Luc be unfettered and led with Aimée to another room, where they would be kept under lock and key, until they could be moved elsewhere the next morning.

* * *

After the door slammed shut behind them, they fell into each other's arms. They sat tightly huddled together, leaning against the rough stone wall of the cellar, each drawing strength from the other. Aimée was shaking with overwhelming emotion, tears pouring down her cheeks. Luc cuddled her, as he would have done a baby, stroking her hair until he gradually felt her settle and begin to calm down. He raised his head and stared around the room. He saw nothing in the impenetrable gloom. Not even the thin slits of light, either side of the door, could make any impression on the darkness of their prison.

'Who are you?'

The voice, emanating from another part of the pitch-black cell, made Luc's hair stand on end. The shock of finding that they were not alone was compounded by the voice itself. It elicited a sudden electric reaction in the girl. She sat up so abruptly her head hit Luc's chin. Both of them recoiled in pain. Then, through the pain he heard her desperate whisper. She was close to hysteria.

'It's him. It's him again. I would know his voice anywhere.'

Her voice rose dangerously. Luc continued to stroke her hair with his free hand in an attempt to stop her from losing control altogether. He, too, had realised who it was. He groped in vain for his dagger.

'If you can reach it, there's a torch and tinderbox to the right of the door. I've seen them use it.'

It was indeed the same voice, but the cocky confidence had gone completely. In its place was resignation and fear. Luc helped Aimée to her feet. He kept one arm around her shoulders while he ran his other hand along the wall until he hit something at shoulder height.

'Aimée, I've found the tinderbox. I'm going to need two hands. Are you going to be all right if I remove my arm for a moment?'

He heard a faint murmur in reply.

Carefully, lest he should drop the tinderbox and its all-important flint into the straw on the floor, he released his hold on her. He fumbled until he was able to strike first one, then a stream, of sparks. He was relieved to see them catch. The tar of the torch caught and was soon well alight. He took it in his hand and raised it as high as he could. With his other arm he gripped the trembling girl as he stared around the room.

The cell itself was similar to the one they had been in before. It had a slightly lower ceiling and a bigger window opening at the far end. The rough marks on the walls, where it had been hewn out of the bare rock, were still clearly visible. Lying on the floor, directly across the room from them, was the bandit leader himself. Luc saw the unnatural angle of the legs, and the pain on his grey face. The man spoke in a weary voice.

'They broke my legs, so I couldn't get away.'

The man was in deep shock. There seemed no recognition of either of them in his eyes. A raw, red, broken end of bone protruded through his bloodstained breeches. The pain must have been excruciating. But then, through the haze of suffering, a glimmer of reaction showed. Moments later it was followed by full recognition. But instead of anger or even fear, his expression was one of relief.

'It's you. The heavens be praised. I was afraid it might be some cowardly little runt in here with me. I'm truly relieved it's you. Will you kill me, please?'

His request was serious, totally serious. Aimée's shivering stopped. She clutched Luc's hand so tightly as to dig her nails into his palm. For his part he found himself torn. A few hours, even minutes earlier, he would have had no compunction about killing this foul creature. Now, here, things had changed. Firstly, they were all prisoners and in a sense they were brought closer together by adversity. Second, it had never been his way to kill another human being in cold blood. Add to this the fact that the only way of killing him would be by strangling him with his bare hands and it was unthinkable. He started to tell him so, but the man's brain was still working.

'The window; it looks big enough to get through. I imagine there's a long drop below it. Just help me to get through and I'll do the rest.' He panted as he spoke. His words were slurred. 'Help me. I beg of you. You'd do it for a dog.'

His tone was pleading. The complete change from man of action, evil or otherwise, to pathetic wreck was all too evident.

'Do it.'

Luc looked round in surprise at the sound of Aimée's voice. She took a deep breath and repeated her words.

'Do it. Help him.' Her tone was insistent.

Luc looked closely at her face and saw the determination. For a moment he still hesitated. Then he gave her an encouraging squeeze and made his way over to the window. It was wide enough for even his broad shoulders. He leant out as far as he dared, straining to see what lay below. After the glow of the torch, he could see nothing but blackness. He turned back, pulled a handful of straw from the floor, held it to the torch until it flared, and then threw it out. He followed it down with his eyes, watching the flame fall away into space, while he started to count. He reached eleven before a brief shower of red sparks showed where it hit the ground, hundreds of feet below.

'It's a very long way down.' He was speaking more to himself than to the others. He looked back at the two of them. On the one side stood the victim, physically and mentally scarred for life by an act of barbarism. On the other side lay the crumpled remains of the cause of her grief. He cleared his throat.

'I won't be a party to murder, whatever the justification.' His voice gained in strength, as his thoughts cleared. He met the eyes of the bandit leader. 'However, I will help you to take your own life. At the same time I'll give you the opportunity to help in some way to make amends for the terrible scars you've left on Aimée, and who knows how many other victims.'

The man, whose initial reaction had been one of abject despair, looked back at him in gratitude. 'Anything. I'll do anything.'

Luc had been thinking fast. The straw on the floor came from a bale in one corner. Maybe, just maybe, it might work. He outlined his plan to both of them. He was gratified to see immediate agreement from the man on the floor. More importantly, there was a new sense of purpose on the face of the girl.

'Listen, as a plan it's risky in the extreme, but we've run out of options. Aimée and I will somehow contrive to hide ourselves under the remains of that straw. Once we're covered, that's where you come in.' He looked down at the agonised face of the bandit. 'You'll throw yourself from the window. But you only jump after making enough noise to alert and bring the guards. Is that clear?'

The other man nodded twice, rapidly, comprehension on his face. 'How do I get over to the window?' His eyes flicked down to his grotesquely angled legs.

'I'll carry you over and put you on the windowsill. But remember I'm counting on you to get the guards in here first. They need to believe that the three of us have jumped to our deaths. All right?'

He knew it was a long shot, but anything was worth trying. If all went well, the soldiers wouldn't spot their bodies under the straw. It was tentative, to say the least.

They had some good luck when he found that the cave floor sloped away to one side. This formed a depression, where they would be more likely to pass unseen. He helped Aimée to stretch out as far into the corner as possible, and scattered straw loosely over her. He stepped back and looked down critically. She might just about escape a hurried glance, but a dedicated searcher wouldn't be fooled for long. Knowing there was no other option, he shrugged and prepared a line of straw beside her, which he would do his best to scatter over himself as he lay down. Then, finally, he went over to the other man.

The bandit's face was chalky white and his eyes unnaturally bright. Luc stared down at him for a moment, but there was no answering glance. There was no point in waiting any longer so he bent down and lifted the man by the shoulders and thighs. The sudden pain must have been unbearable and the man fainted. Quickly, before he returned to consciousness, Luc carried the body across the room and propped it right in the window frame itself. It would take only a slight effort to slip through and over the edge. He was turning to check his hiding place when the bandit stirred, emitting a long, low moan of agony. His face screwed up. He tried to move a leg. The stab of pain, caused by the movement, opened his eyes.

After a momentary delay, while his brain came to terms once again with his surroundings, a look of understanding and relief crossed his face. He caught Luc's eye and spoke hoarsely.

'You're a good man. You've kept your word. Now I'll do what you want me to do. I hope it helps you to make good your getaway. Don't look so worried.' His tone was momentarily sharper. 'I'm not going to ask you for your forgiveness. Now give me the torch and lie down and hide.'

Luc spread straw over himself and did his best to squeeze into the inadequate depression in the cave floor. After a few moments he heard the screams and watched the ensuing scene out of the corner of his eye. The man by the window screamed and shouted, louder and louder, until the sound of running footsteps was heard in the corridor. As the door burst open, the bandit turned towards the window.

'Wait for me.' And he launched himself into the void.

'May God have mercy on his soul,' Luc murmured to himself as he hugged the ground.

The group of soldiers ran across to the window. One peered out, just in time to see the blazing torch smash into the rocks below, still in the hand of the bandit.

'Good God Almighty. They've jumped. Quick. Tell the archbishop.'

They streamed back out as fast as they had come in. No sooner had the footsteps receded, than Luc was on his feet. He pulled Aimée roughly with him, his arm round her waist, half-carrying her. They ran out of the door and into the corridor. They raced up the stairs that still echoed to the sound of the guards' boots until they found themselves once more in the main entrance hall. Mercifully it was empty at this time of night. The main doors were solidly bolted and any attempt to open them would have taken time and made a lot of noise. More importantly, it would have alerted the soldiers to the fact that he and Aimée were, in fact, far from dead.

The sound of approaching voices came drifting down the corridors and he made up his mind. 'This way. Hold tight to me and run, Aimée, run for your life.'

He dragged her down the corridor, past the refectory and the cloister until they reached the door of Brother Michael's cell. Running footsteps in the main hall told him they had no time to lose. Without any preamble, he threw open the door, pulled her into the shadowy interior, and closed the door softly behind them.

'Brother Michael. Are you there?' His voice was an urgent whisper. There was a movement and then, to his immense relief, he heard the old man's voice.

'May the Lord be praised. He has delivered you from the valley of the shadow of death.'

There was a rustling sound, then a small oil lamp flared into light. The old man's eyes glittered in the orange glow, his face split by a smile, which went from ear to ear. He leapt up and came over to them, hugging them emotionally. 'As soon as I heard about your capture, I ran to tell the abbot what was happening in the storeroom. Now I was on the point of trying to organise your rescue. I was just wishing I'd let you tell me who your other contact here at San Juan was. That would have made two of us.' He laughed shyly. 'Well, one and a half really. I never have been much of a man of action. More of the contemplative cleric, myself. Anyway, I was all set to try, although I fear I wouldn't have furthered your cause to any great extent.'

Luc clapped his hands around the old man's shoulders. 'Brother Michael. I thank you from the bottom of my heart. You've saved our lives tonight.' Then he moved on to more pressing matters. 'I would imagine we have a few hours, maybe even until first light, before they discover that there's only one, not three bodies at the foot of the cliff. At that point, the first thing that will happen, I feel sure, will be a thorough search of the monastery. Our luck won't hold for long.'

'You're right, my son. There's been terrible trouble here all evening with the King of France's lackey, the archbishop, pressing for a full search and although our abbot has resisted strongly, it'll be a different matter in the morning. I'm fortunate to have neighbours who are older and deafer than I myself and I have little fear of detection. However, I had a moment of blind panic a short while ago, when I found your cloak on my shelf.'

With an embarrassed grin he handed over the heavy leather cloak. Luc was about to put it on, as the temperature in the old man's cell was close to zero, when he noticed that Aimée, who had lost her cloak, was shivering with cold. He made to hang it over her shoulders, but the old monk was ahead of him.

'No, Luc. Keep your cloak. For your friend, I would humbly offer this.'

He reached for what turned out to be a thick oiled wool cloak, lined with silver fur. He wrapped it round her, and saw the look of gratitude on her face as she felt the thick fur against her skin. 'Thank you, Brother Michael.' Her voice was husky.

'Bless you, my child. Bless both of you.' The old man turned to Luc and asked in a businesslike fashion, 'So, tell me now. What do you need from me?'

Luc's answer came back immediately. 'Food, drink and a hiding place. Somewhere we can remain undiscovered for at least a couple of days, until the hue and cry dies down.'

Brother Michael's smile didn't leave his face. 'I know just the place.'

After waiting anxiously for the noise of footsteps in the corridor outside to subside, the old man opened the door. When he was satisfied, he led the two of them back towards the main entrance. Before they reached the hallway, they turned off into the refectory. At the far end they saw a lighted doorway. Steps led down to the kitchen where the pile of blazing logs in the fireplace cast enough light for them to make their way safely around the tables. They tiptoed past the barrels and open sacks. Luc cradled Aimée's head so as to avoid the festoons of onions and garlic, cooking pots, sausages and hams, all hanging from the vaulted ceiling. Aimée heard scurrying by her feet and she realised that the paws responsible for it were surely bigger than mice. With a shiver, she pulled her cosy new cloak tighter round her and gripped Luc's arm. Then they suddenly stopped.

Brother Michael caught Luc's eye and pointed across towards the fireplace. Slumped back on a grain sack was a young monk, his sleeves rolled up, his forearms still covered in flour and dough. He was fast asleep. Although he looked as if nothing short of a peal of bells would wake him, they tiptoed past, trying not to make a sound. He didn't stir.

They passed from the kitchen into a storeroom. At the far end of the room, there was a hatch, set in the wall. Michael went over and pulled it inwards. It slid smoothly open on well-oiled hinges. Cold air came rushing in. Luc realised this was an outside wall and the hatch the main rubbish shoot. He leant out and peered around, dreading what he thought he might see. He was not disappointed.

The clouds had cleared and the moon had risen, bright in the sky clear, illuminating the scene he had feared. The hatch opened onto a steeply sloping wooden ramp that stuck out from the sheer cliff face. Down this, the monastery refuse would slide freely, before dropping vertically hundreds of feet to the rocks below. He felt the familiar knotting of the stomach muscles that his fear of heights always produced. Instinctively he clutched the sides of the hatch and stepped back.

'That's the way, my son.'

Brother Michael's hand was pointing straight out of the opening. For a moment Luc found himself wondering if the old man had lost his reason. Their eyes met in the twilight and the old man chuckled.

'Look up, Luc, not down.'

Hesitantly Luc leant out again and obeyed. Above him a series of metal brackets were set into the cliff, leading up from the opening, but it was too dark to see where they led. There seemed to be little more than bare cliff above them. Once again he felt the dizziness of fear. It took all his strength to speak normally when he ducked back into the kitchen.

'Where do the steps lead?'

'About twenty or thirty feet above us there's a path.' Brother Michael could read the fear in Luc's eyes, so he hastened to reassure him. 'A good, wide path, Luc. It runs around the cliff for a few hundred feet before disappearing into the trees. About halfway along there's a hermit's cell. It was part of the original monastery hundreds of years ago, before this building was constructed. It's dry and you'll be comfortable there for as long as you want. When you feel the time is ripe, you can walk round the path and make your escape. Will it do?'

'It'll have to do.' Aimée's voice held none of the fear that she knew Luc was feeling. 'If it's a choice between falling off a cliff, or being mutilated by the archbishop and his soldiers, I'll take my chances with the cliff any day. Right, Luc?' She raised her face towards him.

Put in those terms, there was no doubt about it. Since childhood Luc had suffered from acute vertigo. Through adolescence he had hoped it would improve but, if anything, it had got worse. He remembered his early years in the Order, moving from castle to castle in the deserts of the Holy Land. Many times he had been more afraid of the view downwards from the battlements than the hail of arrows launched towards them by the enemy hordes. Aimée's hand tightened on his arm. 'Don't worry, Luc, I'll go first.' Her voice was quiet, but quite level. 'If I can do it, anybody can.'

She pressed her head against the side of his chest. Her face turned up towards him, the flickering of the fire highlighting her cheekbones. He pulled himself together.

'You're right. It's the only way. I'll go first, don't worry, but before that I need a few bits and pieces.' He roused himself and set off round the storeroom and kitchen, searching carefully in all the drawers, until he found the cutlery drawer. Gently, so as not to wake the sleeping baker, he sifted through the different knives until he found what he wanted: a replacement for his lost dagger. He pulled out a vicious carving knife with a bone handle. Its blade was honed almost crescent-shaped by years of sharpening. The firelight flickered on the blue steel as he felt the edge appreciatively. Turning back towards the others, he tucked it out of sight into the sheath in the fold of his sleeve, where it lay snugly.

'Here, Luc, take this bread, cheese and sausage. Enough to last me a week or two, but surely enough to last even a big man like you a few days.' The old man's eyes shone out at him from the shadows. Luc gripped him warmly by the shoulders.

'Brother Michael, you're a good man.' He meant it. 'When all this is over, I'll come back to thank you properly.'

'It will never be over, Luc.' There was deep sadness in the old man's tone. 'It can never be like it was again. The forces of the Antichrist have triumphed and there's no going back. Before you or any other Templars have the right to return, I'll be long dead. Make yourself a new life far away from here, Luc. Make good your escape, deliver your most precious of cargoes. Then spend the rest of your life in safety and peace, far away from your oppressors. And make sure you take good care of this courageous and beautiful lady.' His voice broke, and he wiped his face on his sleeve.

'Did you say beautiful?' The mischief in Aimée's voice snapped both of them out of their melancholy, and spurred Luc into action. He shouldered the bag of food, along with a wineskin and a couple of gourds full of water. He kissed Brother Michael on the cheeks and then forced himself to lean out of the opening. He stood there for a few moments, one hand still firmly gripping the window frame, his wounded shoulder throbbing.

The cold night air drifted gently up the cliff face and brushed his face. It brought with it the smell of the forest, so many hundreds of feet below them. A wave of sickness swept over him. It took all his determination to reach upwards with one hand, until he made contact with the first of the iron steps. At least it felt solid. He kept a tight hold on it as he ducked his head back into the kitchen.

'Till we meet again, Michael.'

'Not in this life, Luc. Of that I'm sure. But I know we'll meet again in the house of our Father. Look after this lady, look after yourself and may God's blessing be upon you.'

Aimée hugged him tightly, and then they were off.

It probably took less than a minute to climb to the top of the iron steps, and another two or three minutes at most from there to the cave, but to Luc it seemed like eternity. He clutched the rungs of the ladder so tightly as he climbed up that his fingernails drew blood from the palms of his hands. When he reached the path, he made his way along it on his hands and knees, crawling along like a man possessed, which in a way he was. He even went straight past the narrow entrance to the hermit's cell without noticing it. It was Aimée's low call that stopped him in his tracks.

'It's here, Luc. Back here, I've found the entrance to the cave.' Her voice became more indistinct as she disappeared inside the opening. He shuffled backwards along the ledge, terrified of trying to turn on the narrow path, until he heard her voice beside him. He opened his eyes enough to be able to make out the dark opening in the sheer cliff face. For the first time, he realised that his eyes had been clenched tightly shut throughout the whole climb.

'In here, Luc.'

He saw her in the shadows and crept across to her. She reached out and caught him in her arms, pulling him to her side and, this time, it was she who comforted him as one would a child. Slowly, gradually, he regained control. He opened his eyes and looked around the cave curiously. The moonlight was filtering in through the doorway. As his eyes got used to it, he found he could see reasonably clearly.

The first thing he saw was a crucifix on the wall by his head. Turning towards it, he murmured a prayer of gratitude to the Almighty, for saving them from the very jaws of death. Aimée joined him in the Lord's Prayer. Afterwards, she fell silent, grateful for their deliverance, and thankful they were back together. He remained kneeling, facing the crucifix. She could hear him murmuring as he prayed. It was strange for her to hear him reciting the prayers like a priest, and she had to bear in mind that he was a member of a monastic order. Once again she felt almost improper snuggled up against him.

'Aimée.' His voice was low and tired. Suddenly she realised how tired she, too, was feeling. 'There's a bunk over against the wall. You should go and lie down. There's good dry straw on the floor beside it, where I can sleep quite comfortably.' She heard his hands feeling around the cell. He reached into the far corner and pulled out a dusty sack. 'Unless I'm mistaken, these are blankets.' From it, he produced three crumpled, but still serviceable, woollen blankets. Maybe the mice and rats didn't get up here.

'Here, take these blankets and cover yourself. If you're as tired as I feel, you'll probably sleep until sundown.' He, too, felt exhausted.

'Will you be beside me?' she asked hesitantly, her hand gripping his, in spite of her feeling of impropriety.

'Right beside you. Now go and sleep.' His voice was kind and caring, like a parent to a child.

She released her hold on him. The narrow bed was quite unexpectedly comfortable. Wrapping herself in the wonderful new fur-lined cloak, she lay back on the soft straw. She heard him moving about. There was the smell of cheese as he pulled the bag off his shoulders. Then the events of the last few hours finally caught up with her and she fell into a deep and well-earned sleep.

18

SPANISH PYRENEES, APRIL 1314

It was getting dark by the time Luc eventually saw the roofs of a hamlet, little more than a big farm. He heard the crowing of a lone cockerel, along with the bark of dog. He and Aimée crouched behind a wall for some minutes while he studied the scene, before he finally decided it was safe to venture in amongst the houses. The dog, a large mongrel, came running out at the sound of their approach and Luc gripped his stick warily. The dog was, however, closely followed by an old man, who called it off with a sharp command as he came forward to meet them.

'Pilgrims?'

Not unfriendly, just curious. Luc thought for a moment, before opting for the truth, or at least a version of it.

'Yes, sir. We're just about the first pilgrims to come over the Somport this season. We're on our way to Santiago.'

The old man spat carefully into the clump of weeds by his left leg.

'Not the first. There was a group through yesterday morning, and another group last night. Three groups today. The season's started again all right.' He shrugged as if announcing the arrival of rain. 'You'll be staying the night here, I'll be bound.'

Luc nodded. 'If that might be possible.'

The old man pointed to a large stone barn down by the river. 'That's for the use of you pilgrims. There's no charge, but you could say a prayer for us when you get to Compostela. Yes, say a prayer for us.' He turned to go, but Aimée's voice interrupted him.

'Have you been to Compostela yourself?'

She wasn't sure why she asked him the question. Maybe just because he sounded a good, fair man. Maybe because she was longing for some conversation after the long silent day's hike. The old man turned his attention upon her. His voice softened as he replied.

'Yes, I have. I went many years ago, when my children were still young. My wife stayed at home to look after them. I went with a group of monks from Jaca. It's the most wonderful place in the world.' His tone was awed, still now after the passage of so many years. 'There are buildings twice, three times the size of our castle of Javier. The smoothest stone slabs cover the streets and the cathedral, ah, the cathedral... It is surely the tallest, most wonderful, the most majestic building in the whole world.' He reached out a paternal hand and patted her shoulder.

'Just wait till you stand under the Pórtico de la Gloria and look at the carvings and statues. Nowhere will you see their like. Even the Moors come up from their lands down south to admire their beauty. Take my word for it, my dear, you'll never see a finer sight.'

With these words, he tipped his hat courteously and returned to his home. Luc glanced across at her face. He wondered whether the use of the word 'see' might be bothering her, but her face looked untroubled.

The two of them headed down to the barn-like construction. It turned out to be dry, comfortable and empty.

'By the look of it, we are going to have the whole place to ourselves.'

Both of them were delighted to have found a comfortable place of rest after a long, hard walk down from the hermit's cell that had been their home for two days and nights. Here, at least, Luc could stand upright and there wasn't a terrifying drop right outside the entrance.

Luc set down his pack and led Aimée to a huge tree trunk that served as a bench. The shiny surface attested to the constant passage of pilgrims over many years. There was ample space in the barn for thirty or forty to sleep in comfort. There were even the glowing embers of a fire in the hearth and Luc managed to restart it without much trouble. No doubt, once the season was further advanced, the pilgrims passing through would increase to a steady stream.

'This place is terrific, and there are even cooking pots and pans.'

Luc's attention was suddenly caught by a noise at the door. He was already on his feet, reaching for his knife, when it opened and a young boy came in. Luckily the knife was still out of sight up Luc's sleeve, and the child noticed nothing untoward. From a sturdy wicker basket, the lad produced two large duck eggs and a fresh loaf of bread. He held them out to Aimée. Luc reached across and took them, thanking him warmly.

'My grandfather thanks you for saying a prayer for him at your journey's end.' He had learnt the speech well and delivered it without hesitation, before scuttling off.

'Fresh bread and eggs,' Luc announced grandly. 'With the remains of the sausage, and some fresh water from the fountain, we have a feast fit for a king.'

He busied himself preparing the food. A well-used pan was perfect to fry the sausage and eggs.

Aimée smelt the tempting kitchen smells. 'I used to be a good cook, you know.'

'You don't need to tell me. I've been fed by you on many an occasion. I always thought that Bertrand was a lucky man, in more ways than one.'

He looked across at her but she didn't react, except to murmur, 'Bertrand, lucky?'

She left the question floating in the air. He was suddenly pleased to have to return his attention to his cooking, as the eggs spat and hissed. He pulled an egg out onto a plate and handed it to her, along with sausage and bread. He ate out of the pan, happily mopping up the sausage fat he had used to fry the eggs.

She wondered whether he would say grace before eating. She even hesitated until she heard him chewing, for fear that he might start a prayer after she had begun to eat. Once again, she found herself trying to analyse her feelings for this wonderful man, who had appeared from nowhere to rescue her. Of course, it was right and proper to be grateful to him. But she knew it went deeper than that. She nourished a deep and increasing affection for him. This could so easily have blossomed into more, had it not been for the constant reminders that he was a man of the cloth. *Luc is a monk,* she told herself. *Remember that. His life is devoted to the Almighty.*

It was not going to be easy to accept. Hopefully, as each day passed, she would better be able to come to terms with the reality of the situation. She ate her food in silence. Finally, inferring from his lack of movement that he had already finished, she contrived to leave a piece of her bread and most of the sausage.

'Luc, would you like to finish mine? I'm full.'

He made a weak attempt at protest and then accepted it gratefully. Finally, he voiced something that had been bothering both of them for days.

'Just what do you think it is that we're supposed to be carrying? Brother Michael was quite adamant. He said we already have it.'

'We, or you?'

'I can't remember. I think he said I had it. But he wasn't surprised that I was travelling with you. Maybe he knew all along that you'd survived and you're the one bearing the secret.'

'Luc, all I've got are the clothes on my back. No jewellery, no lucky charms, nothing in my bag but the remains of yesterday's bread and a few personal things.'

'And it's the same for me. I've even lost my trusty old knife that was given to me in the Holy Land. There's nothing else.' As he spoke, he suddenly realised that this wasn't quite correct. 'Wait a minute, there's the cloak the abbot of Santa Cristina gave me.' His voice rose in pitch. She caught his arm and squeezed.

'Shush. But you're right. Come to think of it, I've got this lovely fur cloak from Brother Michael. Maybe the secret's hidden there.'

They reached for the two garments and spent an age running their hands over them, probing every fold and pocket. They found nothing. Luc pulled out the kitchen knife he had taken from the monastery and used it to make a series of cuts in the lining of both. There was nothing in his, apart from the layers of cloth that made up the insulation. Beneath the fur lining to hers, there was nothing at all. Finally they had to accept the inevitable conclusion. Whatever the old monk had said, they were not carrying anything of value. There had to be more to it than that. Then Aimée had an idea.

'So it's definitely not on us, but what about in us? In our heads?'

Luc looked at her for a moment before he realised what she meant. 'You mean something we know?'

'Yes, Luc. Now, I definitely don't know the location of any treasure, or any great secret. I'm sure of that. What about you? You were a high-ranking member of the Order. Might you have knowledge in that head of yours that makes you so important?'

He frowned to himself. 'Nothing that makes me any different from dozens of others. All right, my brother was Preceptor of Normandy, but he never told me any deep, dark secrets.'

She reached over and gripped his hand. By now, she knew all about his brother and the Master being burnt at the stake. 'But are you sure? Nothing at all?'

'Nothing.' He sounded miserable.

'Maybe Brother Michael is just being secretive. Maybe we have yet to pick it up, whatever it is. He was very insistent upon us following the Pilgrims' Way, after all. Maybe we'll get it further along the way.' An idea occurred to her. 'Maybe that business about wanting you to return the cloak to Ponferrada was a discreet way of telling you the secret will be given to you there.'

Luc snorted in frustration. 'God only knows.' After a while, he turned to more pressing matters. 'When we leave here, we've got a couple of days' walk downhill, then we'll be back on the Pilgrim's Way. Then, safely hidden in the anonymity of the crowd, we head westwards.'

'When do you think we'll get there?'

He did a bit of mental arithmetic. 'If all goes well, some time around Pentecost.'

'So, what's that, about five or six weeks? Well, Luc, we're going to know each other very well indeed by then.' She reached out, found his hand and squeezed it. 'I hope I don't turn out to be too much of a nuisance.'

'Nuisance, you?' He snorted. 'Just promise me one thing. As we are supposed to be a married couple, please don't nag me too much.'

'Just you make sure you wash the pots properly.'

He grinned at her and cleared the dishes, taking them outside to the riverbank to wash them clean. After he had finished, he washed his shirt, keen to be rid of the bloodstains he had picked up in his fight with the bandit at the inn and then at the hands of the archbishop's men in the monastery. These would be bound to arouse suspicion among fellow pilgrims. He replaced the pan and plate where he had found them, and then he hung the clothes to dry by the fire. He glanced at Aimée, feeling embarrassed to be bare-chested in her presence, even though he knew she couldn't see him. She was still sitting on the log, facing the fire, and she looked miles away. She didn't turn around towards him as he moved about. Determined to cleanse himself fully, he slipped outside again. Pulling off his boots, and unlacing his breeches, he stripped completely. Then, gritting his teeth, he waded into the freezing water. It was so cold, it took his breath away.

He splashed about in the rushing stream, rubbing himself and his clothes vigorously until he felt clean once more. Climbing out, he patted himself dry. Then he wrapped himself in a blanket, hanging his wet trousers on a bush. It was a clear night and the stars sparkled out from the deep velvet of the sky. The snowy mountain tops reflected enough light from the near full moon to provide a luminous frame to the scene. A sensation of the majesty and grandeur of what he was observing, compared with the total insignificance of the players in this tiny human drama, himself included, hit him hard. Ignoring the cold, he sank to his knees. Softly, he began to pray, his hands clasped in front of him. His eyes were fixed on the starry firmament above and around him.

He prayed out loud, but in a low voice, little more than a whisper. He prayed for help and for guidance, for the strength to finish his mission. He prayed for the future of the Order and he prayed, above all, for Aimée, that she might survive the present danger, and live a full and happy life. As always, when he found himself in close communion with his Lord, he drew immense comfort from the nearness he felt to God. When he finally bowed his head and said, 'Amen,' he felt purged, restored and fortified. It came as a surprise when he heard her quiet 'Amen' just a few feet from his side. He hadn't heard her approach.

'Thank you for letting me be part of that.'

Her voice was low and warm, maybe even respectful. He turned his head and saw her outline against the flickering silver reflections of the moon on the river. He moved across to her and stretched his arm around her shoulder, feeling her head against his chest. He raised his other hand and tilted her face towards him, his hand on the side of her cheek. He gently touched her sightless eyes.

'May the Lord protect you and keep you, Aimée. May he give you happiness and peace to the end of your days.'

He felt her nod, her lips mouthing the 'Amen'. His eyes went up once more to the starry sky. He found himself smiling into the glittering heavens.

'It's good to be alive, Aimée.' He pressed her head to his chest.

'If I am, it's thanks to you.' Her arms gripped him tightly as she spoke into his shoulder. 'You brought me back to life. I owe you everything. I would give you anything, everything.' She held onto him as if her very life depended upon it. Then, she raised her face towards him, her expression now deadly serious.

'Luc. Can I ask you something, please?' He could feel her trembling.

'Anything, just say it. I would do anything for you, you know that.' He raised his hand and stroked her cheek. The only response he elicited was a stream of tears. It took a while before she managed to calm herself enough to speak. He hugged her to him, wondering what was coming next.

'Anything? That's good, Luc, because what I have to ask won't be easy.' She rubbed the tears angrily from her eyes. 'If they... if we are ever captured again, I want you to kill me. Will you promise to do that, please?'

She was gripping his arm tightly. He had to struggle hard to chase the grey, pain-racked face of the bandit leader from his mind as he listened to her words. He tightened his arms around her thin body.

'I would give my life gladly to protect you. You know that. But I couldn't kill you, Aimée, any more than I would agree to kill that worthless murderer back there in the monastery. It's not my way to kill in cold blood.' It was the truth, and a pious, maybe even a little pompous, speech. Her expression didn't change.

'Could you bear the thought of them torturing me with those terrible things? Could you?' Her words cut him like a knife. 'They told me all about them in foul, disgusting detail back in there while they were mauling me with their hands.' She did her best to suppress a shudder of shame and disgust. 'Hot coals, hooks, whips... Could you? Could you, Luc?' She shook herself out of his arms. Gripping his shoulders with both hands, she trained her sightless eyes upon his face. 'I'm asking you, Luc, to save me. I'm asking you to give me the one thing that will save me if ever we have the misfortune to find ourselves in a situation like that again. Please, please say you'll do it.'

He was stunned. All his training had told him that killing was only to be tolerated as a last resort, and only on the field of battle. How could he do something like that? Then he saw again the trestle table spread with the obscene implements of torture and he knew he would do what she asked. He could never let her go through that. At whatever personal cost to himself, he knew that he would do it.

'I promise.' His voice was low. She barely heard his words.

'Do you truly promise?'

'I truly promise,' he repeated miserably.

She let herself collapse against his chest and gave free rein to the floods of tears that had been building up inside her for days. He held her lightly, and let her purge herself through her tears. When she finally recovered enough to set about wiping her face and blowing her nose, it was clear that a weight had been lifted from her mind. He, on the other hand, suddenly found himself feeling even more troubled. He had just realised that, under the blanket, he was completely naked.

He gradually disentangled himself from her. Collecting his boots and breeches, he headed inside. He was still in the process of lacing himself up, when he felt a gentle touch on his bare shoulder. He jumped.

'Well, you smell a lot better than you did. I think I might have a bath as well.' She was sounding much happier now.

He blushed red, grateful she couldn't see his embarrassment. Or so he thought. 'Erm, yes. That's a good idea.'

'Are you embarrassed, Luc?' Her voice was positively mischievous and, in spite of his embarrassment, he was glad to see her happy again. 'I promise I won't look.' She giggled.

He did his best to recover his composure. 'It's all right, I'm quite decent.' He wrapped the blanket back around his shoulders and led her out to make sure she got her bearings.

'Be very careful, Aimée. The river's quite deep here, and it's running very fast at the moment. Stay close to the bank. Shout if you get into difficulty.'

She gave him a smile and she kicked off her shoes. He hastened back into the barn, terrified that she would call him to assist her, and plunge him into even more embarrassment.

Five minutes later she came back into the barn, decorously wrapped in a blanket.

'I wonder if you'd mind hanging my clothes up to dry. I'm afraid I might set them, or myself, on fire.' She passed him her wet dress and sat down on her cloak. After a bit, she handed him the blanket to hang up to dry. Although he averted his eyes, he couldn't help noticing she was only in her undershirt. He looked away, rolled himself into his cloak and did his best to dismiss the image from his mind.

In spite of being tired, he lay awake for a while, thinking of what she had said and the promise he had made. He knew that there would be danger lurking ahead of them every step of the way, and he prayed he would never have to fulfil his commitment to her.

19

SPANISH PYRENEES, APRIL 2016

The drive down from the monastery to the floor of the main valley involved hairpin after hairpin and it was approaching noon by the time the road levelled out. The April sun was already hot enough for Luke to feel grateful for the cold air from the air-conditioning unit blowing in his face. High summer here would be very, very hot.

'So is it all downhill from here?' Amy reached for her bottle of water and took a mouthful. 'I'm not sure my stomach can cope with any more bends for a while!'

'You and me both. As for downhill, I suppose it'll be pretty much gently downhill now for a day or two. But then it all gets hilly again as we start going west, into the Rioja region and on through the Montes de León.' He spotted a filling station ahead and pulled over. 'Not the most modern-looking petrol station. Mind you, at least there's little shop next door. I'll see if I can get us something for lunch.'

'Remember, no beer.' She was enjoying her role as medical supervisor.

'Yes, Doctor.'

The attendant came to serve them and Luke jumped out into the surprisingly warm noonday sun to ask him to fill the tank. It was probably ten degrees warmer down here than up by the monastery. While the Range Rover was being filled up, Luke bought a chorizo sausage, some Manchego cheese and two enormous bread rolls from the shop. He used a sponge in a bucket to clean the windscreen, the lights and the number plates. The rest of the car remained a muddy brown colour after their days on the snowy roads of the mountains. He paid for the fuel and rejoined her.

'I think I'll run us through the next car wash we come to.' A glance around the bare hillsides in all directions prompted him to add, 'Though it might be a while before we find one of them.'

'Pretty remote up here?'

'A few sheep, the odd crumbling barn and that's about it. Probably not substantially different from what it looked like in the Middle Ages.'

The valley was wide and the valley floor sloped down so gently it appeared almost flat. As for traffic, there was little or nothing on the road. Luke could easily have put his foot down and sped along. As it was, he chose to take his time, savouring the clear blue sky and the warm sunshine and trying to be as graphic as possible in his description to her of their surroundings.

Amy listened with interest as he described the spectacular snow-capped chain of the Pyrenees behind them. 'It's like a great white-topped wall. It's exceptionally clear today, after the recent snow. You can see for miles in all directions.' He did his best to convey the sense of sweeping vastness that Spain always aroused in him. The dusty fields without hedges to divide them stretched out as far as the eye could see.

Amy enjoyed listening to his voice and, in spite of her resolve, found herself wondering what she would feel, and what she would do, when this wonderful journey finally finished. Back to the huge, elegant, but empty house in London? Somewhere else? She still had the house in the Alps, although she knew she would need all her strength before she could go back there to confront the ghosts and the memories. Maybe if Luke came with her. There, she had said it. She wanted his support. There could be no doubt in her mind how close she was getting to him. How, she wondered, did he feel about her?

They arrived in Sangüesa at six o'clock that evening. It had been a fascinating, if tiring, day. On their way down the valley from the mountains onto the plains they had visited everything worth seeing – and for two people with a special interest in medieval history, that had meant an awful lot.

When they finally got there, Luke booked two rooms at the Hostal Santiago. Unsurprisingly, almost every town along the Pilgrims' Way had a Hotel Santiago or a Hotel Compostela. This one was very simple, but it was clean and the man on the reception desk very friendly. And it was slap bang in the medieval centre of this historic town. Luke accompanied Amy to her room and gave her the usual tour.

'Not the height of luxury, but quite comfortable. And definitely a lot more comfortable than the pilgrims' hospice where our man would have stayed.'

'You mean I don't need to sleep on the floor and share a hole in the ground as a toilet with a couple of hundred people?' She was smiling at him.

'Not unless you want to.' He glanced at his watch. 'What do you feel like doing?'

'I'm determined to wash some underwear before I run out completely. Give me an hour or so.'

'I'll go and take a look round town. I'll come back for you at, say, eight-thirty.'

Outside the hotel Luke turned right and walked down the long, narrow Rúa Mayor until he reached the crossroads at the end by the river. There, dominating the scene, was the Collegiate Church of Santa Maria la Real, its sandstone walls glowing in the rosy light of the setting sun. After pausing to stare in silent appreciation at the wonderful medieval figures carved around the portal, he entered the church.

The church was empty, silent except for the cooing of doves high up on or, more probably, in the roof. The altar was a simple affair surmounted by a delicate statue of Our Lady of Rocamadour, showing the close links all these different stages on the Pilgrims' Way had with the lands north of the Pyrenees. He had told Amy he wasn't religious and he wasn't. He found it impossible to study the crimes committed by the medieval church, let alone the atrocities still being committed by Man all over the world today, and still retain a belief in a kind, merciful god. But he did appreciate the atmosphere of peace and tranquillity to be found in many churches, and this one was no exception.

He sat down on a pew in silent contemplation for many minutes, thinking back on all his troubles, his depression and despair. These past few weeks with Amy had been the brightest point in his recent past and he knew he was growing ever closer to her, whether or not he should be. Her presence had cheered him and helped him, and his life would never be the same again as a result. Maybe, just maybe, he was finally on the way out of the abyss in which he had been stuck for so long. After quite some time alone with his thoughts, he stood up. There was something he had to do. He turned and made his way out of the church.

Outside, the sky was still and clear, the sun just dipping below the horizon. Luke sat down on a stone bench in the main square, pulled out his phone and dialled. Father Tim answered straight away.

'Hi, Luke, great to hear from you. Where are you and how's everything going?'

'Hi, Tim. We're in Sangüesa, not far from Pamplona, and I've got a bone to pick with you.' His tone belied his words.

'With me? What've I done?'

'You know full well. When you put me and Amy together, it wasn't just so we could talk about history, was it?'

'I don't know what you mean.' Father Tim wasn't a very good liar. 'So, does this mean you two are getting on well together?' His tone betrayed more than casual interest.

Luke told him the truth. 'We're getting on very well together, just like you knew we would. She's a lovely, bright girl and I feel I'm getting closer and closer to her. And it's all your fault.'

'I'm delighted to hear it.' Tim sounded delighted for them. 'So where do you go from here?' Luke knew he wasn't talking about their route, but he chose to interpret it as that.

'We start going west now, through Burgos and León towards Santiago. Depending on what stops we make, I reckon we should be there in a couple of weeks.'

'And what then, Luke?'

'That's what I'm trying to work out.'

Luke went on to tell Tim that he was feeling better than he had in years and the reason for this was, without question, his proximity to Amy. They chatted for some minutes and when the call ended, Luke definitely felt brighter, more cheerful and reassured. He slipped the phone back into his pocket and stood up.

All around, people were finishing their day's work. The bars were already starting to fill, as men and women met to talk over the day and relax. He thought about stopping off for a beer, but a glance at his watch made him realise that he had left Amy alone long enough. He headed back to the hotel.

He knocked a couple of times, but she wasn't in her room. Coming back down the stairs, he met the proprietor.

'Señor Patterson, I have a message for you.' The man smiled broadly and pointed back up the road. 'Your friend thought you might be in one of the bars, so my daughter is walking with her down the Rúa Mayor to look for you.'

He was a kindly looking man fighting, in common with so many restaurateurs, against the steady and inevitable expansion of his waistline. He proudly sported a moustache worthy of a Mexican bandit. He proceeded to curl it up almost to his eyebrows as he gave Luke a conspiratorial grin.

'My wife is also often checking up on me too. It is their way.' This observation was accompanied by an expansive wave of the hand that conjured up generations of wives checking on their husbands, and the husbands in turn telling other men, who would in their turn be checked up on by their wives, and so on throughout an eternal cycle.

'She's not my wife.' Before he could stop himself, Luke added, 'Yet.'

'But she will be.' The hotelier was quite sure of his prediction. 'And she is already starting to check up on you now.' He chuckled and spread his arms wide once more. 'It is their way.' With a bow he returned to his kitchen, leaving Luke still stunned that he had chosen to use the word *yet*.

He found them almost immediately. They were sitting in a renovated bar halfway along the street, just before the medieval square. Amy was sipping a glass of Cava. Beside her, the hotel owner's daughter, who was about twelve, was demolishing a huge multicoloured ice cream, topped with whipped cream and adorned with a pink parasol. Luke squeezed past a group of young men by the door and made his way down to their table. As he materialised alongside them, he laid his hand on Amy's shoulder and she looked up with a happy smile.

'Hi, there. Good walk?'

'It's a lovely little town. How's the ice cream?'

'Lourdes here says it's great, but tells me the ice cream at her father's restaurant is even better.' In halting, but comprehensible, Spanish she repeated her remark. The girl giggled into her sundae.

'What about you? Ready for that beer?'

He studied her reflectively. She looked lively, contented and relaxed. In particular he was struck by the happiness in her face, especially when he compared it to the bleak loneliness of her expression when they had first met. He realised that the sense of optimism he had felt in the church was here to stay, and he came close to reaching out and hugging her but, as ever, he resisted the temptation.

'Definitely a big beer. I'm feeling very good this evening.' There was no doubt at all. Compared to his mood over the past few years, he was indeed a happy man. 'I really am. I haven't been happier for years and years and years, and being here with you is what's doing it.'

The waiter passed and asked briefly if they needed anything. Quick as a flash Amy caught his attention and ordered confidently.

'Una cerveza mas, mas grande.'

It must have done the trick. Shortly afterwards, Luke found himself on the receiving end of a huge German-style litre mug of beer. Goodness only knew how it had ended up here. Amy reached out and felt the dimensions of the glass for herself before murmuring an appreciative grunt. The little girl watched goggle-eyed as Luke lifted the mug to his lips and looked disappointed that he didn't drain it in one mouthful. The sundae now demolished, she dedicated herself methodically to the assorted nuts and olives that arrived with the beer. Luke wondered absently how these would lie with the ice cream and whipped cream in her stomach. Wisely, he decided that this was up to her to discover for herself.

'Anyway, talking of happiness, you're looking radiant and cheerful tonight. I was just thinking how different you look and sound compared to the first time I met you.'

'If I look it, that's because I am. I couldn't ask to be anywhere better than this. The atmosphere's good, the wine's good and the company's very good. And I'm not just talking about Lourdes here.'

He would have reached over and taken her hand, but again he resisted the urge. Instead, he looked at his watch. 'What say we head back for dinner? If for no other reason than to stop this young lady from exploding. The consequences in this crowded room could be catastrophic.'

Amy giggled and asked whether he had finished his beer. He hadn't, but he did so in record time, gaining an admiring look from the little girl as he did so.

The restaurant in the hotel was about half full by the time they got back. Lourdes disappeared into the kitchen, only to emerge seconds later with a huge plate of meat and potatoes that she set about with the same gusto she had shown earlier. Luke and Amy sat at a table in the corner of the utilitarian dining room and he described the other occupants of the room to her.

'They look like mostly commercial travellers, with one or two locals thrown in. There's a family celebration of some sort on one long table in the centre of the room. Six or seven adults are surrounded by about twenty children.'

'My ears had already worked that out.'

The restaurant owner came over to their table, bearing a bottle of Cava. He opened it with a flourish and placed it on their table, giving them both a big smile.

'My daughter's thanks for the ice cream and my good wishes for your future together.' He made the announcement grandly and swirled off into the kitchen once more.

'Are you blushing too?' she asked timidly.

'I do believe I am,' he answered. 'I wouldn't want you to think that I'd given him the wrong idea about us.' She could even *hear* him blushing now.

'Wrong idea?' she asked innocently. Luckily at that moment food started to arrive and he sounded relieved to revert to his usual tour-guide mode.

'Black olives looking lovely and fat, probably still with stones in them, so watch your teeth. The bread's in a basket bang in front of you.'

He reached over and poured some of the wine into their glasses. As he did so, two huge plates of mixed salad arrived.

'Green salad, red salad, two or three other types of crinkly stuff, some sort of dandelion leaf shaped, some normal, onion rings, a boiled egg and a load of tinned tuna.' Amy couldn't help smiling.

'I must give you a guide to salads one of these days. "Crinkly stuff", indeed?'

He laughed back at her, the spell broken. 'Sorry, I'm afraid I'm not getting any better. I'm good at dates, though, and popes. I can recite them backwards from now to the early Middle Ages.' He would have launched into a demonstration, but her finger reached out, found his face and sealed his lips.

'I'll remember that next time I order a plateful of popes.'

They ate in silence for a while before he picked up the conversation again. 'I've been thinking seriously about a lecturing position.'

'I would imagine you'd go down a bundle with the female students if you choose that career path.' He choked on his tuna and she was able to go on unopposed. 'With your background and qualifications, I am sure you could get yourself a lectureship without too much trouble.'

He drained the glass of water, glad the tuna hadn't gone down the wrong way. 'I already have an offer.'

This was news to her. 'I didn't know. That's terrific. Where?'

'Boston.'

She took the news expressionlessly. 'That's not the one in Lincolnshire you're referring to, I imagine?' He grunted. 'Starting when?'

'Start of the next semester, if that's the path I choose to follow.' He resumed his assault upon the salad.

She slowly digested what he had told her.

Of course life had to go on; his and hers. Wonderful as this interlude was, she could hardly expect it to last forever. It would end. It had to. And when it did, there was every chance they would each resume their individual, normal lives. In spite of herself, she felt a chill run through her. What was normal life? Would she really return to the empty house and resume her dull, dry and sensible existence, wanting for nothing that money could buy? But all the time she knew she would be longing desperately for laughter and, yes, for love.

'Aren't you going to finish your salad?' His voice cut in on her thoughts. She shook her head. 'When we get home I promise I'll take lessons in identifying different types of lettuce. Honestly.' His hand reached across and gave her hand a quick squeeze. She looked up and smiled.

'And desserts.' He waited while a young waitress cleared their plates before continuing.

'And cheeses. Anyway, I said I'd had an offer. I haven't accepted it yet. Besides, Land Rover reckon these diesel engines are good for hundreds of thousands of miles. We could always go on from Santiago to Rome and from there to Jerusalem. Maybe then we could try Mecca, although they wouldn't let us in. From there it's only a short step to Amritsar then Lhasa. Come to think of it, we could carry on round till we reach Graceland. Let's not forget the modern-day pilgrimages.'

She laughed in spite of herself and realised, as if she needed to, that she would miss the fun of being with him.

'You make me laugh.' She banished the future and tried hard to concentrate on the present. She dearly wanted to save the moment in her memory forever. 'Save to disk...' she murmured, and then made the whirring sound of the computer doing its work.

'Hard disk?' he enquired gently, continuing her train of thought.

'CD-ROM, of course. Read-Only Memory. Can't delete it, can't change it. Keep it in a little plastic case and trot it out whenever I want to. The ultimate computer game. Virtual reality.' The words were light, the tone wasn't.

'Virtual?'

'That's not up to me.'

20

SPANISH PYRENEES, APRIL 1314

The next morning dawned bright and clear. Both Luc and Aimée had slept for almost twelve hours. When he awoke, warm and comfortable, the first thing he saw was Aimée, lying on her cloak, only a short distance away from him. A shaft of sunlight streamed in through the gable doors, lighting up the whole barn. The residual heat, cast by the embers of the fire, still warmed them both and she had cast off the cloak. She was only wearing her under-shirt, her shoulders bare, the gentle swell of her breasts clearly visible.

She stirred and stretched. He watched her emerge from the depths of slumber and gradually awaken; this time not rudely into a hostile world, but gently and willingly into an environment that was no longer so threatening. He reached over and touched her lightly on the forearm. Her left hand caught his and drew his fingers to her lips.

'Good morning.' His voice was warm.

'Good morning to you.' She kissed each of his fingers in turn and held his hand to her cheek. 'Is it my imagination, or is it late?'

He wondered how she could tell. In fact it had been light for some hours, by the angle of the sunbeams.

'No imagination. The sun through the windows is already quite warm.' He looked down at her, affection brimming over at the sight of her. 'I don't need to ask whether you slept well last night.' She grinned, and stretched like a cat.

'So, what's the plan today? Another route march, or have you something more interesting in mind?' She relinquished her hold on his hand and sat up, reaching up to tidy her hair. She seemed oblivious to her state of undress, and the effect it was having on him.

'You heard the old man last night.' He did his best to sound businesslike. 'There are already a number of groups of pilgrims on the way. If this sunshine keeps up, the snows will soon melt away and then the numbers will increase enormously. I would think the safest thing to do would be to head for the next big town. I think that's Sangüesa. It's about twice the distance we did yesterday.'

He saw the expression on her face, and hastened to clarify.

'It's all right. We'll do it in two days. I'll ask the old man for directions. Maybe he can suggest somewhere suitable to stay tonight. Once we get to Sangüesa, we should be able to join a group of pilgrims. We stand a much better chance of getting through to Compostela unharmed if we blend in with the local colour. Does that seem like a reasonable idea to you?'

She stretched again and reflected that if he had suggested crawling to the next town on hands and knees, she would most probably have gone along with it. She felt safe and secure once more. Her faith in his ability to look after them both was stronger than ever.

'The fire's still throwing out quite a bit of heat,' she observed gratefully. 'Have the clothes all dried?'

He got up and went over to the line. The clothes were all dry and warm. He collected her dress and brought it to her.

'Thank you. That feels lovely. Tell me, Luc, are we staying for breakfast?'

'We certainly are, if I can find any. I'll throw a few more logs on the fire and then I'll leave you here to get ready, while I go and see what can be found in the way of food.'

He pulled on his shirt and jacket, relieved to be clean once more. He soon had the fire burning up nicely. With a last glance at the girl, who looked as settled and contented as he had ever seen her, he headed out of the barn.

She got up in her turn. As she buttoned up her dress, she reflected on the previous evening. On the one hand, she knew she had to come to terms with the fact that Luc was a monk, with all that this entailed. On the other, she knew that she had enjoyed herself immensely flirting with him. In fact, she had enjoyed herself more than she had for months. The thing was that, somehow, she knew she had always loved him. Even though Bertrand had been her husband, she had felt an attraction to this handsome man ever since the first time she had met him. She remembered that moment as if it were yesterday. He had been thrown off a horse in training and was bleeding profusely from the side of his head but, even so, he had given her a warm smile when Bertrand had introduced him to her. Of course, her love for Bertrand had been strong and her relationship with him had been paramount, but deep, deep down, the seeds of love had been sown. Now, under these intimate circumstances, she knew that it would take very, very little for them to grow and blossom. She shook her head helplessly. It wasn't easy.

She rolled up their blankets, trying to squeeze them tightly so they would occupy as little space as possible in the pack. As she folded his, she felt something caught up in it. Reaching in, she pulled out his heavy wooden crucifix. She took it in her hands and pressed it to her cheek. The wood was still warm with his warmth and she could smell his body on it. She let the crucifix slide down her cheek and touch her throat. She still felt the warmth of it as she slipped it under her shirt, and pressed it to her heart. The touch against her bare skin sent a thrill throughout her whole body. She gave a guilty start, pulling it out and laying it once more on his cloak. Hastily, she gathered her skirt around her and made her way out of the door, towards the unmistakable smell of the latrines.

When she got back, she could tell immediately that he had found fresh bread. He caught her arm and led her to the log by the fire.

'A real treat today, Aimée. We have fresh bread, fresh butter, honey and cow's milk. Here.' He pressed a mug of warm milk, sweetened with honey, into her left hand. A rough chunk of fresh, warm bread was pushed into her right. 'I doubt whether the King of France himself is enjoying a better breakfast!'

He sat down beside her and they ate heartily. She felt warm, cared for and carefree.

'How're the feet?' The previous day had been hard on her after weeks of immobility.

'Fine. No serious blisters, and the stiffness in my ankle's gone. How far are we going today?'

He had been calculating. 'An easy day's walk to our overnight spot, according to the old man. But you know these country folk. They'd probably walk from here to the top of the Pyrenees and back in a day. But supposing we get away fairly soon now, I would hope we'd be there by late afternoon, blisters permitting.'

'And the archbishop and his men?' Her voice was lower now. 'Are we sure we can avoid them? After all, doesn't Sangüesa lie just inside the boundary of the kingdom of Navarre, with its French ruler? It's a major stopping point on the Pilgrims' Way. Wouldn't that be a logical place to wait for us?'

'Well, that's not till tomorrow night.' Luc did his best to sound confident. 'The old man tells me there's a little hamlet by the river for tonight, with a similar set-up to this. It's so small it doesn't even have a name. I imagine we'll be as safe there as we possibly could be.'

She finished her food, drained the milk and sat upright. He took the empty mug from her and swilled it with water.

'Come on.' He reached for his pack. 'Let's get going. The sooner we start, the sooner we get there.'

They made good time down the valley. The sunshine was making short work of drying the fields and they were able to negotiate all but the deepest fords without difficulty. They reached their next way station in the late afternoon. Locating the farm and outbuildings, as indicated by the old man, turned out to be quite straightforward. Although it was a bit smaller, they were warm and comfortable once more. Luc was also able to buy cheese, ham and bread from the farmer and they ate well that night.

At some point during the following day, they must have crossed the boundary between friendly, or at least neutral, Aragon and far more threatening Navarre. And here, Luc had no doubt that King Louis' men would be on the lookout for them. In the fields there was no sign of any frontier, but the tension began to mount in both of them. The day turned out to be a lot longer than the previous one and it was almost completely dark by the time they climbed the last slope before Sangüesa.

The lights of the town were bright and it looked lively. The sounds of voices, domestic animals and carriages were audible even before the walls of the town came into view. They stopped on the outskirts and Luc pressed Aimée into hiding.

'If you stand tight against this tree, you're in thick shadow. You'll be fine here while I go and take a look. I'll be back in a few minutes.'

She took cover as instructed, while he slipped forward in the darkness, to check whether the king's men were in evidence. The sense of abandonment set her heart racing, but he was as good as his word and returned almost immediately.

'Aimée, I'm delighted to say that everything looks peaceful: no soldiers, no cavalry. We should be fine. Now let's see if we can find lodgings.'

He led her along the darkest side streets, until they reached what looked like the poorest hostelry in the place. Cautiously, he peered in through the thick curtain hanging inside the door. He saw only some pilgrims, eating at a long table, and, beyond them, a big open fire. He turned back to Aimée and whispered.

'Not a lot going on here, by the looks of it. No soldiers, and it's certainly not the sort of place an archbishop would stop in. I think it's worth taking a chance. Let's try to make contact with some of these pilgrims, in the hope that we'll be able to join a group tomorrow morning.'

She nodded her agreement, keen to rest her weary feet. He pushed the door open and they slipped into the big room and made for the corner. They were only halfway across the floor, when Luc heard a booming voice.

'Well, hello again, Luc. We thought we'd lost you.'

He wheeled around, his left hand pulling Aimée tightly to him. His right reached for the carving knife. Mercifully, he had not pulled the weapon out when he recognised the owner of the voice.

'Friar Laurent. How wonderful to see you again.' He squeezed Aimée's hand encouragingly, as he relaxed his right. 'When did you come over the pass?'

The friar smiled broadly and pointed along the table. Amongst them Luc recognised the peasants from Champagne, the pessimistic stonemason and the baker, together with his family. He couldn't, however, see any trace of the snooty nuns.

Friar Laurent came over and the two men embraced.

'Ah, Luc, we were truly blessed. The snow stopped just as we reached the top. We were able to make it up and over to the valley beyond without stopping. But what about you? We wondered if something had happened to you in Oloron.' His expression was benign, but his eyes were watching shrewdly.

Luc's immediate reaction was one of relief. The group hadn't stopped at Santa Cristina. That was good news, because there was every likelihood that the tale of his escape from the king's men would have been common knowledge to anybody going through the hospital for weeks, if not months, to come.

'Let me introduce you to Aimée. She's a good friend of mine.' He was racking his brains for a reasonable explanation for why he had left the group. In the end he opted for a version of the truth. 'I had to go and look for Aimée. I was told she was in the area. The problem was, I wasn't given specific directions how to find her. I do hope you didn't waste time waiting for me.'

'Not at all, Luc. As it was, we got held up for hours by the army. They were looking for some criminal or other.'

Luc's ears pricked up as the stonemason from Beauvais chipped in.

'Looking for one of those damned Templars, they were. Bastard escaped the medicine all the others were getting. They were trying to catch him before he disappeared off across the border like a scared rabbit.'

He turned his head and spat into the fire. He missed, reached out absently with his boot and smeared the spittle into the tiled floor. Friar Laurent winced. He gave Luc a look that indicated graphically that the mason had not developed into any better company.

Luc and Aimée settled down on a bench with the rest of the group. They drank gratefully from the jug of wine that the friar pushed across to them. The baker's wife gave him a bright smile, while his daughter gawped at Aimée with disbelief. Surely a blind woman wouldn't be able to undertake this long and arduous journey? Luc reached for Aimée's hand under the table. As she leant towards him, he put his mouth up against her ear and whispered.

'I think we're all right. If they'd been told about us, it would show, I'm sure.' He drew away again and spoke in a normal voice. 'What would you like to eat?'

'Isn't this your chance to have a hot meal, Luc? I'll have what you're having, but less of it.' Her voice was tired.

He smiled and got up. He went off to look for the landlord. He found him just coming out of the kitchen with half a roast chicken on a plate. It was the work of a moment to ask for the other half. It was brought to their table along with bread and wine and they enjoyed an excellent evening meal.

'Will you join us when we set off in the morning, Luc?' The friar sounded keen. Through her tiredness, Aimée realised why he wanted Luc's support. This would further strengthen their chances if bandits should descend upon them.

'We'll be pleased to, Brother.' Luc glanced across at Aimée. She looked half asleep. Her cheek was on her forearm, and her eyes half closed. 'What time are you setting out?'

'First light, or as soon after as we can manage. I'll ask the landlord to wake us when he rises. All right?' Luc nodded and took Aimée's hand, leading her to the next room. It was a communal dormitory. Straw-filled mattresses were scattered across the floor.

'At least there's one advantage to being among the first pilgrims this year.' He lowered his voice. 'The mattresses look clean and well filled. We should get a good night's sleep.'

'I feel so tired, I am sure I could sleep on a stone floor.' She sounded it.

With the help of the baker's wife, Aimée had no trouble in locating the latrine. It felt strange, and very reassuring, to have female company once more. It came as a relief after months in an all-male environment and, although she was tired, she enjoyed the opportunity to chat. Beatrice, the baker's wife, was a cheerful soul, who was only too happy to help. Finding Luc again in the crowded room, scattered with sleeping bodies, would have been difficult, but Beatrice led her across to him. She squeezed Aimée's arm before leaving her.

'We'll be travelling with you all the way to Compostela, Aimée. You can count on me.'

Aimée thanked her, her spirits buoyed by the simple friendship. Luc was delighted to see the smile on her face.

'Here, there's space for us over here in the corner.'

He had picked the spot well away from any door. It was within easy access of a window, in the event of their having to make a break for freedom in the course of the night. They lay down close to one another and rolled up in their blankets and cloaks. His hand reached out and brushed her face.

'Sleep well.'

She caught the hand and held it tightly, wishing she could be more to him, closer to him, forever.

21

NAVARRE, NORTHERN SPAIN, APRIL 1314

The next few days with Friar Laurent and the other pilgrims passed uneventfully, in spite of the fact that they were deep in the territory of the King of Navarre, none other than the son of the French king. Even so, with every step they took, Luc felt more able to relax his vigilance. Their group blended ever more into the flow of pilgrims. From a trickle a few days earlier, it was already fast developing into a powerful stream. Every evening it became more difficult to find suitable lodgings for the group. Parties of pilgrims from as far away as England and Holland regularly beat them to it. While this competition for accommodation was a serious source of concern and irritation to Friar Laurent, Luc was secretly happy as the protective walls of bodies around them thickened.

He and Aimée talked a lot now. This part of the Pilgrims' Way brought them down from the mountains into the river valleys that then fed out onto the dry plains beyond. The going was not difficult and they could walk side by side on decent roads. As well as talking together, they spent time talking to their fellow pilgrims. With the exception of the stonemason, they were all in fine spirits now that the Pyrenees were behind them. Even the baker's daughter gradually shed her scepticism as she saw Aimée take everything in her stride.

The weather stayed good as they dropped down onto the high lands of northern Spain. Although still the month of April, the sun already carried considerable warmth. By mid-afternoon most days, they were searching for shade and stopping regularly to fill their gourds and skins with water. The stonemason refused to drink water, claiming it was bad for him. Instead, he slaked his thirst with the local wine. In consequence, by late afternoon most days, he was almost asleep on his feet.

'At least it keeps him quiet,' Friar Laurent fretted as the mason's drinking slowed them down, but the blessed silence made a very welcome change.

After a few days, they reached the busy market town of Puente la Reina, with its magnificent stone bridge. The flow of pilgrims suddenly swelled again. It was here that the two branches of the Pilgrims' Way joined up. Large numbers of pilgrims had crossed the Pyrenees at Roncevaux, further to the west. That was a lower, easier crossing than the Somport, and consequently more popular. From now on, there would be only one route to follow all the way to Compostela. Luc became more wary. That night, as he and Aimée lay close beside each other in a huge hostel, tightly crammed together in the midst of a hundred other people, he whispered in Aimée's ear.

'If you want to catch a rabbit, you put the snare across the path he has to follow, not the one he might take. I'm afraid it's not over yet.'

She gave no answer. She just reached over and gripped his hand.

There were few minutes in the day or the night when they were not together. They walked arm in arm for most of the daylight hours. In spite of the difference in their respective heights, they developed an easy pace. When obstacles presented themselves, he was able to encircle her waist with his arm and guide her through, if necessary lifting her off her feet.

The group would stop every few miles for a brief rest, and for longer around noon to eat lunch. Luc bought new packs for both of them in Puente la Reina; large for him and smaller for her. Although they both carried some cheese and sausage for emergencies, it was easy to obtain food from the houses they passed along the way. Everywhere they went, from isolated farmhouses, to rows of inns lining the route in bustling towns, they could always rely upon somebody being around to sell them something.

Every evening they would lay out their bedrolls side by side, for all the world like a married couple. If either of them heard the occasional grunts and pants from those lying around them during the night, neither of them commented. They would almost always fall asleep hand in hand, but neither of them dared to step beyond their state of innocence.

The friar was the only one who worried Luc. There were occasions when he would sense eyes observing him and, turning, he would find himself face to face with Friar Laurent. The monk's expression remained benevolent, but the curiosity in his eyes warranted caution. And, over the past seven years, Luc had become very cautious.

Things came to a head a few days beyond Puente la Reina when they reached a small town called Torres del Río. In the middle of town was a fine church, whose style was unmistakably Templar. As they trudged up the narrow street towards it, Luc could feel the eyes of the friar on him. He was sure Laurent was watching to see whether the beautiful octagonal building would have any effect upon him. Although he knew he was under observation, Luc found it hard to keep the emotion off his face, particularly when he saw the Templar splayed cross carved in the stone of the doorframe.

'What is it, Luc?' Aimée could feel his tenseness through the sleeve of his jacket. Although her voice was low, her solicitous tone was probably audible to Friar Laurent. Luc was quick to reassure her.

'Something I ate last night probably. It's just as well we're stopping for lunch here. I could do with a visit to the latrines and then something warm to drink.' He made sure his voice was loud enough to carry.

They continued past the church, but it looked deserted, much to Luc's disappointment. Fortunately, there was an inn only a hundred paces further on and Friar Laurent called a halt. The members of the group filed in gratefully for a drink. Leaving Aimée with Beatrice, Luc headed out of the back door. Ostensibly he was on his way to visit the latrines. In reality he wanted to find out whether there might still be any Templar presence in the town.

It was fairly simple to slip out of the yard gate and double back to the church. He circled round it, full of admiration for the simple elegance of the design. Like other Templar churches, it was quite evidently modelled upon the Church of the Holy Sepulchre in Jerusalem, where Luc had prayed in person years before. So many memories came flooding back as he scanned this little church for signs of life, but the doors were firmly locked. He was scouting about for a friendly face, to see if he could get news of the Order, when a voice from behind him made him jump.

'A truly beautiful piece of architecture.' It was Friar Laurent.

Luc did his best to assume an air of nonchalance but had little doubt that the friar had formed his own conclusions. He made no comment. Both of them continued around the building until they reached the solidly closed front door, set in its surprisingly simple frame.

'Now where have I seen a design like this before?'

Luc had little doubt that the friar was toying with him, but he did his best to play dumb.

'Saintes, I think it was. There was a much bigger version of this in the main square, I do believe.' He shot a glance across at the other man and was not reassured by what he saw.

'What was it you said you did for a living, Luc?' The friar's voice was harder now, in spite of the benevolent expression on his face.

'I didn't.' Luc had had enough of being a fish on the end of a line. With a shrug of his broad shoulders, he turned back towards the inn, followed by Friar Laurent. Maybe the time had come to leave Friar Laurent and his group.

As they came level with a narrow alley between two houses, Luc suddenly scented danger. He was already reaching up his sleeve as two men leapt out in front of them, swords unsheathed in their hands. Luc stopped and tensed his muscles, studying the two carefully.

'Money. Give us what you've got. Do it now, or you'll be dog meat.'

The taller of the two, a near toothless character with a mop of carrot-coloured hair, shouted the command, his fetid breath reaching across the gap between them. Luc felt the friar bump into his back and heard a sharp intake of breath. For his part, Luc made no move, but eyed the men closely. They were both filthy and unkempt, with the look of men who had been sleeping rough for some time. Their swords were streaked with rust and the hand of the smaller of the two was shaking visibly. Luc straightened up to his full height, gratified to see fear in both sets of eyes, and released his hold on the handle of his dagger. There was no need to reveal his secrets to them or the friar unless it was absolutely necessary. He smiled and spoke kindly.

'Leave us, brothers. We mean you no harm. Put up your swords and return to wherever you've come from. Please.' He was being reasonable and generous, but he could tell from the nervous panting behind him that Friar Laurent clearly thought he was out of his mind.

'Give them what they want.' Friar Laurent's voice had suddenly become falsetto. 'Here, take this.' Luc felt the purse pass his arm and drop on the street in front of the two attackers. The taller of the two ducked down to retrieve it. In a flash, Luc's new staff caught him behind the ear with a heavy thud, laying him out, unconscious. Seeing one man down, Luc transferred his attention to the other. For a moment their eyes met. Then there was a clatter as his battered sword landed on the cobbles and the man turned and disappeared back up the alley as if the devil himself were at his heels. Luc grunted with justifiable satisfaction and picked up the friar's purse.

'Here. You don't want to be too generous, you know.' He smiled encouragingly at the monk, whose pasty face still expressed bleak terror. Luc held out the leather pouch and Friar Laurent took it from him as if in a dream. It was only when Luc bent to retrieve the fallen swords that he managed to find his voice.

'It's you, isn't it?' Luc froze, the swords still in his hands. The friar stared at the blades, mesmerised, as he repeated, 'It's you. You're the Templar knight they're looking for. I knew it.' He wiped his face with his sleeve and managed to slide his attention from the swords to Luc's face. His voice was hoarse as he continued.

'My God. Those two bandits. They could feel it too, and you didn't even have a sword.' As if realising for the first time that Luc now held the weapons, he reached out his hands towards him. But it was not in supplication. The gesture was one of thanks. Luc let him take his left hand in both of his and pump it up and down gratefully. After a glance over his shoulder, Luc threw the swords up and onto the roof of a low barn on the other side of the road. There was a clatter as they landed, then silence.

'So what do you intend doing about it?' Luc's tone was light, but his thoughts were anything but. Automatically, he found himself thinking that he could very easily break the friar's neck, if it came to it. The presence of the unconscious bandit would ensure that no eyebrows would be raised. However, the thought of doing it filled him with regret, not least because he had come to like Laurent. Besides, even though he knew the friar was the most likely to betray him of anybody in the group, he recoiled at the thought of cold-blooded murder.

'Logroño. That's where they're waiting for you.' Luc listened intently to the friar's words as they came rushing out, barely louder than a whisper. 'The priest back at Los Arcos told me that there are soldiers checking all pilgrims going into Logroño. You'll have to skirt round the town and meet us the other side.' He still had hold of Luc's hand and pressed it to his own chest. 'Upon my honour as a man, and upon the holy cross of Christ, I swear I will not betray you.'

Luc felt the touch of the crucifix beneath the rough habit. He relinquished the friar's hand and smiled. 'Isn't it your holy duty to tell your superiors of the presence amongst you of a foul idolator, who's probably a blasphemer and a pederast to boot?' He prodded the unconscious man on the ground with the end of his stick and was reassured to see him still out cold.

'Forget for a moment that you have most probably just saved my life.' The monk was regaining his composure. 'When I came out looking for you a few minutes ago, I had already decided to warn you of the trap ahead.'

Luc's expression was one of surprise. Friar Laurent explained.

'I've seen you with Aimée. Her whole life revolves around you. She loves you with an obvious fervour that even we men of the cloth can admire, and maybe envy.' His voice faltered a little. Luc flushed in spite of himself. Friars like Laurent, after all, were bound by the same rules of celibacy as Templars. 'The way you look after her, that's not the behaviour of a pervert or a blasphemer. Nor is the way the two of you pray together every night and morning. No, if the Templars are really as evil as the king would have us believe, then you're an exception. If the Order of the Temple is as virtuous as it claims, then you're the living proof. You can trust me.'

Luc's heart sang, not just for the lifeline Friar Laurent had thrown him.

'Laurent, my friend, you bring joy to my heart and your words give me hope. It's been all too easy for me and my companions to fear the worst over the last few years. Listening to you, I know all is not lost.' He smiled broadly and caught the friar in a bear hug. 'I believe the others have ordered us a drink of wine, Laurent. Come, I feel we've earned a little relaxation.' Clapping his arm around the other man's shoulders, he led him back to the inn.

22

PILGRIMS' WAY, NORTHERN SPAIN, MAY 1314

Friar Laurent's group reached Logroño late in the afternoon. They were all tired, the stonemason in particular. He was being chivvied along by the rest of the group but, even so, he was a long way behind. Luc, Aimée and the friar, on the other hand, had deliberately pushed on ahead. It had been the hottest day so far and there had been precious little shade. The town looked very welcoming, spread out along the south bank of the vast Ebro river. As the setting sun dropped to the horizon, the smooth water of the river turned blood red. Luc took another cautious look around and prayed that this was not an omen.

'The bridge is only a few hundred paces from us now.' They had been told about the famous Puente de Piedra, the only bridge for many a long mile in either direction. From the shelter of a bank of reeds, they could clearly see knots of men at arms on either end of the bridge. Even without Laurent's warning, Luc would have realised that this was the perfect place to lay, and then spring, a trap. The river was wider even than the Seine at Paris and the magnificent bridge was composed of no fewer than eight massive arches. Although Luc could swim, Aimée could not. But, even if she had been able to, it was a still very, very long way to the other side.

'Aimée and I will leave you here, Laurent. You're right; it's pretty clear the soldiers are checking everybody as they cross the bridge. We'll find another way and, once we're over, we'll avoid Logroño completely. We'll hope to meet you in Navarrete the day after tomorrow.' They had discussed the best course of action the previous night. If all went well, they would stay on the north bank and follow the river westwards until they found a quieter crossing point. 'If we're late, don't worry about us. You carry on, and we'll meet in Compostela.'

'God protect you both.' Laurent reached across and traced the sign of the cross on Aimée's forehead.

'Thank you for all your kindness.' Aimée reached out and gripped his arm. 'If there were more like you in the Church, the world would be a better place.'

'God bless you, Aimée. Now you'd better hide. The rest of the group will be coming round the corner behind us any minute. Godspeed.'

Luc led Aimée away from the road, down into a small copse of trees. From there, they waited and watched the others pass by and onto the bridge.

'I hope we see them again.' Aimée kept her voice low. 'Beatrice has been such a good friend to me in the short time that I've known her.'

'I'm sure we will. Now, come on and let's head west. Once we're out of sight of the city, we can look for a place to stay.'

'Have you still got money to pay for an inn?' Aimée had realised months ago that she had no money at all. Luc took her arm and led her back onto the track and across it, onto a smaller path that ran alongside the river.

'Money?' She heard him laugh. 'That's the least of our problems. They sewed so many pieces of silver into my breeches and waistcoat that I'd probably sink if I ended up in the water. No, money certainly isn't a problem.'

In fact, the next two days turned out to be very pleasant. They found accommodation for the next two nights in wayside inns in reassuringly quiet little villages well off the Pilgrims' Way, far from the eyes of the archbishop's men. The only rather unsettling thing, at least as far as Luc was concerned, was that on both occasions they were provided with their own room and, in both cases, only one bed. As had happened up in the Pyrenees, Luc had woken early to find the warm, soft body of Aimée draped across him. Now, however, in spite of his scruples, he hadn't made any attempt to extricate himself.

For Aimée, being able to share a bed with him had been a source of considerable pleasure and an equal amount of frustration. She was ever conscious that he was a monk and the vows he had taken meant that relations between them had to remain pure and chaste. Each night, she did her best to stay away from him as she drifted off to sleep, but each morning she found herself clinging to him as if her life depended upon it. The conflicting emotions this aroused in her occupied her mind for most of the day and, from the silence coming from him, she got the impression that he might be harbouring similar thoughts. Rejoining Friar Laurent's group the next night and once more sleeping in a crowded room came as both a disappointment and a relief.

Beatrice was delighted to see Aimée again and was quick to take charge of her, leading her off to the dormitory, while Luc sat down at table alongside Laurent and stretched his back.

'Wine?' Friar Laurent pushed a mug of wine across the table to him. Luc took it and drained it. As Laurent leant over to give him a refill, he lowered his voice and asked: 'How did it go?'

Equally quietly, Luc gave him a brief account of their journey along the north bank of the Ebro. Then he took another mouthful and leant back. 'So, Laurent, were there really soldiers waiting for us there?'

The monk nodded. 'Yes, but not Spaniards. Remember, we're no longer in the Kingdom of Navarre, so the locals bear no allegiance to the French king. But there were several dozen French soldiers and, in their midst, an archbishop, no less.'

Luc caught the attention of a serving girl and ordered soup for Aimée and meat for himself. This news did little to improve his appetite. He looked back at Laurent and shook his head wearily.

'They don't give up so easily, do they?'

'Why do they want you so badly, Luc? Surely it isn't normal for troops to follow a fugitive all this way from one country to another? And in the company of an archbishop?' Luc could hear from his tone that the friar was seriously worried.

'I've no idea, Laurent. Maybe it's because of my rank.' Luc had never told him anything about himself before, but now it made little difference. 'My brother, Geoffroi de Charny, died at the stake alongside Jacques de Molay. I suppose my capture would be a feather in the archbishop's cap.'

Laurent looked up, a half-smile of recognition on his face. Luc spoke hastily, his voice a low whisper. 'Don't ever mention that name, Laurent. I'm just Luc. All right?'

The monk nodded. 'I knew you weren't just anybody. So I've been travelling with a celebrity, have I?'

'Please keep that to yourself, Laurent. I would imagine that the price on my head would keep any one of these pilgrims happy till the end of his days.' He knew he was taking a chance revealing his identity. Nevertheless, it was better if the friar thought his pursuers were after him for himself, rather than for what he might be carrying. If, indeed, he really was carrying something precious. He found himself wondering yet again how on earth he could have something without realising it.

'Here you are, sir. Chicken soup and a plate of stewed beef.' The serving girl leant across him and deposited the food on the table. He gave her a silver coin and received a handful of copper in change.

'Save my seat, Laurent, will you? I'll just take the soup to Aimée.' He carried the bowl through to the next room. It was a long, vaulted barn of a room, with bunks and mattresses scattered across the floor. Half were already occupied. He saw Aimée, Beatrice and her daughter in one corner. Stepping carefully, he made his way across to them.

'Here, Aimée, I've brought you something to eat.' She was looking comfortable and relaxed, sitting on a bench as she waited to be allocated a mattress. The other two made room for him beside her.

'I'm not really very hungry, Luc.' They had been eating well over the past two days.

'I thought you might say that so I just got you some soup. It'll do you good.' She gave him a smile and he handed the bowl down to her. 'Is there anything else you need?'

She stretched out her hand. 'No, thank you, Luc. With Beatrice and Jeanne looking after me as well as you, not even the Queen of France could be better cared for. You must be starving. Go and eat. All I ask is to have you beside me when you come back here to sleep.'

He squeezed her hand and left her with the ladies.

The beef was hot and tasty. As he ate his way through it, the friar outlined their plans for the next days. By this time they had realised that it was easy to get news of the route ahead by swapping experiences with pilgrims who had already completed their pilgrimages and were coming back in the opposite direction.

'Tomorrow's an easy day. We should be in Nájera by midday.' Friar Laurent sounded glad. He and all of his group were feeling the strain after weeks on the road. 'And if anybody's feeling a bit under the weather, we'll be heading on from there to Santo Domingo de la Calzada.'

Luc had already heard of that town. Many pilgrims had spoken about it and he knew it was the site of a famous pilgrims' hospital. 'I'm sure we'll all welcome an easy stage for a change. We've done a lot of walking.' He finished the last piece of meat and mopped up the gravy with his bread. 'I think I'm going to turn in now. I just hope that the archbishop and his men spend the next month in Logroño, waiting in vain for us to pass.'

'If I hear anything, I'll tell you. You can depend on me, Luc.'

At that moment, the door opened and a last pilgrim pushed his way in. He was carrying a heavy pack and he looked tired. Luc stood up from the table and pointed to the place where he had been sitting.

'Here, there's a seat if you want it.'

The man shrugged off his pack and gave a sigh of relief.

'That's very good of you. I'm worn out.'

'I recommend the stewed beef.' Luc clapped the newcomer on the shoulder, picked up his own bag, and made his way through to Aimée.

At first he couldn't find her and he looked round in some alarm. Had the archbishop's men sneaked her away while he was eating? Then, mercifully, he saw Beatrice waving, beckoning him over.

'I'll take you to your room, Luc.' He looked up in surprise. Private rooms were not normally found in pilgrim hostels. Beatrice smiled. 'Looks like you're the lucky ones tonight. You're through here. Come on, I'll show you.'

She led him to the other side of the room, weaving in and out among the bunks and palliasses before stopping at a low doorway and waving him inside. It was a good, clean room with two comfortable-looking beds, side by side. Aimée was already in one of the beds, a candle lantern hanging from the ceiling. Beatrice caught his arm and whispered, 'If you need anything, you know where to find me.'

'Thanks so much, Beatrice.' She turned and left.

He sat down on his bed and pulled off his boots. Then he removed his jacket, blew out the candle and stretched out on the bed alongside Aimée. He reached across and took her hand. She didn't stir.

Luc found it hard to get to sleep. At first he wondered if it might be the stew, but he didn't feel any digestive problems. As he tossed and turned, he gradually realised what was stopping him sleeping. It was his mind. Thoughts kept sweeping through his head. And what these thoughts kept telling him was that there was something wrong. He couldn't put a finger on it, but something wasn't right.

Always one to trust his instincts, he slipped out of bed and padded across to the door. Gripping his knife in one hand, he used the other to ease the door open. The big dormitory was peaceful, if you ignored the snoring. The snores of the stonemason were unmistakable; Luc had heard quieter battle cries in the Holy Land. Nevertheless, the pilgrims all around were fast asleep, the fatigue of their daily march rendering them immune to interruptions. A single lantern gave just enough light for him to see around the room and he noticed nothing untoward.

He closed the door once more. This time he wedged a chair against it. He took the other chair and placed it against the wall, below the high window. Climbing up, he was able to see out. He found himself looking into the yard of the hostel, where two or three dogs were also fast asleep in the moonlight, tethered to rings set in the walls. This, more than anything else, reassured him. The dogs would be woken if anybody came into the yard and their barking would be sure to wake him. He returned to bed and finally managed to drift off.

23

PILGRIMS' WAY, NORTHERN SPAIN, MAY 1314

Luc was woken at daybreak by a cock crowing in the yard, followed by a cacophony of barking. He jumped out of bed, climbed onto the chair and looked out again. The reason for the barking was immediately visible. A scrawny tabby cat was walking disdainfully across the yard, just out of range of the dogs. Somewhat reassured, he climbed back down and returned the chair to its original place. The other chair was still wedged in position. Easing it out of the way, he opened the door a fraction and glanced out. The pilgrims in the big room were beginning to stir and everything looked normal. He closed the door and sat back on his bed. He was relieved, but the feeling of uncertainty remained.

'Good morning.' He felt her hand rub against his arm. He turned towards her.

'Good morning to you. Sleep well?'

'Mmmh. I slept like a log. You've got nice warm hands.' She sounded blissfully content. He smiled with her. Maybe they had truly left the archbishop and his men back in Logroño.

'So, are you fit enough for a short walk? Today's only half a day.'

'That sounds wonderful after all the walking we've been doing. Now if you'd just point me in the direction of Beatrice, she promised to look after me this morning.'

There was almost a holiday atmosphere among the members of their group that morning, knowing it would be a short day. The terrain made for easy walking, too, as the track weaved its way through vineyards and almond groves and there weren't even any hills of importance. The weather was calm and clear, the sun warm on their cheeks. Aimée walked arm in arm with Beatrice and her daughter while Luc followed twenty or thirty paces behind. As they passed alongside a low hill, Friar Laurent dropped back to talk to him.

'You always like to be at the back of the group, don't you, Luc?'

'I suppose I do, Laurent. In my fighting days, I always chose to ride at the tail, rather than up in the vanguard. In my experience, more attacks come from the rear than from straight ahead.'

'And your fighting days, Luc, are they over now?' The friar gave him a searching look. 'I was wondering what future a warrior monk might have, now that his order has been abolished.'

Luc was prevented from answering by the sound of hooves coming up the track behind them. Ever vigilant, he swung round to check. It was a single rider. Even from a distance, it was clear to see that he was mounted on a mule, the long ears sticking out like horns either side of the beast's head. Definitely not the mount an archbishop would choose. Luc relaxed as the rider approached.

'Good morning. *Buen camino.*' The man gave the traditional pilgrim greeting. Luc nodded but stayed silent, letting the friar reply.

'And *buen camino* to you, my friend. We're nearly at our destination for today. Where are you bound on that fine mount?'

'Santo Domingo de la Calzada. They tell me the cathedral was built by the saint himself. I hope I get there in time to see all the sights.'

'That'll depend on the state of the roads, I suppose. They've been good so far.'

'The cavalry platoon I just overtook told me the Pilgrims' Way's good all the way to the mountains of León and they're much further on. Well, I wish you all the best.'

'May the love of God go with you.'

The man gave a wave and spurred the mule into an ungainly trot. As the man overtook the rest of their group and disappeared into the distance, the friar turned to Luc.

'Cavalry? Fancy that?' There was a twinkle in his eye. 'You know, Luc, I think this might be a good time to stop for a little break. I can see the roofs of a village off to the right down there. It should offer refreshments, although it'll force us to make a short detour. Would you object to leaving the Pilgrims' Way for a while?'

Luc gave him a broad grin. 'Laurent, you're a fine man.'

Friar Laurent hastened to rejoin the rest of their group. Unsurprisingly there was general agreement to the idea of stopping for a break. They took the next turning to the right, heading down towards the houses. They had just reached the little hamlet when the sound of horses and a plume of dust back on the Pilgrims' Way told Luc the cavalry had passed. He and the friar exchanged glances.

The village didn't have an inn, but a stall in the middle of the cluster of houses offered wine, ham and bread. The stonemason's eyes lit up as he spotted the flagons.

'Excellent choice, Friar. I think I'll just fill my water bottle.' He headed over to the wine stall eagerly.

'He's put enough red wine in there over the last couple of months to rot the leather.' The friar sat down in the shade next to Luc.

'Think what it must be doing to his insides.' Luc lowered his voice. 'In answer to your question back there, I really don't know what I'm going to do next. I suppose I'll have to find a way of earning my living.'

'But you come from a noble family. You are...'

Luc held up his finger. 'I'm nobody, Laurent. I'm just Luc. Remember that. Whatever my background, that's all finished now. I can't return to my place of birth to reclaim what's rightfully mine. The king and the archbishop would have me in irons. No, my future, I fear, will have to be outside France.'

The friar heard the sadness in his voice. Before he could offer consolation, they were interrupted.

'Friar Laurent, could I join you? The sun's hot for this time of year. Shade's in short supply.'

Luc looked up. It was the man who had arrived late the previous night. He was stockily built, maybe five years younger than the friar and him.

Obligingly, they squeezed along the bench and made room for him on the end, just out of the direct sunlight.

'Thanks a lot.' He held out his hand to Luc. 'I'm Thomas. That's the second time you've given me a seat.'

'And I'm Luc. Good to meet you. Have you come far?' The feeling of suspicion was back again.

'I started at Saintes a month ago. I thought I was going to get held up in the mountains, but the big thaw started just in time.'

'Did you come over the Somport pass?'

The other man shook his head. 'No, I took the easy option. Starting at Saint-Jean-Pied-de-Port, I was over the top in a day's walk.'

Luc was relieved to hear that. He had no doubt that his escape with Aimée from the archbishop would still be big news at the abbey of Santa Cristina.

'So why are you doing the pilgrimage, my son?' Laurent asked everybody that.

Just for a moment, Luc thought he spotted slight hesitation before Thomas replied to the friar's question. 'Just something I've always wanted to do.' He began to sound more confident. 'My brother did it a few years ago. He's told me of the many wonders along the way and, of course, the magnificence of Compostela itself.' He looked directly at Luc. 'And what about you?'

'It's more for Aimée, really. She needs someone to accompany her.' Luc had already used this explanation more than once. 'Who knows? She might get a miracle from the apostle's tomb.'

'She's a brave woman. I know plenty of sighted people who would hesitate before undertaking something like this.'

'It's funny. You seem familiar. Have I seen you before?' Luc could still feel that same sense of unease.

The man's eyes flashed for a second. 'Not that I can recall. Where are you from?'

'Paris.' It was sufficiently vague as an answer. 'And you?'

'Me too. Maybe we met in a market or something.'

The friar squinted up at the sun. The sky was still cloudless and it was getting hotter out there by the minute. 'I don't reckon we've got more than another hour to go. I suggest we get on with it.'

The others, seeing him rise to his feet, followed suit. Luc walked across to Aimée and took her arm. She smiled at him.

'Hello there. Did I hear you making new friends?' She caught his hand and squeezed. 'Tired of me already?'

'I'll never tire of you, Aimée.' He saw the joy in her face. As they started walking back up the track towards the main Pilgrims' Way, he found himself turning over in his mind something the friar had said earlier. If the Order of the Temple had been abolished, then did that mean that Luc's vows no longer applied? Did that mean that his relationship with Aimée could develop?' He swallowed to remove the lump that had formed in his throat and did his best to banish the thought. At least for now.

As usual, he took up station at the rear of the group. As they walked, he pulled Aimée closer and whispered to her about the cavalry. She remained resolutely optimistic.

'It might not have been the archbishop's men, Luc. Maybe it was just a local troop patrolling the Pilgrims' Way.'

Maybe she was right. He had no way of knowing who they were, but he still nursed this feeling of insecurity. And, somehow, he felt that the new man, Thomas, might be involved. However, he decided not to burden Aimée with his worries that might well prove to be unfounded.

24

PILGRIMS' WAY, NORTHERN SPAIN, MAY 2016

As Luke and Amy drove further westwards, the countryside became much flatter and the vegetation ever more sparse. The snows of the Pyrenees retreated to a distant memory as unbroken spring sunshine sent the temperature rising.

'Hardly a tree to be seen for miles. Summer here must be brutally hot and arid, even though the mountains aren't far away.'

Luke found he enjoyed his role as tour guide more and more as the days went by. Amy listened attentively, enjoying his company and the historical background he was able to provide. The roads were wide and good. European Union subsidies had flowed abundantly for many years and the infrastructure had benefited immensely, but now, since the economic downturn, everywhere he looked, he saw unfinished buildings and empty shops. Amy was a perfect companion and he knew he was feeling ever closer to her.

After visiting Logroño, where they admired the magnificent old bridge over the River Ebro, they decided to stop for the night at the Parador in the centre of Santo Domingo de la Calzada. Like most of this famous state-owned chain of hotels, this one had been created inside a historic monument. For people with an interest in the Pilgrims' Way to Santiago, it couldn't have been more appropriate. The building, erected on the site of an ancient palace of the kings of Navarre, had been a hospital and shelter for pilgrims back in the Middle Ages.

A policeman directed them into the very heart of the beautiful medieval town and across the square in front of the cathedral. A porter came out to take their bags, while another volunteered to take the car and park it for them. Inside, the hotel was splendid. The hall on the ground floor had presumably been the main part of the pilgrims' hostel. It was a delight, with Gothic arches, sculpted stone and medieval statues. As they checked in, Luke did his best to describe the place to Amy.

'Subdued lighting, antique rugs, leather armchairs and oak tables, hanging baskets and some spectacular wooden statuary. I've never been in a hotel like this anywhere before in all my life. Certainly a bit different from some of the places I stayed in when I was in Africa.'

'When we've changed, can we come down here for a drink?' Amy was breathing in the atmosphere of the place. 'I've been to a few good hotels in my time, but there's something very special about this one.' She tried to place it. 'Maybe it's the sense of peace and tranquillity.'

Luke looked across at the row of keys in the pigeonholes behind the reception desk and concluded that there were very few guests in the hotel. No doubt that added to the sensation of calm. He handed over the passports and signed the registration forms. A porter appeared to collect their bags and lead them to their rooms. These were on the first floor, at the head of a magnificent stairway. The thick pile of the carpet at their feet absorbed the sound of their passing and added to the sensation of peace and quiet.

Just over an hour later he led her back down the ornately carved wooden staircase. She was dressed more elegantly than he had ever seen her before. She wore a white linen blouse and her black skirt was breathtakingly short, emphasising her long legs. Her hair was tied up formally, but with a few long strands hanging around her face. She looked immaculate and he wondered at how she had managed it without being able to see her reflection in a mirror. He felt positively scruffy in a pullover and jeans – clean jeans but still jeans.

Downstairs it was immediately evident that his initial suspicion that there might be very few other guests was correct. There were no more than half a dozen people in the spectacular vaulted bar. He led her across to a table by the fireplace. Settling her into a deep leather armchair, he described their surroundings in more detail.

'All very tasteful. Lighting that highlights the arches and columns all through the room. It's like being in the crypt of a church or in a Turkish harem. It wouldn't surprise me if a mysterious veiled lady didn't materialise to take our order.' He looked across at her.

Feeling herself observed, Amy pulled a few loose strands of hair across her face and asked huskily, 'Does Effendi like what he sees?'

'Effendi certainly does.' At that moment, a matronly Spanish lady appeared to ask what they would like to drink. Without hesitating, Amy ordered a bottle of champagne, explaining to Luke that anything less wouldn't have matched the surroundings. The waitress disappeared and Luke continued to describe the polished floor, stone walls, bread ovens either side of the fire, the massive oak chairs, and the multitude of plants. Amy sat back happily, a smile firmly on her face. She was listening with only part of her brain. The rest of her was concentrating on committing this place, the smell of leather, the distant notes of the 'Concierto de Aranjuez' coming from the speakers and the sound of his voice to her memory forever.

'There's something about this place. And present company, of course.'

The head waiter himself arrived with the champagne in a regal-looking bucket. He opened the bottle without more than a slight hiss from the top as he drew the cork. After filling two delicate tall flutes with wine, he withdrew. He was immediately replaced by the waitress, bearing a tray loaded with food.

Luke waited until she had left and then launched into guide mode. 'Huge green olives, the biggest crisps I've ever seen in my life, two or three different types of nuts in a bowl, two slabs of tortilla, deep-fried squid rings and a couple of huge prawns in batter. If we eat this lot we probably won't need to eat dinner at all. Here.' He passed over a frosted glass of champagne and let his glass lightly touch hers. 'Here's to you.'

'And to you, Luke. Thank you for everything.'

Amy sipped the cold wine and tapped along to the classic guitar music with her fingers, clearly enjoying the place immensely. Neither of them spoke for quite a while. Finally, Luke made up his mind. He had something to say and this was the right place and the right time.

'I need to talk to you.' She made no reply so he waded on. She could hear his uncertainty and gave him an encouraging smile. 'I've been trying to find the courage for days now.'

She smiled a bit more broadly. 'Am I that scary?'

'No, it's me, not you. The fact is, my confidence has taken a bit of a bashing over the last few years, so I'm sorry if I seem a bit hopeless and pathetic.'

'Two words I would never associate with you, Luke.' She was still smiling and he took heart.

'There's a lot I've got to tell you. I can't keep putting it off any longer. You've got to know the full story.' He kept his voice studiously level, but there was no mistaking the emotion barely held in check in the background. She reached out, found and gripped his hand. He hardly noticed.

'For what it is worth, you're just about the first person who's ever heard the full story.' She squeezed his hand as he steeled himself for what he knew he had to tell her.

'Apart from Father Tim.'

'Yes, apart from Tim. He's a very, very good friend, you know.'

'And to me. He helped me so very much.'

'Amy, it's like this.' He cleared his throat. 'When I finished school, I didn't go to university to study history. I actually studied medicine.' He paused and she found herself digesting the news.

'Medicine? So does that make you a double doctor?' She was trying to keep the tone light.

'It does indeed. MD and PhD.' He hesitated, then managed to carry on. 'I qualified and went straight into one of the big London hospitals. It was hard, tiring work, but I learned a lot, and people told me I was good at my job.'

Amy was sitting quietly, wondering why it had taken him so much effort to tell her this. Somehow, she had been expecting something much more dramatic. So he had been a doctor. It was a bit of a surprise, but so what? She waited for him to continue his account, wondering what was still to come.

'Then, one day, I made a decision that would affect my whole life. Have you heard of *Médecins Sans Frontières*?'

'Yes, everybody's heard of Doctors Without Borders. Did you join up?'

'After a few years working in London, I knew I wanted a change and I felt

I could be most useful in a Third World country. So I applied to MSF and they took me.' There was a pause. 'I was sent to Africa.' His voice tailed away, and he lapsed into a silence that lasted several minutes. Finally, Amy tried a gentle prompt.

'And something happened over there, in Africa?'

'Something happened.' There was another pause before he picked up his story once more. 'Have you ever heard of *Boko Haram*?'

'That's the Islamist terrorist group, isn't it?' Amy began to get a feeling she knew where this was leading.

'Yes.' Another pause. 'Anyway, it happened five years ago now and I'd been in Nigeria for a couple of years. Things were going really well for me. I was working in a hospital in a little town in the north of the country, not far from the border with Niger.' There was another long pause before he started again, the strain in his voice all too evident. 'I'd met a girl. Her name was Nicole. I loved her very dearly and we were going to get married.' He paused again, clearing his throat before resuming. 'Although the conditions over there were pretty tough and the workload relentless, I was just about as happy as I've ever been in my whole life. Until now, at least.'

Amy squeezed his hand again, dreading what was to come next.

'One day, while I was operating on a woman who needed a Caesarean section, I heard gunfire.' He stopped to take a deep breath. 'Gunfire wasn't that unusual up there and, at first, we weren't too worried. Anyway, I was in the middle of the operation and couldn't stop, even though the shooting got nearer and nearer. Finally they reached us, the door was kicked open and a hail of gunfire came pouring in. The nurse beside me was cut to pieces before my eyes and I was hit three times. I was thrown back onto the floor, ending up under the operating table, covered in the blood and body parts of the two nurses and the other doctor.' Another pause and then, when he started speaking again, his voice was totally devoid of any emotion. 'The other doctor was Nicole.'

'Oh, Luke.' Amy was appalled and didn't know what to say. She could imagine the horrific bloodbath and could only begin to guess at the effect it must have had on Luke. She squeezed his hand again but felt no response.

'It must have been the fact that I was hidden under the other three bodies and covered in their blood that saved me from being hacked to death with machetes. I passed out and when I came round, the men had gone, I was alive, and everybody else in there was dead, including the patient on the operating table along with her unborn child... and Nicole.' For the first time, Amy felt his hand grip hers. 'I can't even begin to describe the scene that greeted me when I tried to stand up, although I'll never forget it.'

She heard him pick up his glass and take a mouthful. 'Anyway, I was very lucky. Two of the bullets passed right through the tissue of my upper arm without touching the bone and the third must have hit one of the other victims first, because it entered my chest cavity and stayed there.' He cleared his throat and explained. 'AK47 rounds tend to do most damage on the way out. They can literally blow a chunk of body away. The fact that I was hit by a spent round saved my life. Like I say, I was very lucky; at least physically.'

'How long did it take you to recover?'

'Physically, not so long. A month, two maybe. They flew me back to Abuja and from there to London and I got the very best care available. The trouble wasn't with my body so much as with my mind. I'm afraid that, psychologically, I went to pieces.'

'I can well believe it.' Amy was appalled at his story, particularly the fact that his fiancée had died in the attack and her blood and body parts had covered him. It didn't bear thinking about. She squeezed his hand again. 'I can't begin to imagine how awful it must have been for you.' She had a thought. 'So, did you meet Father Tim in Africa?'

'Yes, and then again when I was in the hospital in London. He'd returned to the UK by then and when he heard about what had happened to me, he came to visit me in there and then, later, at the mental health hospital.' Luke took another mouthful of wine. 'He helped me a lot. You see, ever since that day, I haven't been able to pick up a scalpel, put on a surgical gown, or even sit down with a patient. It's as if my whole being has rejected my former life. Even if I wanted to go back to medicine, my brain refuses to let me.'

'Luke, you can stop talking about it now, if you like. Don't let the memories stress you out any more.'

'I've almost finished, Amy, and, anyway, everybody tells me it's good to talk about it. The fact is, like I said, you're just about the first.'

'Thank you.'

'Amy, you needed to know.'

'So when did you decide to go for medieval history?'

'I'd always been interested in history and you won't be in the least surprised to hear that it was Tim who pushed me into doing something about it.'

'Just like he did to me.'

'I owe Tim a lot. When he saw the way things were going, he told me to get myself back to university. He got me to face the fact that I needed to make a change from medicine. So that's when I chose medieval history.'

'And after the PhD, what happened?'

'You happened, Amy.' She heard him pause again. This time it was a long pause. 'Tim took me to one side and told me he thought I needed a break; time to decide on my future. He told me about this brave girl who'd been dealt a pretty poor hand.' She felt his fingers tighten against hers. 'And he put the two of us together. He's a lovely man, but he's a conniving, scheming plotter, you know.'

'You said it. Without his insistence, I'd never have gone ahead with this trip and I'd never have met you.'

'I think we both owe him a lot.'

'Amen to that.'

'Thank you for listening. I'm sorry it's taken me so long to summon up the courage to tell you my story.'

'Nobody could accuse you of lacking courage, Luke. Thank you for telling me and remember the old saying, a problem shared is a problem halved. I'm here for you any time, you know that, don't you?'

Amy knew, without a shadow of a doubt, that a watershed had now been reached. Getting him to start to open up about his life was a massive step forward for him. The next step, she fervently hoped, would be for him to begin to process whatever feelings he might be harbouring towards her. It wouldn't be long before they reached the end of their journey and the spectre of losing him from her life was haunting her more and more as the days went by.

25

PILGRIMS' WAY, NORTHERN SPAIN, MAY 1314

It was the hottest part of the day. Looking down from the hillside, they could just make out the roofs and towers of Santo Domingo de la Calzada before them. In less than an hour they would be there and the group was strung out over several hundred paces. The friar was up at the front, while Luc and Aimée were joined at the rear by the stonemason.

'You didn't waste much time, did you?' The mason's voice was slurred, his breath toxic.

Luc ignored him, hoping he would lapse into drunken silence. But the stonemason's brain, unusually at this time of day, was still functioning.

'You didn't wait long to get the little lady into bed with you, did you?'

Luc bit his tongue and feigned deafness.

'Good in bed, is she? Even if she's blind, she's got all the right bits, I'll be bound.'

This was too much. Drunk or not, the man had overstepped the mark. Luc stopped in his tracks. The mason stumbled past him. Luc pushed out his foot. The man tripped, falling headlong onto the dusty track. He roared in anger, flailed about, and pulled himself to his knees. Heads turned in the group ahead. Luc stepped forward as the man struggled to get to his feet and caught him by the scruff of the neck, holding him down on his knees. He spoke quietly and firmly, the menace clear in his voice.

'Mason, you really should watch what you say. One of these days you're going to say something rude to somebody less forgiving than me and you'll get into trouble, serious trouble. You'll remember that now, won't you?'

He released his hold and turned dismissively away. He caught Aimée's arm again and set off towards the others once more. He had taken only a few steps when he heard a familiar noise. It was the unmistakable sound of a blade being drawn from a sheath. He whirled round, protecting Aimée with his body. He found himself confronted by the mason holding a vicious-looking knife, the point aimed at Luc's chest. The man's face was covered in dust from the path, his knuckles bloodied, scuffed from his contact with the ground.

'Nobody does that to me. I'm going to slit you from ear to ear.' The man's voice was heavy with rage as well as drink.

'Aimée, take a couple of steps backwards. You'll be fine.' Luc pushed her gently backwards and she did as she was bidden, fear etched on her face.

'Luc, be careful.' He could hear the anxiety in her voice.

Luc didn't take his eyes off the stonemason. He heard running feet behind him as the others came back to see what was happening. The mason, seeing that he had an audience, and seeing no weapon in Luc's hand, took a pace forward.

'You're drunk, mason. Don't do anything foolish.' Luc's right hand was on the hilt of the hidden dagger. For the moment, it remained concealed in his sleeve. 'Put the knife away, apologise to the lady and we'll forget the whole thing.'

'From ear to ear, you Templar bastard.' He must have seen the shock on Luc's face. He raised his voice. 'You heard me. I know what you are. You're a cowardly Templar, escaping from justice. You've probably got a sack of gold in your pack. It'll be a pleasure to do the executioner's job for him.'

Luc heard intakes of breath from behind. He kept his eyes on the point of the knife, his mind racing. Just then he heard a movement and Friar Laurent pushed past, deliberately stepping in between them.

'Get out of the way, monk. This is between me and him.' The mason's voice was a snarl.

'You're drunk, man. You could be arrested for pulling a knife on a fellow pilgrim. Wound him, and they'll string you up. Listen to me, will you?'

'String me up? I'll probably get a medal for killing a Templar.' The man was sounding less drunk now. His eyes were unnaturally bright, but he was in control of his faculties. Luc caught the friar by the arm.

'Be careful, Laurent. The man's off his head.'

The baker and the new man, Thomas, appeared alongside the friar. The stonemason, relishing the audience, stepped forward once more. Luc knew he was still out of range of any but the most desperate lunge, so he kept his knife hidden. The best way of convincing the other members of the group that he was not a Templar was to appear helpless. He took a step back. The stonemason crowed.

'That's right, you coward. Back away. But it won't do you any good. This blade's got your name on it. Right now!' He leapt towards Luc, his teeth bared in a wicked grin. But as he started moving, just as Luc was about to pull out his knife, the new man, Thomas, reacted. With lightning speed, he reversed his heavy staff and lashed out. There was a sickening thud as the solid end of the wooden staff crashed into the base of the stonemason's skull. He went down like a stone, headfirst into the dust.

There was stunned silence. Luc looked down at the stonemason, but the violence of the blow, and the precision with which it had landed, told him the man was dead. The friar dropped to his knees beside the body and laid his hand on the mason's throat. After a few moments he looked up.

'He's dead.'

Aimée gave a little cry and ran forward, tripping as she did so. Luc reached out and swept her into his arms before she could fall. 'It's all right, Aimée.'

She gripped him tightly, an expression of overwhelming relief on her face. 'Thank the Lord. I didn't know, I didn't know.' The thought of losing him from her life was too terrible to contemplate. She burst into tears and Luc cradled her against his chest.

'Well, there's nothing more we can do for him now.' Friar Laurent made the sign of the cross over the dead man and looked up at Thomas. The other pilgrims had all backed away, unsettled by the savagery of his attack. 'Thomas, you were acting to protect an unarmed man. The authorities won't worry you, once we tell them the circumstances.' He pulled himself to his feet. 'Luc, I believe you owe your life to Thomas.'

As his blood began to cool, Luc was rejoicing. This intervention by the new man was a godsend as it allowed Luc to remain anonymous. He held out his hand. 'I thank you with all my heart, Thomas.' He kept his voice suitably humble. 'It's ironic he accused me of being a Templar. I have a horror of weapons and all forms of violence. You saved my life, and I'm in your debt.'

'You're very welcome, Luc. I'm just sorry I seem to have hit him too hard.' Thomas neither looked, nor sounded, contrite. Luc studied him carefully. As a soldier himself, he knew full well how carefully executed the murder had been. And he had little doubt that it had been murder. For some reason, as yet unfathomable, Thomas had deliberately killed the stonemason.

'Luc, perhaps you would stay with the body, while I take Thomas to the authorities in Santo Domingo to explain what happened. I'm sure they'll send a cart to collect and bury the mason. When you get into town, one of us will be waiting for you in front of the cathedral. Otherwise you won't know where we're lodged.'

Luc nodded in agreement.

The friar knelt down once more and searched through the mason's clothes until he found his purse. From it, he removed, and carefully unfolded, his pilgrim's passport. 'Louis Dubois of Beauvais. I never knew his full name.' He straightened up, tucked the purse into his pocket, and looked round.

'Should we move him off the road?' Luc did his best to maintain the impression of a helpless victim, unfamiliar with violent death. 'What if a cart were to come along?'

The friar nodded. Together with Thomas, Luc lifted the dead man and moved him into the shade of a scrawny holm-oak tree at the side of the road. Then he and Aimée waited alongside the corpse as the others set off. In the shade of the tree, there was a large rock, its smooth surface testimony to its regular use by passing pilgrims in search of shelter from the relentless sun. Luc led Aimée to it and they both sat down. She kept hold of his hand.

Once the group was out of earshot, he recounted what had happened.

'So you're saying that this Thomas man deliberately killed the stonemason?' Aimée's voice was sceptical. 'Couldn't it just have been a lucky blow?'

'It might.' Luc sounded even more sceptical. 'Except for the speed of it. You didn't see it, but Thomas was like a striking serpent. I was reaching for the knife I keep up my sleeve. Before I could draw it, he had swung and connected, and with deadly accuracy.'

His eyes flicked down to the body beside them. The stonemason's head was lying at an impossible angle. The blow had broken his neck. It could almost have been the work of the infamous Assassins. For a moment, Luc's thoughts flashed back to his fighting years in the Holy Land. He had seen more than his fair share of violent death over there, but rarely as perfectly executed as this.

'He meant to do it. Believe me, I know.' He squeezed Aimée's hand.

She bowed to his superior experience of these things. 'All right, he deliberately killed him. So tell me why.'

'I don't know.' Luc's voice betrayed his mystification. 'If we accept my theory that he knew what he was doing, then it's indisputable that he has to be a professional.'

'A professional what, Luc?'

'Either a professional soldier, or a professional killer.'

'A professional soldier who just saved your life.' She was turning the idea over in her head. 'Does that mean he might be a Templar like yourself?'

He gave a sigh of frustration. 'I've been wondering that. It wouldn't surprise me if the men who sent me on this mission had arranged to have me shadowed, in case I might need help. But surely they would have told me. What's the use of a bodyguard if you don't know who he is?'

Aimée shook her head. 'Think back to the abbot of Santa Cristina, Luc. You remember what he said about links on a chain, don't you? If you're unaware of the identity of your guardian angel, the archbishop and his men would be unable to make you reveal anything about him.'

Luc reflected on her words. 'You're right. And if I failed, he would still be able to step in to help complete the mission.' He gazed down at her tenderly. 'You're a clever woman, Aimée.'

She gripped him more tightly. 'Of course, you said a professional soldier or a professional killer. What if he's a killer working for the archbishop? Maybe he deliberately sacrificed this unimportant pawn so that you would believe him to be on your side. Then, when your guard's down, he'll pounce.'

Luc turned this other hypothesis over in his mind. It was a sobering thought. He was still reflecting on it some time later when a municipal official arrived to retrieve the body of the stonemason. The driver offered them a lift into town and they were happy to accept. He dropped them off in front of the cathedral and, as promised, Jeanne, the baker's daughter, was waiting for them. She ran over and took Aimée by the arm, leading them along a narrow street to the hostel. It was a simple inn, small and crowded, but Luc preferred it that way. If the archbishop's men were already in the town, he and Aimée would be less conspicuous here than in the big pilgrims' hospice.

'Luc, Aimée, you're here at last.' Friar Laurent was sitting at a long table, a plate of sausage and ham in front of him. He waved them onto the bench beside him. 'Sorry it took so long. There was no problem with the authorities. Everybody here would appear to sleep from lunchtime till late afternoon. Anyway, they've accepted the witness statements. Thomas is in the clear.' He leant closer to Luc. 'And your name wasn't even mentioned.'

Luc gave a satisfied nod. So the stonemason incident had not caused a stir. He glanced around, checking the faces in the room, recognising a few, but not many. He searched for Thomas, but there was no sign of him so he allowed himself to relax. Catching sight of the innkeeper, he ordered a jug of wine and some food. The wine arrived almost immediately. Luc refilled the friar's mug, then took one for himself and one for Aimée. He pressed it into her hand.

'Here, have some wine and then we should get some sleep. I don't know about you, but I'm really tired tonight.'

'It isn't everyday somebody tries to kill you. That might have something to do with it.' Her tone was dry, but he could hear that she was still disturbed by the events of the day.

'The important thing is that he didn't succeed.'

The innkeeper returned with a steaming bowl of thick vegetable soup with dumplings. Sight of food reminded Luc he was hungry.

The innkeeper straightened up and looked across at the friar. 'Are you Friar Laurent, by any chance?'

The monk looked up. 'Yes. What is it?'

'Message for you. The bishop wants to see you. You're to go to the Bishop's Palace as soon as possible.'

'The bishop wants to see me?' Laurent was amazed. 'But how does he know I'm here?'

'No idea. The messenger was here five, ten minutes ago, but he left.' The innkeeper shrugged and returned to the kitchen.

Luc's appetite suddenly left him. That same sensation that all was not well was back with him again. He watched as the friar jumped to his feet, agitated at this summons to such an august personage. Before he could set off, Luc caught his arm, lowering his voice to little more than a whisper. 'Laurent, do you want me to come with you?' He really didn't want to leave Aimée, but this summons could mean danger for the friar.

'No, of course not.' The friar smiled down at him. 'Maybe my abbot wrote to him about our pilgrimage. He did tell me he knew people along the way.'

'Well, if you're absolutely sure...'

'It's fine, really, Luc, thanks for the offer. Anyway, it's not far. The palace is right beside the cathedral.' He turned and disappeared out of the exit.

'What do you think that's all about?' Aimée was as puzzled as Luc.

'I don't know.' Luc looked around, subjecting all the other people in the room to close scrutiny. He saw nothing untoward, but his instincts were still screaming caution. He took his time, waiting to see if his feelings changed before making a decision. At last he made his decision. He rested his mouth against her ear and whispered. 'Listen, Aimée, do you think you'll be all right if I leave you here with Beatrice and Jeanne? I'm worried for Laurent. How did the bishop know about him? How did he know he was here, in this little inn, and why today? How do we know the messenger was even sent by the bishop anyway?'

She nodded, feeling his lips rub against her ear as she did so. In spite of the circumstances, she felt a thrill at his touch. 'I'll be fine here, don't worry. What're you going to do?'

'I owe, we owe, Laurent a lot. He's gone out on a limb for us and he deserves all the help I can give. I'll head for the Bishop's Palace and check on him.'

'Promise me you'll be careful.'

'I promise. Oh, good, here's Beatrice. I'll be back before long.'

Aimée listened to the sound of his feet and then the squeak of the hinges on the heavy door as he left the inn. All afternoon, since the death of the stonemason, she had been thinking about Luc and the importance he had now assumed in her life. Of course, on the one hand there was the practical consideration that he was her eyes and, without him, she would be in dire straits, but there was so much more to it than that. The moment she had heard the words 'He's dead' and had feared the worst, the realisation had descended upon her that she was deeply and irrevocably in love with him, and of that there was now no doubt at all. She had already lost one man she had loved dearly. To lose two was unthinkable. If Luc were to die, she knew she would follow him. She pressed her hands together under the table and prayed silently to herself for his safe return with the friar.

Outside, the narrow streets were dark. Night had fallen and the moon had not yet risen. Luc stood in the shelter of a woodpile and waited until his eyes adjusted. Apart from the hum of conversation from the inn behind him, all was quiet. Gradually, he began to distinguish things in the gloom. He could see the street leading back to the cathedral, down which they had come, with two other streets running off it. Ever cautious, he avoided the direct route and made his way there along narrow side alleys.

It was not a big town, and he soon found himself back at the cathedral. There were no lights around this side of the building, and he was able to cross to the deeper shadow of the cathedral wall without fear of being seen. Hugging the stone, still warm from the residual heat of the sun, he headed for the front. Arriving at the corner, he peered cautiously round. Apart from a lantern over the main portal of the cathedral, and another by the Bishop's Palace, there were no signs of life.

He calculated that the friar, by coming straight up the road, would have arrived five or even ten minutes earlier, so he settled down to wait for him to come out. Within a very short space of time, he heard marching feet. He shrank back into the shadows and looked on as four soldiers appeared, one of them carrying a lantern. Although they bore swords, they were not wearing chain mail and their weapons were sheathed. It looked clear that this was the local militia, patrolling the streets. After a brief pause in front of the cathedral, they set off down a side street to continue their rounds and Luc breathed a sigh of relief.

No sooner had the sound of their feet receded, than he heard a loud creak. The Bishop's Palace door was pulled open and a cowled figure emerged. The man closed the door behind him and locked it. Luc clearly heard the jingle of keys. Cupping the lantern against his hand, the man blew out the flame, plunging the building into darkness. Luc heard his footsteps recede along the main street, until all was silent once again.

Luc's mind was racing. The Bishop's Palace was dark and, presumably, empty. Where was Friar Laurent and where was the bishop? And, he wondered with a shiver, where was the Archbishop of Sens? If Laurent wasn't here, where was he? Was all this an elaborate ploy to get him away from the inn, and both of them away from Aimée?

He didn't hesitate. Casting a wary look round, he emerged from his shelter and ran across the square into the street leading directly to the inn. Apart from an occasional flickering candle in a window, it was pitch dark down there. He hoped he wouldn't trip over anything as he hurried through the shadows back to the inn. The road curved slightly to the left and he saw a lantern up ahead, with shadows moving around it. He slowed up and felt his way hesitantly along the wall, until he could see and hear men talking.

'How long do you think he's been dead?'

'Not long. He's still warm.'

Luc realised that the night patrol had found a corpse. His immediate reaction was one of relief. They were talking about a dead man, not woman. The body couldn't belong to Aimée. But could it be the friar?

'We'd better get him off the street. We'll go and get the cart. Who's going to wait with the body?'

There was silence. Clearly none of them fancied standing around in the dark with a dead body, and a murderer on the loose.

'All right then, we'll all go. He isn't going to move, after all.'

There was general agreement. Luc heard them move off, their shadows flickering against the walls of the shops and houses as they disappeared. As soon as they were out of sight, he slipped down the road to the body. His heart sank as he saw the dark monastic habit. There was no doubt about it. It was definitely the friar. He reached down and around the body, searching for the cause of death. A first pale glimmer of moonlight began to shed some illumination on the scene. All at once he saw what had happened. Friar Laurent's head had been twisted viciously round, so that it was past his shoulder. His neck had been broken. Silently, ruthlessly and professionally.

He laid the friar gently back on the cobbles. Raising his hand, he made the sign of the cross over him and murmured a prayer. Then he stood up and set off at a run.

He reached the inn within two minutes. Aware that the killer might be lying in wait for him with a bow, he steeled himself and ran the last few steps in a crouching zigzag. He reached the door unscathed and burst in. Inside, everything was calm and still. Most of the pilgrims had retired to bed and there were only a few men left around the table, drinking wine and talking in low tones. They looked up in surprise at his abrupt entrance. Hastily, he made his way across the room towards the group where, to his immense relief, he saw Aimée leaning against her pack, chatting to Beatrice.

'Everything all right?' Beatrice took one look at his face and realised that all was far from well. Aimée, hearing him approach, turned towards him with a smile.

'Did you find Laurent?'

He sat down beside them and took a deep breath. Somehow, the enormity of the crime made it hard to accept, and even harder to describe.

'I'm afraid I have bad news, very bad news.'

He noticed a few heads around them look up, among them Thomas, looking sleepy. Luc paused for a moment, his mind struggling to make sense of this. Of all the things he had expected to find in there, Thomas in his bedroll was not one of them.

'I'm afraid Friar Laurent's dead.' He heard sharp intakes of breath around the folk in this corner of the room. More people stirred. The family from Champagne peered out of their beds like chicks in a nest. To Luc's amazement, the oldest of them spoke. None of them had been heard to utter more than a syllable at a time for weeks now.

'How did he die?'

The question, coming from such an unexpected source, only served to further confuse Luc. His head was spinning. Mechanically, he recounted the facts.

'I found him lying in the road. He was savagely attacked. His assailant broke his neck. At least that means he would have died instantly, and without suffering.'

'But who would want to kill the friar?' Jeanne stared helplessly at her mother.

'My dear girl, there are some terrible people in the world. May God have mercy on his soul.' Beatrice was weeping. As the news sank in, others followed suit. Laurent had been well loved.

'Have the authorities been informed?' Thomas pulled himself out of bed and came over to stand beside Luc. Luc found himself inching away from him.

'The nightwatchmen found him before I did. I heard them say they were going to get a cart.' Luc glanced at the man beside him. The very professional nature of the killing had immediately stirred Luc's suspicions that it might have been the stocky man's handiwork, but his face gave nothing away. Thomas was fully clothed, but that meant nothing. Most of the pilgrims slept in their clothes, only removing jacket and breeches if it was exceptionally warm. He felt Aimée's hand on his arm.

'You were right in your fears for him, Luc.'

'What fears?' Thomas sounded interested.

Luc told them all about the messenger and his doubts as to how the bishop could have traced Laurent. 'I went to the Bishop's Palace to look for him, but it was closed up and dark. I don't think he even got there. I'm afraid it looks like the killer, or killers, were lying in wait for him.' He was still racking his brains for a motive. The friar's death made no sense.

'Have you asked the innkeeper about the messenger?' Aimée was practical, as always. 'Did he recognise the person who delivered it? This isn't a big town. I'd imagine the innkeeper would know most of the people here.'

'That's a good thought, Aimée. I'll go and ask him now.' Luc turned and made his way back across the room. As he reached the other side, he realised that Thomas was right behind him. Reaching a quiet corner, Luc stopped and turned.

'It's about time you and I had a word.' He kept his voice low, although there was nobody within earshot.

'Always pleased to talk, Luc.' Thomas affected a relaxed, cordial tone, but Luc could see he was very much on guard.

'Tell me, Thomas, how long have you been in here this evening? I went out less than an hour ago and you weren't here then.'

'That's funny. I got here almost exactly an hour ago. We must have missed each other by seconds.' Thomas met and held Luc's eye. 'Why do you ask?'

'It just seems like a big coincidence that the friar and the stonemason were both killed in the same way. A very professional way. You're clearly an expert.'

'Professional? Expert? Thanks for the compliments. But—' Thomas's voice dropped even lower '—if there's a professional killer here, are you so sure it's me? It's you, and you know it.'

Luc stepped slowly back, until his shoulders touched the stone wall behind him. He began to ease his right hand towards his sleeve as Thomas continued.

'You're big enough and strong enough to have killed the monk with your bare hands. I dare say you've done that sort of thing before.' Thomas was staring at him with an ironic smile. 'Just like I know you think you could kill me with that dagger you keep up your sleeve, if you wanted to.' He did not, however, roll up his own sleeves and Luc watched his hands very carefully.

'Who are you?'

'Thomas. I already told you that.'

Luc glanced around. They were still clear of prying ears. 'Did you kill the friar?' He kept his tone level. The other man's stare didn't waver.

'What if I did?'

'Are you telling me you killed Friar Laurent?'

'I'm just saying, why should that bother you if I did? He represented the Catholic Church and the Pope. Everything you hate and fear.'

'Why should I hate and fear the Church?' Luc glanced around again. This conversation was moving into dangerous waters.

'We're neither of us children, Luc. I know who you are. You can probably guess who I am. You're a fugitive. And it's the Catholic Church, my Catholic Church, you're running from.' His expression hardened. 'And the Catholic Church is going to get you, and get what you're carrying. You can't escape. You and the girl are pawns in a much bigger game; you must know that by now.'

Luc tensed his muscles. He could feel the blood pulsing in his throat. The other man smiled and took a half-step back.

'Before you launch yourself at me, Templar, remember this. You're getting old now. You're no longer as fit and fast as you once were. You've been running and hiding for too long. Me, I'm a specialist. Try me, if you like, but don't forget you've been warned. You won't get your knife out of its sheath.'

They stood like that for a full minute, without another word being uttered. Finally, Luc dropped his shoulders. When he spoke, his voice was little more than a croak. He saw the triumph in the other's eyes.

'So why kill the friar? Surely he's one of your own?'

'He was, but he was weak. He took a liking to you, or more probably to the pretty girl. As a result, he betrayed the trust placed in him by His Holiness. He betrayed the Church, my Church.' Thomas's voice was harder now. 'He died so that you could be arrested and tried for his murder.'

Luc was genuinely surprised now. This man, this assassin, was prepared to kill a member of the Church just like that? Thomas was happy to explain.

'Today, on the road, everybody in our group heard the stonemason accuse you of being a Templar. By the way, my compliments on your acting skills. What was it you said? "I have a horror of weapons and all forms of violence." I almost laughed out loud. I killed the mason, because I didn't want you to be killed by him. We want you alive, you see?'

Now Luc did. It made perfect sense. The friar had been killed while Luc was away from the inn. He had been alone and so had no alibi. The stonemason had accused him of being a Templar in front of the friar. There was a macabre logic in the idea of Luc killing Friar Laurent before he could reveal what he had heard to the bishop. The other man's eyes were watching closely. He saw the comprehension dawn on Luc's face.

'That's right. All it'll need now is a word or two from me, and all these fine pilgrims will turn against you. Without us having to dirty our hands, or, more importantly, show our hand, they'll denounce you to the authorities. They'll have you in chains in the wink of an eye.'

Luc had no illusions as to his fate if that ever happened. His thoughts turned to Aimée. It was too horrible to contemplate. He hung his head in sheer dejection. Thomas laughed and wiped his mouth with his right hand.

Luc had been waiting for just such an opportunity. He leapt forward, making no attempt to reach for his hidden dagger. He saw the other man's hand snake down from his face to his side and the knife appeared like magic. But the extra distance his hand had to travel meant that Thomas was still lifting the point upwards when Luc's left hand slammed into his windpipe. This was followed by Luc's right palm that thudded into the man's nose with brutal force. The nose shattered under the effect of the blow and Luc pushed it upwards, into the man's brain. Thomas died on his feet.

Luc caught him before he could fall and rested the body against the wall. There was a faint clink as the knife fell out of the dead man's hand. Luc scanned the room anxiously, but nobody in the shadows of the dormitory appeared to have noticed anything.

He returned his attention to the dead man. His face was red with blood, but the flow had stopped as soon as it started and the ground around them was clean and unmarked. Luc waited for a few moments for his breathing to slow down, then he tore a piece of cloth from the dead man's shirt and used it to clean the blood off the lifeless face. Satisfied with the result, he took the dead man's left arm and pulled it across his shoulders, catching hold of the hand in his own left hand. With his other arm, he gripped the man tightly around the waist. In this way, he managed to frogmarch the lifeless body past the few remaining drinkers in the next room, without attracting their attention. Drunkenness was no cause for alarm. He struggled with the door handle for a moment. Finally, he pulled it open and they disappeared into the night.

Outside, the moon had risen and illuminated the scene. He swung the body over his shoulder in a more comfortable fireman's lift and set off down a side road. He met nobody, but he scanned every shadow apprehensively. After three or four minutes, he emerged on the riverbank. The river was wide and deep at that time of year. Most importantly, it was flowing away from the town centre. Luc slid the body off his back and into the water, watching as it floated off into the night.

He fell to his knees and gave thanks to the Lord for his salvation. Leaning forward, he scooped a handful of water out of the river. As he splashed his face and wiped the sweat off his brow, he found that his hands were shaking. He wasn't surprised.

Collecting himself, he set off back up the dark street to the inn. He let himself in the door and was pleased to see that the drinkers had all retired to bed. He managed to return to the dormitory without trouble and found that the other members of his group had all gone back to bed. Aimée was left sitting against her pack, listening nervously for his return. He slipped off his jacket and lay down beside her, hugging her warmly. He pulled her ear close to his mouth and covered them both with the blanket. In the darkness, he whispered the events of the last ten minutes.

'So he was a Church assassin?' She turned towards him, whispering in her turn.

'Yes, Aimée. He knew all about us, and he knew we're carrying something precious.'

'Well, that's more than we do.' For a moment she allowed herself a flash of frustration. 'So they appear to know our every move?'

'Yes, so far. Anyway, for the moment, the initiative's with us. At least until they find Thomas's body.'

'So what do we do now?'

'We get out of here. We get out of Santo Domingo and we find ourselves another bridge. And from now on, we don't join any other group of pilgrims. We keep ourselves to ourselves. All right?'

She murmured her agreement.

'Right, pack up your things as quietly as possible. Try not to wake anybody else. There's just one thing I must do first.'

He slipped out from under the blanket and over to the spot where Thomas's pack and bedroll still lay. He and Aimée could gain a few precious hours if the others thought Thomas had already left. He lifted both and carried them out to the latrines. By the light of the moon, he dropped them one by one into the depths of the reeking pit. Returning to Aimée, he picked up their packs. Taking her hand, he led her on tiptoe out through the rows of sleeping pilgrims and into the cool night air.

'Right, from now on, we're on our own.'

She reached up on her toes and whispered in his ear. 'Well, there's nobody I'd rather be with.' And she kissed him softly on the neck.

26

PILGRIMS' WAY, NORTHERN SPAIN, MAY 2016

Luke and Amy didn't reach Ponferrada until early evening. The weather had changed and the day spent driving over the mountains brought back memories of the Pyrenees. Both of them had to dig out jackets they hadn't expected to use again that trip. The temperature at the top was close to zero and piles of dirty snow at the sides of the road attested to the long hard winter the region had suffered.

Luckily, the rain stopped long enough for them to be able to add their stones to the huge cairn at the top. Alerted to the tradition by his guidebook, they had collected one each from a dried-up stream bed a few hours earlier. Up here in the unrelenting downpour, all the stream beds were anything but dried up.

'They don't call this region Green Spain for nothing. North-west Spain has more rainfall than some parts of England.' Luke had to shout to make himself heard over the roar of the wind. In the distance he spotted a couple of stalwart pilgrims, struggling up the hill towards them, enveloped in bulky yellow capes.

'There are two pilgrims over there.' He gave Amy a brief description. 'They're heading east. That means they've been to Compostela already and are on their way home. At least they'll have the wind behind them.'

'Is there a good view from up here?' Amy was hanging onto his arm with her free hand.

'View? Maybe on a clear day, but, today, about one or two hundred yards at most. I think we've ascended into the cloud base. Here's the cairn. It's enormous.' He helped her scramble up the massive pile of rocks, until they were on top of it. The mound was made up of thousands upon thousands of stones of all shapes and sizes, deposited there over the centuries.

'So, is this the top of the pile?' She raised her face towards him, her expression bright and cheerful. He reflected that her face had been bright and cheerful for the last few weeks now, so different from only a month before. Mind you, he thought to himself, he couldn't remember being so happy for years either. Particularly since summoning up the courage to tell her about the events in Nigeria, he felt a weight had somehow been lifted from him. He gave her hand a squeeze.

'This is it. You're at the top of the cairn.'

'Do we just drop the stones on the pile?'

'Unless you want to say a few words.' He was joking. The weather conditions didn't invite lingering in the open. To his surprise, that was exactly what she intended to do. She took his stone from him and crouched down. After laying both on the pile she stood up again, her head bowed.

'We know you got this far. Only a few more days, and you'll be at your journey's end.' She turned back to Luke and caught hold of his arm with both hands. 'We owe them that. They deserve a bit of good luck for the last part of what's been a long, hard journey.'

He marvelled at her involvement with the story. But then, he thought to himself, didn't he also feel the presence of their medieval counterparts? He dropped his eyes to the stones and murmured, 'Good luck to you both.'

'It must have been tough for them having to trek all the way up here. But this is the top, isn't it? Is it all downhill from here to Ponferrada?'

'As far as the road's concerned, yes. This is the top of the pass, but the mountain stretches on up into the mist. I don't know how much higher. Here, we're at fifteen hundred metres. That's almost the same as the Somport pass.'

At that moment, a squall came rushing across the mountainside, bringing another downpour. Luke grabbed Amy round the waist and together they rushed back to the shelter of the car. He received a wave from the stoical pilgrims, whose pace didn't falter, in spite of the rain. He waved back with his free hand, part of him wishing he, too, were making the journey on foot. However, the more rational part of him welcomed the blessed warmth and protection as they slammed the Range Rover doors behind them.

Amy struggled out of her jacket and threw it onto the back seat. She raised her arms and fiddled with her ponytail, the curve of her throat and the outline of her breasts producing an instant reaction in him. For once, he didn't lift his eyes from her. He just sat there looking at her, a feeling of happiness spreading throughout his body. At long last, after five years of grieving, he knew he could now move on and there was only one person with whom he wanted this to be. Deep down inside he had known this for weeks, but he was finally able to admit it to himself and act upon his feelings. He cleared his throat. 'Amy.' He reached across and took her hand in his. She turned her head towards him in surprise, but he took heart from the smile on her face.

A blast of wind rocked the big vehicle on its suspension and rain battered the windscreen. Amy hardly felt the movement. She sensed that the time had come and her whole body, her whole being was desperate for his touch, desperate for his love. She found herself having to struggle to control her racing heart and spinning head.

'There's something I've been meaning to say to you for a long time now, Amy. I've been putting it off for fear of what you'll think, but it's no good, I've got to tell you.' His voice was hesitant, even shy. 'We share so much, get on so well, and I think about you all the time.' She felt a rush of emotion and had trouble keeping from jumping out of her seat as she heard him begin to say the words she had been waiting to hear. 'Even when I was lying in my bed in Jaca feeling like death, I was still thinking of you. I find you fascinating, beautiful and...' he hesitated, searching for the right word '...and desirable, very, very desirable. After Nicole's death, I never thought I'd ever feel that way again, and yet, it's happened. It's a very disconcerting feeling. I want you to believe that.'

He stopped and she held her breath, wondering what was going to happen. After a few agonisingly long seconds she heard his voice once more. 'I just had to tell you.'

She reached across towards his face, letting her hands rest against his cheeks for a few moments, before pulling him gently towards her until their lips met.

It wasn't a sensuous, passionate kiss; rather a soft and tender joining of two people. Even so, the intimacy of the touch drained the depths of her emotions and she felt her head swim. As she pressed against him, she felt tears start to trickle down her cheeks. Here, at last, after five long dark years, was her return to happiness. Then she felt him take a deep breath and heard his voice, chock full of emotion.

'Oh, Amy...' She felt a movement and his hands caught hers and squeezed them gently. They sat there in silence for some time until she felt she had better say something.

'If you only knew just how long I've been dying to do that.' She sensed his relief at the sound of her voice. Then he surprised her.

'Amy, but there's something else I've really got to say.' He stopped again and she heard him take another deep, apprehensive breath. For a moment she found she couldn't breathe, terrified that he might be about to plunge her back into loneliness and misery. She tried hard not to squirm in her seat as she waited for what he might have to say. She heard him clear his throat. 'I have to warn you that this may well be a big, big mistake for both of us. For you in particular.' She didn't release his hands, but she was listening keenly. 'You're in a very impressionable state and I may well appear to be much more appealing than I really am. This is, after all, just about the first outing of any length that you've had since the accident. I speak the same language as far as our interest in history's concerned, we like many of the same things, and, of course, I'm your guide. Did you ever have a crush on any of your teachers as a young girl? Well, that could be what's happening here. Are you with me?'

She had started breathing again some seconds earlier and she now felt almost relaxed once more. She found herself smiling at him. She heard him swallow hard and try to finish.

'What I'm trying to tell you is that this may be nothing more than an inevitable and predictable mistake for either or both of us.' She made no comment, letting him say what he wanted to say, knowing how she felt and becoming more and more confident that he felt the same way. 'What we feel for each other now, what I feel for you and whatever you may feel for me, may well turn out to be just the product of the particular circumstances in which we find ourselves. What I'm trying to say is that you, we, have both got to think this thing through carefully. Try to think logically about our situation before we do something we might regret.' His voice tailed off, his words at odds with his feelings.

She ran her hands back up to his face, passing her fingers gently over his eyes, then his ears and then she slipped them around his neck. She pulled gently and he bent forward, making no attempt to resist as she kissed him again. Then she crushed her face into his collar and spoke.

'I wouldn't regret a thing, Luke. Believe me, I would swap the whole of the last five years of my life for this moment with you right now. I mean that. If you then dumped me here and disappeared, it wouldn't matter. It would break my heart, but it wouldn't alter the joy of this and any other moment we can be together like this.' She let her lips rest against his neck for a few moments. 'I'm grateful to you for your warning, but I'm ready to take my chances on this just being a quick holiday romance, or some kind of predictable physical occurrence. I don't happen to think that it is but, like I say, I'm prepared to take the risk.' To reinforce her words she reached up and kissed him lightly on the cheek then ran her fingers across his face once more. When they got to his mouth she could feel the smile on his lips. 'I'm glad you're smiling. Take a look at me, Luke. I'm smiling too.' She sat back, happy and contented.

'I phoned Tim earlier this evening.'

Amy wasn't surprised. She listened carefully, keen to know what had transpired between the two men. There was a pause while he searched for the right words. 'I spoke to him for quite a long time. I told him more about our trip so far and I told him about you. In particular I told him about my feelings for you. He didn't seem very surprised.'

This came as no surprise to Amy. Their cunning friend had known what he was doing all along. 'So just what, exactly, did you tell him about your feelings for me?'

Luke answered immediately. 'I told him I was hopelessly in love with you, and I hoped you felt the same way about me.'

The joy she had been feeling suddenly overflowed. Tears flooded her eyes once more and rolled down her cheeks. She snuggled even more tightly against him. 'Luke, I need you to hold me tight, please.' She heard the leather upholstery creak and his arms envelop her even more tightly, pulling her halfway out of her seat and across the centre armrest. She sank her face into his shoulder and sobbed her heart out.

'Are you all right? Is something wrong?' She could hear the concern in his voice. 'Is it something I've said?'

She pulled her head from his chest and reached for his face with her hands again. She drew him so close to her, she could feel the warmth of his breath on her cheek.

'Yes, Luke, it's something you've said.' She was smiling now, even though the tears still ran. 'You've said the words I've so longed to hear from you.' She kissed him hard on the lips and felt him respond. She hugged him tightly to her for several minutes before she finally, reluctantly, pulled back and set about mopping up her tears. It took her a while before she could talk properly once more.

'It's all right, Luke, I'm all right. In answer to your question, yes, I love you dearly. Be in no doubt about that.'

Unable to resist, he leant across and caught hold of her again, pulling her gently towards him. She raised her head as she stretched her arms around his neck and kissed him, loving the feel of his hands on her. She abandoned herself against him as the rain beat down and the wind whistled round the car. It was a long while later before they both paused for breath.

Her heart sang. The impossible had finally happened. The gloom that had settled upon her in the wake of her plunge into blindness suddenly lifted. She felt happy, no, she told herself, that was too weak a word. She felt totally, overwhelmingly, earth-shatteringly imbued with a new sense of purpose, of satisfaction and of hope, all brought about by a few words from this wonderful man. She savoured the moment before straightening up and returning to her side of the car. She ran her hands across her hair once more and down over her body, tidying her rumpled jumper, sensing his eyes upon her. Now it was her turn to swallow hard as she knew that another watershed had been crossed and another was surely approaching. They sat in silence for a few minutes until a particularly hard gust of wind reminded her of events outside the warm interior of the car. She turned towards him, deeming it time to return to more mundane matters.

'Here we are in the month of May and it's like winter out there. Brr, I bet our couple found it hard going if the weather was like this.' She reached over and took his hand again. 'I suppose pilgrims died in conditions like this way back then.'

He gave her fingers a squeeze in return. He had to clear his throat before he could respond, and she was delighted to hear the emotion still there as he tried to sound normal after their moments of passion. 'Not just way back then. Every year there are a number of fatalities on the Pilgrims' Way. There's even a special mass to remember them. No, you need to be pretty hardy to do the whole thing on foot. The couple of pilgrims we saw out there on the road have disappeared into the mist.'

'But our two managed it all right.' She had no doubts. 'I'm sure of that. Maybe we'll meet up with them again at Ponferrada.'

The journey down the other side of the pass was like driving through a river in full spate. Streams and drains overflowed, and spouts of brown water gushed out onto the road. Mud and loose stones were washed into their path. It wasn't an easy drive and Luke was very glad to be in a big, solid vehicle with four-wheel drive.

Their accommodation for the night was outside the town in an old farmhouse, set on the side of the hill, with a view down over the town to the magnificent old Templar castle. Fortunately, by the time they got there, the rain had eased and the cloud had lifted. There was no doubt, however, that the view beyond the town, over the jumbled mass of hills ahead of them towards Compostela, would certainly be daunting for people on foot.

'We have a sunset.' Luke's voice sounded cheerful. 'After all the rain and cloud up on the pass, we appear to be getting some better weather down here.'

'What's the farmhouse like?' She stretched and reached for the door handle.

It was magnificent. The Casa Rural had recently been converted into very comfortable accommodation. They were shown to their rooms by a charming Romanian woman whose English was as fluent as her Spanish. The rooms were side by side and they were the only guests. The Romanian woman accompanied Amy to her room and showed her how everything worked. Luke left them to it and went into his room, closing the door behind him and throwing his bag onto the large bed. He heard Amy's door shut as their hostess departed and he was about to go out into the corridor to her door to see if she needed anything when he heard a gentle tap on the wall. He glanced round and discovered a cunningly concealed communicating door that he unbolted and opened. Behind the door was another door on her side that she had opened.

'Clever, eh?' She ran one hand up the shiny surface of the door and reached out for him with her other. 'Our own private entrance.' Stepping aside, she beckoned to him to come into her room. Being here with him like this heightened the intimacy of their relationship and she felt a knot in her stomach. When they were standing in the middle of the room, directly in front of the huge double bed, face to face, she wondered if similar thoughts were going through his mind. She felt nervous, shy even, but also excited. For the first time, she felt a real sensual wave come over her in his presence and she actually felt her knees go weak. She swallowed hard, unsure what was going through his head.

'Do you want me to go?' He coughed, cleared his throat and had two or three tries before he managed to get the words out. Amy realised with a rush of affection that he was similarly affected by the situation. She pulled him towards her until they were touching, her head level with his shoulders. She reached up and put her arms around his neck, bending his face down towards her. His lips touched hers, his arms encircled her waist and he straightened up again, lifting her feet from the floor and pressing her whole body against his. They kissed with a passion that confirmed, if confirmation were required, that their relationship had progressed to another level. She abandoned herself against him and let the warmth of the embrace reach down inside her, sweeping away the pain and sadness and replacing it with a glow of joy.

Eventually he set her back down on her feet again and sat on the edge of the bed, pulling her gently towards him until she, too, reached the bed. She climbed onto his lap, straddling him with her legs, and pushed him gently back until he was sprawled on the bed. She felt his arms reach round behind her and crush her to his body. She hoped he could see her face. She knew she was smiling from ear to ear.

27

PILGRIMS' WAY, NORTHERN SPAIN, MAY 1314

It was early evening and the sun had long since disappeared behind the hills that encircled the town. It would soon be dark enough for them to risk an approach. Both of them were tired after a relentless series of wearying marches and Aimée had developed a persistent hacking cough over the past few days in the high mountains as they climbed up and over the Monte Irago Pass. It was terribly exposed and windswept up there and Aimée had been exhausted by the time they reached the summit, and Luc little better. Although the road was clear, drifts of snow still filled the ditches, and it was freezing cold. As they began the long descent, the rain started. The next day, the fever struck her and Luc realised that she needed shelter and rest, very urgently. He uttered heartfelt prayers that the castle at Ponferrada would still have friendly faces waiting for them.

Now, finally, they were in Ponferrada. At long last, the castle was within reach. Luc was pinning his hopes on what the abbot of Santa Cristina had told him as he passed on his leather cloak to Luc. The first thing to do was to establish whether or not the Templars were still there. Aimée was lying stretched out beside him in the sodden heather, wrapped in her fur-lined cloak. She was half asleep, regularly wracked by violent coughing fits. He stole a worried glance across at her, before concentrating his attention on the castle, barely visible in the twilight as dusk fell.

It was set in a dominating position, partway up the hillside overlooking the river. It was massive, and reminded him of the enormous crusader castles that had sheltered him in the Holy Land. There were two lines of defensive walls, both crowned by battlements and walkways for the defending troops. A massive stone keep, quite literally a castle within a castle, rose up at the highest point. Such a fortress would be virtually impossible to storm. His hopes rose that he might indeed find other remnants of the Order inside.

There was another painful bout of coughing from the little figure beside him and he realised that time was not on their side. If she didn't get into the warm soon, he could see her condition deteriorating more and more. He reached down and laid his hand on her hair.

'It's time for me to go and look for our friends.' His voice was deliberately more confident than he felt. She wasn't fooled.

'Have you seen any signs of Templars?' Her voice was a croak.

'No.' He answered cautiously. 'But I haven't seen any signs of the enemy either. In fact it looks pretty dead. What I'm hoping is that there's a rearguard of Templars left behind. Hopefully, the main garrison escaped to safety, maybe to Portugal where we're supposed to be heading.' He stroked her hair as she broke down into a fit of coughing once more, her whole body shaken by the force of the attack. Finally she rallied enough to be able to murmur:

'Take care, Luc. They may be waiting for you. Please God you may succeed.'

'Amen,' he murmured in his turn and added quietly, 'Don't move from here. Stay wrapped up and try to keep warm. I'll be back shortly.'

He bent and kissed her on the forehead. Then he straightened up and started to make his way down the hill. Aimée curled herself up as tightly as she could into her cloak and did her best not to give way to the shivers that threatened to engulf her. What if he was intercepted and captured? Could it be that he had just walked out of her life forever? Would he find what he was seeking and would he be able to find her again when he came back? She bit her lip to hold back not only the shivering but also the tears that were oh so close to flowing.

The sky was overcast and there were neither stars nor moon to light his way. His progress was hesitant. Every now and then he stopped to check his bearings back up the hill towards the spot where he had left her. He was all too aware of how easy it would be to miss her in the darkness. The wind was icy and he wrapped his leather cloak tightly around his shoulders, hoping that she would be warm enough until his return. The huge bulk of the castle loomed closer and he smelt the burning tar of torches at the gate. He crept closer and closer until he was less than fifty paces from the heavily fortified entrance. He sank down behind a rock and searched the shadows for any signs of life. He looked for any clue as to the present occupants of the castle. Nothing moved.

He looked down the hillside and saw a series of low-roofed houses just above the riverbank. From the end one he could just make out a flickering light. Silently, he slipped away from his boulder and down towards that light. Approaching the house, he saw that it was candlelight, escaping through a broken shutter. He crept to the window, easing himself up until he could look inside. At first he could distinguish little, apart from a fire burning brightly in an open fireplace directly across the room from him. Then he saw a slight movement. He realised that someone was sitting directly in front of the fire, shoulders to the window. It was impossible to see whether this was a man or a woman or, indeed, whether there was anyone else in the room, outside his field of vision.

He crouched down and thought hard. The darkness around him was total, his night vision temporarily ruined by the candlelight. It was probably this as much as anything that made his mind up for him. He reached out, slipped his hand through the broken plank and was pleased to feel the wooden bar that held the shutters together. With a jerk he wrenched it out of its brackets and pulled the shutter outwards towards him. He sprang up and leapt into the room feet first, his knife in his hand. Pulling the shutter closed behind him to protect his back, he straightened up.

The figure in the chair started to move, but slowly, terribly slowly. Luc stepped forward, the flames of the fire reflecting off the vicious blade in his right hand. He was barely a few feet from the back of the chair. He knew that he could slit the other's throat without difficulty if it came to it. The candle-light struck the side of the face that turned towards him and he stopped in his tracks. The face before him was that of a woman. More than that, it was the face of an old woman, her hair white as snow. Her cheeks were deeply wrinkled, and her skin looked like dry parchment. He lowered the point of the knife so as not to terrify her any further. Then she spoke, and the surprise was his.

'Luc? Luc? It is you, isn't it?' Her voice was stronger than her outward appearance. He was stunned. 'Come here into the light and let me see you again. Come.'

She held out her hands towards him. He felt himself drawn irresistibly across the room to the fireside.

'God be praised. It is you.' Her voice was awestruck. 'You did it. You managed to get here. May the Lord God Almighty bless you and keep you, for you are our salvation.' As she spoke, the memories came rushing back. He saw her face, this same face, refined and elegant, framed by the branches of an olive tree, the burning sun of Cyprus casting a moving pattern of light and shade across her. And alongside was her brother, Theobald Gaudin, the previous Grand Master of the Order. Luc sank to his knees, slid the knife out of sight up his sleeve and prayed aloud, the words of the 'Gloria in Excelsis' coming spontaneously to his lips.

'Glory be to God on high...' As he recited the words, she joined in and they both crossed themselves thankfully. Finally he opened his eyes and saw her holding out her hands to him. He knelt before her and let her encircle his shoulders with her arms. She didn't rise. From the walking stick beside her chair, he could see that this would be difficult for her. He stood up again, warmed by the fire and heartened by her unexpected presence. His joy was short-lived.

'They've all left, Luc.'

He felt he had been slapped across the face. His hopes, so wonderfully raised, were now suddenly dashed. He sat down heavily on a stool by the fireside.

'My Lady Alice, would you tell me all you know, please?'

'The whole garrison left the castle some months ago. Now it's nominally in the hands of the King of León, but in fact there's nobody left, apart from half a dozen caretakers. Those who could headed west towards Santiago de Compostela. From there they hoped to continue down the coast into Portugal. Those who were too old, or too sick, entrusted themselves to the king's men.' Her tone soured. 'In consequence they're now rotting in the dungeons of León.'

'And you, my lady? Did you not wish to follow the others to Portugal?'

'As you know, my dear brother died more than twenty years ago. I was deemed a harmless old cripple, so they left me alone.' In spite of her words, there was a twinkle in her eye.

Luc knew that she had enjoyed a privileged position as confidante to many of the leaders of the Order. This included the last Grand Master, Jacques de Molay, and Luc's own brother, Geoffroi de Charny. Evidently, by virtue of this, she had been chosen to await his arrival.

'So what do I do now?' Luc's voice was low, as was his morale. 'Come to think of it, how could you be sure that I would happen upon you like this?'

'You're right, Luc.' Surprisingly, the old lady's voice was anything but dejected. He looked up in surprise. 'I could hardly count upon your identifying this house and climbing through the window instead of using the door.' There was a dry note in her voice. He glanced across to where the stout wooden bar that served to lock the shutters in place was lying on the floor. He murmured an apology that she either didn't hear or chose to ignore.

'I was relying upon your honouring your promise to the abbot of Santa Cristina.' Luc sat up, wondering how she could possibly have known about that. 'You were to seek out the Master of the castle of Ponferrada to return his cloak to him. That very same cloak that you're wearing now, isn't it, Luc?' He nodded dumbly, his brain working a few steps slower than hers.

A broad smile spread over her face as she continued her explanation. 'I took the precaution of, shall we say, liberally supplementing the income of the caretakers of the castle. They would have referred you to me if you had made contact.' She sat back, hugely satisfied, as he strove to make sense of what she had said. How could she have possibly known what the abbot could have said to him unless... His brain started to put two and two together. Her voice interrupted his thoughts.

'Are you alone, or do you have a travelling companion?'

He nodded, very aware of Aimée's present predicament. 'I'm travelling with the wife of my predecessor, Bertrand. With your permission, my lady,

I'll go and bring her here. I am afraid that she's far from well, having caught a fever some days ago. She's sorely in need of warmth and rest.'

He left immediately, this time by the door.

The wind had started to pick up. It brought with it increasingly heavy rain that beat against the thick leather of the cloak. He picked his way up the hill towards the place he had left her. It took him some minutes to regain his night vision and still longer to get his bearings in the pitch dark. The hillside itself was virtually featureless. He scrambled frantically from one rocky outcrop to another, almost despairing of finding her again. The rain fell harder and harder, drenching him in spite of the cloak. He felt water run down his back and shivered with cold. He spared a thought for Aimée, already cold and sick, and now surely soaked as well.

He quite literally stumbled across her. His foot encountered her soft form and he fell headlong over her. She stirred and unwrapped her head from the waterlogged fur. His relief was so great that he took her face in his hands and hugged her to his chest. She coughed wearily.

'Success?'

'Yes.' He pulled her to her feet and shouldered the two packs. He encircled her painfully thin body with his arm. She was shivering with cold. 'Come on, there's warmth and shelter waiting for us down the hill. Walk with me.'

He led her off down the hillside as fast as he could. She was so weak that he found himself carrying her most of the way, along with the two packs. By the time they reached the house, he felt almost as drained as she did. Lady Alice had been busy and a wonderful smell of mulled wine filled the air. The fire blazed so brightly that the whole room was lit up. He led Aimée in and pulled off her soaking cloak. Lady Alice helped her out of her equally wet dress, until she stood shivering in her shift in front of the fire. The old lady produced a thick woollen blanket and wrapped it round her twice, cocooning her like a newborn baby. Gently Luc helped her onto a deep, soft mattress to one side of the fire and watched as Lady Alice pressed a mug of the hot wine into her hands.

'Take this, my dear. You need something warm inside you.'

Aimée was barely able to hold the mug, but, with Luc's assistance, she drank most of it.

Only then did he throw off his leather cloak and his own soaking tunic. Lady Alice handed him another blanket and a mug of wine. He settled down gratefully on the other side of the fire and savoured the hot, sweet drink. With heavy eyelids, he watched the old lady move around the room, picking up the wet clothes and hanging them to dry in front of the fire. She still had a proud, patrician air about her, in spite of the humble surroundings in which she now found herself. She limped around, tidying the room, for all the world like a menial servant. If she felt any bitterness at her change of station, it didn't show. Indeed, she managed to give the impression that she took pride in what she was doing. In particular, he saw a glow of satisfaction on her face as she picked up his leather cloak. She set it to dry before the fire with a reverence that even his tired eyes couldn't fail to notice.

28

PILGRIMS' WAY, NORTHERN SPAIN, MAY 2016

They almost missed dinner that evening. It was only when Amy pressed her Snoopy watch and heard that it was almost nine o'clock that they roused themselves. She rolled across towards him, relishing the feel of his naked body against hers. Her whole body was tingling with joy and she felt a desire to scream her happiness at the top of her voice. Instead, she managed something far more prosaic.

'Hungry?'

He yawned and stretched. 'You know me.'

She ran her fingers through the hair of his chest. 'I do now, that's for sure.'

He caught her hand in his and raised it to his mouth, kissing each of her fingers in turn. 'I love you, Amy. I love you so very, very much. You can't imagine how much I love you.'

She grinned. 'Well, I love you even more.'

'Oh, no, you don't.'

'Oh, yes, I do.'

'Don't.'

'Do.' She reached up and kissed him gently on the lips. 'So, like I said; food?'

'Well, if you insist.'

Downstairs Anna, the Romanian woman, had prepared an excellent meal for them. Amy insisted on getting him a big beer first, and then they opted for a bottle of Rioja. She felt happier than she could ever remember, as the events of this evening in this magical place had finally chased away so many of the demons of the past. They didn't speak much at first. There was no need. Then, as they enjoyed their starter, the conversation turned, as ever, to their medieval characters.

'I've just had a thought.' His voice was almost apologetic, and Amy pricked up her ears. 'You remember the Holy Grail?' She spluttered into her gazpacho.

'I thought those words were taboo?'

'Yes, well...' Still the apologetic tone. 'I might just have come up with an idea of what our man might have been carrying that was so precious. No,' he was quick to explain himself, 'I'm not coming round to thinking that it might have been the Holy Grail after all. Don't worry. But I was thinking of something similar.'

'Like what?' He had her full attention now. 'What on earth could be similar to the Grail?'

'Well...' He sounded decidedly sheepish. 'Maybe the Holy Shroud?'

'The Turin Shroud.' She was almost scoffing. 'Radiocarbon dating's shown it to be a fake. A medieval fake. A good one, but nonetheless a fake.'

'Or a copy.' He spoke quietly and she stopped in her tracks.

'What did you say?' Her tone had become more serious. He took a mouthful of wine and tried to explain his theory.

'The cloth used to cover the body of Christ, when they took him down from the cross, or so the Church would have us believe. All sorts of experts have studied the cloth. Some have produced arguments to support the hypothesis that blood, sweat and bodily fluids could burn a negative image of a man on a piece of cloth. But the radiocarbon dating showed the one in Turin cathedral to be a thirteenth-century fake, as you say. What if it really did exist? What if there really was a Holy Shroud, or at least a very ancient piece of cloth that they believed to be the Shroud?'

She sat bolt upright. 'But why make a copy, then?' But she was formulating the answer even as she asked the question. 'Of course, so that the original could be taken to a place of safety. But why the Templars?'

'I've been thinking about that.' His voice was less hesitant now. He waited while Anna removed their plates. 'One of the recurring charges brought against the Templars during their trial was that they worshipped a myste-rious head; a head with the power to reduce any who looked upon it to trem-bling wrecks. Nobody has ever got to the bottom of that one and quite a few have tried. What if there really was such a cloth, and the Templars had got hold of it? Such a relic, particularly in the Middle Ages, when relics were big, big business, would have been worth any amount to a deeply religious order like the Templars.'

The waitress returned with two huge plates of food. Luke thanked her and gave Amy a running commentary.

'You've got two hefty pork chops, a whole chicken breast and two enor-mous sausages on your plate. It all looks very good and immensely filling. If you're still feeling hungry after that, there's a mountain of roast potatoes alongside. Everything's very hot, including the plates, so be careful. More wine?'

She shook her head, more interested in his Shroud theory than in food. He went on more confidently. 'The history of the Turin Shroud is only really documented from the Middle Ages onwards. But, if I remember right, there was talk of it once being in the possession of the de Charny family. Geoffroi de Charny is a name you know well.'

She certainly did. 'Knights Templar Preceptor of Normandy. Burnt at the stake along with Jacques de Molay on a little island in the Seine on 18 March 1314. Right back at the start of our story.' Her voice was awestruck.

'Precisely.' He was sounding ever more confident. It really could fit. 'Now, there's no real conclusive proof that the Shroud was in the de Charny family; in fact there's doubt as to which branch of the de Charny family that was anyway, but how about this as a scenario? Geoffroi knows that it's very likely that the Shroud will be discovered and stolen from the Order by King Philip. So he commissions a convincing copy and removes the original. His copy in fact proves to be so convincing that it lasts right up to the present day. In the greatest secrecy, he packs the real Shroud up and sends it to safety in the high Pyrenees.'

Amy carried on the story. 'After the execution of Jacques de Molay and Geoffroi de Charny, a Templar knight is sent to pick it up from there and take it to safety.' Her voice was hushed. She reached across and took hold of Luke's hand on the tablecloth. 'But he's killed before he can collect it, and his wife is blinded in the battle. She takes refuge in the hospice of Santa Cristina.' She stopped, an expression of puzzlement on her face. 'Hang on a minute. That's not right. How can a Templar knight have a wife? They were monks, after all, with a vow of celibacy.'

'That occurred to me too. I've been doing a bit of research. Although Templar knights were monks, as you say, there were also a number of married men among their ranks. These were principally engaged for their prowess on the field of battle. They didn't take religious vows, so there was no reason why they couldn't be married. They were tolerated for their fighting skills, but they always remained, in a sense, second-class citizens.'

Amy nodded, satisfied with his explanation. 'So the first one was a lay Templar with his wife. Our man, who's a full Templar warrior monk, is sent from Paris to take over from his predecessor. He collects the Shroud and the woman. Together, they set out to take the Shroud to safety over the border in Spain or, more probably, Portugal.' She sat back, still ignoring her food. 'That's uncanny. It really could be. In fact it has to be.' She squeezed his hand hard and asked half seriously, half in jest, 'Do you think you might have been a Templar knight in a previous life?'

'*Beaucéant!*' He hissed the Templar battle cry between his teeth and then relaxed. 'Who knows? I've been finding it hard enough sorting out just this one life of mine, without getting drawn into any complications of reincarnation.' He looked across the table at her. There was a broad, satisfied smile on her face. 'Happy?'

'I think I'm going to explode.'

'Don't do that. Think of the mess. Instead, why don't you get stuck into your sausage and chips?'

'Food – is that all you ever think of?'

'Well, there's you...'

29

PILGRIMS' WAY, NORTHERN SPAIN, MAY/JUNE 1314

Luc slept all night and well into the next morning. In the little house, with the shutters closed and the fire glowing brightly, it was true luxury to relax and enjoy the rare combination of warmth, comfort and less than the usual degree of wariness. He was vaguely conscious of the old lady moving around, piling wood on the fire, turning their clothes and preparing hot drinks.

When he finally awoke, he realised that the hot drinks had been for Aimée. She was lying on the soft mattress, swathed in blankets, in spite of the heat of the fire. She was still looking terribly pale. When Lady Alice saw him stir, she pushed open one of the shutters, flooding the room with unexpectedly bright light from a cloudless sky and sparkling sun. Aimée looked even sicker in the daylight. He moved across to her bedside, crouching down beside her and reaching for her hand. Her eyelids fluttered, but she gave no other sign of life. He threw a questioning glance over his shoulder to the old lady, who stood back watching them both. In reply she shrugged.

'She's in the hands of the Almighty.' She kept her voice low. 'She was chilled to the bone when you brought her in last night. She should have warmed up by now, but she's still as cold as death.' Luc shivered at her choice of words, raised his eyes to the heavens, and prayed for Aimée's recovery. He prayed as fervently as he had ever prayed for anything in his life, hands tightly clutched together, beseeching the Lord to help her. Finally he tucked her hand back under the blankets and stood up.

'Here. You must look after yourself as well, Luc.' The old lady thrust a bowl of warm milk into his hands. 'Drink this. I'll bring you food. Regain your strength; you'll need it. For both of you.'

He did as he was bidden and then slipped cautiously out of the back door to the latrines. He washed the sleep out of his eyes with icy water from a wooden bucket and looked around. The back of the cottage was only a short distance from the river. The river was in spate, and the water was rushing past with a powerful roar. The rain of the previous night, coupled with the last of the melting snow from the mountains, had swelled the level to within a few feet of the top of the bank. It was a crystal-clear day and the sky was a deep blue. The sun was warm on his back, although the air was still chill. The house prevented him from seeing the castle, which he knew stood a few hundred paces above him.

He wondered where the Master of the castle was now. This made him think of the abbot of Santa Cristina and his leather cloak. The expression of awe and reverence with which the old lady had handled it came back to him. What was so special about the cloak? He turned urgently back into the house, looking for Lady Alice. She was sitting on one of the wooden benches alongside the kitchen table. Her walking stick was propped against the wall beside her. His cloak lay, neatly folded, on the polished wood before her.

'Is there something special about the cloak?' His pulse beat faster as she nodded.

'What is it?' He could barely keep his impatience under control. His voice faltered. He watched her reach out and start to open the cloak on the tabletop. Her movements were formal and deliberate, almost as if she were completing a ceremony of some kind.

He watched her spread the cloak out, leather side down. She reached for a sharp kitchen knife and ran it up the seam where the lining, now crumpled and soiled after his journey, was attached to the strong hide. She pulled the lining away from the leather and then ran the knife down the other sides. Reaching down, she removed the dirty fabric completely, revealing the folded layers of cloth that served as insulation. Delicately, she separated the layers and, from among them, pulled out a piece of material. With movements ever more respectful, she began to unfold it.

There, before his eyes, materialised the Holy Shroud of the Lord Jesus Christ.

He knew of the Shroud. It had been in their family for generations, before being passed over to the Order. All senior Templar knights knew its significance. He had, however, only ever seen the ornate reliquary, in the shape of a head, in which it was kept. There were those who said that sight of it could kill or worse and he felt a shiver run down his spine. He had never seen or handled it, let alone thought he would ever wear it upon his shoulders. He knelt and kissed the edge of the material. The cloth was long, at least twice his height, and the width of the table. In spite of the long journey, it seemed miraculously smooth and uncreased.

The image of the crucified Christ stood out clearly before them. As Luc's eyes made contact with the face of his Lord, he felt an awesome terror descend upon him and he found himself shielding his eyes from the image. He felt humble and insignificant, overcome by the thought that he had worn the image of Jesus Christ himself, upon his unworthy shoulders. He felt he had defiled it. A sense of shame invaded him.

'Forgive me, Lord. I didn't know...' His voice was a terrified whisper. 'I'm unworthy to even touch this most holy of objects, and yet...' And yet he had worn it, slept in it. God help him, he had even worn it when he used the latrines. He was overwhelmed.

'What you did was the most wonderful thing anybody could have done, Luc. You carried our Lord on your back from a place of danger to a place of safety. You are indeed blessed.' He was startled by the old lady's voice. For a moment, it seemed that the man whose pain-racked image lay before him was speaking. He crossed himself and shook his head incredulously, still unable to accept the magnitude of what had happened. He had carried his Lord on his back. He shivered, in spite of the blazing fire.

'The abbot made no mention of the Shroud when he gave me the cloak. I could have left it somewhere or given it away. And then this most precious of things would have been lost.'

'But you didn't lose it. You honoured his request that you return it to Ponferrada, just as we all knew you would.'

'We all knew?' He stared at her. 'You and others knew he would pass this on to me?'

'Luc, the Shroud is the most precious relic in the whole world. Before the arrests started, seven years ago, steps were taken to ensure the safety of our treasure. There are those who only think of material treasure: gold, silver, jewels. For us, some things are worth much, much more. The Shroud was sent to the safest place we could imagine, as far away from King Philip as possible. We sent it for safekeeping to the far mountains, to the abbey of Santa Cristina. When first Bertrand, and then you, were sent there, instructions were given.'

She could see that he was struggling to comprehend what had happened.

'Here, Luc, help me.' Her voice was strong once more. 'We'll fold the Shroud and I'll hide it among my linen in this chest. In that way I'll be able to take it to Tómar in Portugal without hindrance.'

He looked up as he heard and recognised the name. 'Tómar? I, too, am bound for Tómar. Can't we travel together?'

'I'm afraid I must refuse your kind offer of companionship. I'm instructed to travel separately from you. I will travel down to Tómar by a circuitous route, heading back east and then dropping down into the lands of the Moors.' In answer to something in his eyes, she smiled. 'I'm an old woman; a harmless old woman. I have no fear of attack.'

'So, if you're heading east, which way do I go?'

'Your mission is complete, Luc. Safety awaits you in Portugal. You must go west.' She spoke firmly. 'You go west to Compostela and beyond. From there, you continue to the coast of the great sea. When you reach the coast, you turn south into Portugal and join me, and the others, in Tómar.'

He sat back, digesting what he had heard. Lady Alice didn't give him time to think. 'Come, help me. It's time the Shroud was hidden away from prying eyes.'

Together they folded it. The old lady lifted it gently and limped across to the solid wooden chest, open on the floor. Luc watched as she placed the priceless relic amid a pile of folded sheets and then added more linen on top of it, until the chest was full. Lady Alice crossed herself before lowering the domed lid on the chest. She slid a heavy metal padlock into place on the outside. She turned the key and then slipped it onto a chain around her neck.

'I will leave later today.' He looked up in surprise, but a gesture from her silenced him. 'A carriage is coming to collect me. When your friend is well, you will join us in Tómar. But be careful if you decide to cut south direct from here. That will take you through mountains, away from the Pilgrims' Way, and there you will find all manner of vicious bandits. Better to follow the route west from here through Compostela and beyond.'

He nodded.

'Besides, you both deserve to experience the splendour of Santiago de Compostela. I must give you one word of warning, though. It is my under-standing that a group of horsemen came through here less than a week ago. One of the castle caretakers told me. I am reliably informed that they were sent by that snake, the Archbishop of Sens.'

Luc stopped eating in mid mouthful. The rough-hewn cell at San Juan de la Peña and the table, laid with obscene instruments of torture, flooded his memory. The sensation of the barbed whip against his cheek was so real that he found himself brushing his fingers against his face to remove the irri-tation. He shook himself violently, chasing the spectre from his mind.

'He doesn't give up easily.'

Since leaving Santo Domingo de la Calzada in the dead of night, he and Aimée had had no further contact with the archbishop's men. Indeed, by avoiding towns and cities, Luc had dared to hope that they might have finally escaped his clutches. But it appeared that such was not to be the case. He breathed out in frustration but squared his shoulders and returned to his meal. He and Aimée had evaded them so far. They could do it for a few more days.

The old lady watched him covertly. She felt again the raw fear that this big man had inspired in her the previous evening. She had been woken from a cosy daydream by the appearance of the huge figure with a vicious flashing knife. She thanked the Almighty once again that she had not fainted or died of fright. She also thanked Him for allowing her to maintain a semblance of normality in the face of such naked aggression. She reached across and laid her hand on Luc's arm.

'Choose the way you wish. It would take a brave bandit to tackle you,

Luc. But if you've never been to Santiago before, it's a wonderful and memorable experience.'

He caught her eye and held it. He was on the point of opting for the mountains and the bandits, preferring them to the evil archbishop, when there was a sound from the other side of the room. It was Aimée.

He was at her side in a flash. Her face was no longer deathly pale. To his delight, he saw that a rosy flush had spread across it and sweat was beading at her temples. He laid his hands against her cheeks and was rewarded by the sight of her eyes opening, closely followed by her lips.

'Thank God I feel warm.' Her voice was weak, but comprehensible. He leant closer to hear her next words. 'We will go to Compostela together, after all.'

She drifted off into sleep. Her breathing was regular and she looked peaceful. Glancing up, Luc caught the old lady's eyes. Her hands were clasping the crucifix around her neck and her lips were mouthing a prayer. He stood up.

'We'll take the Pilgrims' Way to Santiago de Compostela as you advise.' His mind was made up. 'Then we'll follow you to Tómar. Aimée is going to get better now. Everything will be all right. Thanks be to God.'

'Thanks be to God.' The Lady Alice repeated his words.

* * *

Aimée made good, steady progress. After Lady Alice had left with her precious cargo, Luc spent time resting and recuperating. He prepared food, acted as nurse to Aimée and tidied the house.

Altogether, they were in the little house for almost two weeks and Luc was delighted to see Aimée get stronger day by day. The old lady had left a leg of ham, two dozen eggs, a string of sausages and a larder full of vegetables, wine, oil and flour. Twice each day Luc prepared hot meals for them. At first he ate most of the food, and Aimée would accept only a little soup. Gradually, as the days wore on, she started to eat solid food again and the improvement in her condition became more marked. He experimented with making bread in the little oven at the side of the fire. By the end of the second day, he was able to produce good flat loaves of unleavened bread.

The fire itself never went out and the pile of wood behind the house shrank visibly. Leave nothing behind, Lady Alice had said. It looked as if Luc would do just that.

It was imperative that Aimée should make a full recovery before undertaking the last part of their journey, so he stoked the fire and stirred the pot, cheered by her renewed vitality and healthy colour. Finally, towards the end of the second week, he pronounced her fit to travel. They would set off the next day.

She took the news with mixed feelings. On the one hand, she was keen to get moving and finish the journey. On the other, there was the ever-increasing worry as to what would happen when they finally got to Tómar. She knew that this place of safety was the rallying point for all surviving Templars. By the sound of it, the Order was still alive and well in Portugal. What if he returned to his former life as a Templar and failed to renounce his vows? To be left alone would be bad enough, but to be separated from the man she knew she loved would be even worse.

The thought of losing him made her physically afraid. Every step towards their destination hastened the day when they might have to part. So she rolled up her belongings that evening with considerable regret. In particular, she regretted leaving this little house. They had lived here to all intents and purposes as man and wife. She loved to talk to him, feel him touch her, stroke her hair or just hold her hand. The thought of losing him was terrifying.

She heard him moving around by the fireside. She made her way over, caught hold of him and burrowed her head into his shoulder. She felt his arms encircle her.

'If I lose you, I'll die.' Her words were muffled by his shirt, and he couldn't hear.

'What was that?' He stroked her hair with his free hand.

'Nothing.' She looked up from his shoulder and smiled. 'I'm looking forward to getting to Compostela.'

30

SANTIAGO DE COMPOSTELA, MAY 2016

Their last day's drive was a short one. On the way into Santiago they paused to search for the spot at Labacolla where the medieval pilgrims would have stopped and bathed. This was a ritual, before embarking upon the final leg of the journey. Unfortunately, the proximity of the airport and a lot of new development made it impossible to get the feel of the place. The ever-increasing downpour hadn't encouraged them to do much tramping about either. Slightly disappointed, Luke turned off the new highway onto the Monte del Gozo. This famous hill was the first vantage point from which pilgrims arriving along the Pilgrims' Way would see their destination.

The hill, when they finally located it among a mass of new development, also turned out to be something of a disappointment. Half of the hillside was a huge sprawling twentieth-century pilgrims' hostel. He described it to her as looking more like a theme park without the big dipper. Then they came out onto the hilltop, and he saw the big dipper itself.

'I'm sorry. I know I should be impressed, but it's awful. Since I was last here they've built a monument. It's to commemorate the Pope's visit, during the celebrations to mark one thousand years of the Santiago pilgrimages, but, oh dear, oh dear. It's sort of a concrete bunker with a huge steel horse-shoe and a plastic cross on top of it. Oh dear, oh dear.'

She insisted on going over to the monstrosity in question and running her hands along it. She pondered for a moment and then turned to him.

'First, it's not concrete, it's stone, and second, you forgot to mention the mosaic on the side. Are you sure it is really so awful?'

He hesitated and then decided to be brutally frank. 'I was sparing you that. The mosaic looks as if the Pope is throwing scallop shells at another horseshoe. Believe me, you wouldn't want it on your T-shirt.'

'Do I hear your "outraged academic" tone, by any chance? Anyway, come on, it's the principle of the thing that counts. For them it was a major event, which had to be marked somehow or other.'

'You're right.' He smiled and gave her a hug, the umbrella spilling a stream of raindrops neatly down his neck as he did so. He shook himself mentally and physically. 'Sorry. I'm just a bit disappointed that the first impression of the city we've been so looking forward to seeing is less than perfect. That's all. Anyway, I promise I won't moan any more. All right?'

In reply she kissed him. Then he walked her across to the edge of the hilltop square and described the view, their hands entwined on the handle of the umbrella.

'Forgetting for the moment the holiday camp below us and the monstr... the statue behind us, the first thing that hits you is the cathedral. Nowadays it's surrounded by a mass of buildings, but they wouldn't have been there in the Middle Ages. It would've looked all the more impressive when it stood more or less alone. Two, three, four spires I can count. A mass of pillars, arches, statues and very fancy stonework.'

He looked down at her, sorry that she wasn't able to enjoy the sight for herself, but her expression was happy and interested, no frustration visible.

'Did the pilgrims come right past here?' She was trying to get the feel of the place.

'Absolutely right past us. Follow this road down the hill and you enter the city through the Puerta del Camino, the main gateway. Pilgrims would have been set upon by people selling everything from new boots to miracle cures, all the way from here to the cathedral itself. Mind you,' he acknowledged with a grin, 'things have changed a lot since then. Just you wait until we get into the centre.'

They returned to the car and he threaded his way into town through the traffic. A helpful policeman indicated the way to the Parador through a Pedestrians Only zone. Feeling embarrassingly conspicuous in the big vehicle, they bumped across the wet cobbles of the narrow streets until they emerged into the magnificence of the Plaza del Obradoiro and pulled up outside the Hostal de los Reyes Católicos, now a five-star hotel.

Half an hour later, the car safely parked in the garage below the hotel, they emerged, suitably kitted out with boots and waterproofs, to see what millions before them had undergone hardship and suffering to be able to see.

Luke led Amy diagonally across the square to the sweeping stone staircases that led up to the jewel in Santiago's crown, the Pórtico de la Gloria, like all the centre of the town, a UNESCO world heritage site. Climbing the steps, Luke navigated his way through the beggars and into the splendour of the cathedral entrance. When they reached the central pillar of the Pórtico, he spoke quietly to a robed cleric standing by the precious carved stonework, indicating that Amy was blind and asking for special dispensation for her to touch the sculpture. Receiving a positive response, he turned to her.

'Here we are. We've done it.' Amy could hear the animation in his voice. 'We're here at the Pórtico de la Gloria. This is the Tree of Jesse. Do you know what you've got to do?'

She reached out confidently. Her hands landed on the sculpted marble depicting Christ's family tree and felt gently up from Jesse at the base, across David and Solomon and up towards Christ himself. The Apostle James smiled down benignly at every pilgrim who entered. Back down again and she found the famous spot. She pressed her right hand against the column, each finger slipping into a depression made by the millions of hands that had pressed upon this selfsame spot in gratitude for having been allowed to complete their pilgrimage.

'Just like they did. They made it here. I know they did.'

The same thought had been going through Luke's head and he grunted agreement. Amy spent a long time running her hands up all the pillars, full of admiration for the brilliantly alive and human carvings of Master Mateo, eight hundred years previously, He described the scenes further up the arches, too high for her to reach. These ranged from Adam and Eve, to the

Deadly Sins and the Final Judgement, all carved in the stone with a lightness and a realism that still shone through after so many centuries. Although he had seen it before, the experience of seeing it again was a joy.

'Can we go into the cathedral now?'

He led her through the doors and they walked slowly down the main aisle. He gave her a running commentary, his mouth pressed right up against her ear as the hubbub of hundreds of pilgrim voices filled the air. There were columns rising up on both sides to a gallery of smaller arches. Above these, the perfect symmetry of the vaulted roof gave an air of lightness and grace to the building. He walked her along to the main altar and they squeezed down the narrow stone steps into the crypt. Before them was the highly ornate silver coffer, said to hold the remains of Saint James.

From there they walked around to the Chapel of San Salvador, where queues of pilgrims were waiting for confession. Luke stood quietly for a moment, watching the crowd. It was then that he began to feel it, just like the last time he had visited the cathedral.

It was a feeling of companionship. It wasn't just from being with Amy, although they were really very close now. As he tried to explain to her later, it came from all the millions who had made this same journey, in order to come to this very spot. It was a feeling that he was a part of a huge, timeless, inexorable wave over the centuries. People of all walks of life, brought together by the completion of this act of devotion. What was it they had talked about high up on the Somport pass? The accumulated joy of millions of people? Would she feel it too?

He looked down at her. There was a light smile on her lips. She looked happy, fulfilled and self-assured. In spite of being dealt such cruel blows, she had managed to come to terms with her handicap and make a new, happy life for herself. Her joy shone forth on her face, just the same as the joy of all pilgrims would shine forth when they finally reached this, their hard-won destination. At first he had pitied her for all that she had lost, then he had envied her for the strength of her resolve. Now, finally, he thanked her for helping him in his struggle to regain his peace of mind and his happiness.

31

SANTIAGO DE COMPOSTELA, JUNE 1314

The golden city was steel grey as Luc led Aimée on the final leg of the pilgrimage. The steady rain, which had accompanied them for the last three days, hadn't let up. They had gradually descended from the gorse and heather of the mountains to the jumble of smaller hills around Santiago de Compostela itself. The sky was gloomy and overcast from misty horizon to misty horizon. The roads ran with water, the gutters and ditches overflowed. The city was barely discernible through the rain. But, in spite of the conditions, there was an air of excitement, anticipation and elation.

Luc and Aimée stood with a hundred or so others on top of the Monte del Gozo, staring for the first time at their goal. Some around them were in tears, some laughing, some skipping about like infants, others kneeling, some totally prostrate in their joy. They had stopped in Labacolla earlier that morning. Along with all the other pilgrims, they had leapt into the icy river water. In the previous village, Luc had bought fresh clothes for them both. He had helped her to strip off the old, travel-soiled dress and shift and immerse herself totally in the river. He hadn't remarked upon her nakedness and, in the midst of all the others, it had seemed quite natural. He had stripped in his turn, quite unselfconsciously. Around them, pilgrims of all complexions had been dancing naked and splashing with noisy glee. They had all been cleansing themselves in homage to the Apostle James, whose tomb was now finally within reach.

Refreshed and restored by the cold water, they had dressed impatiently, infected with the same enthusiasm that had struck their companions. On top of his new clothes, Luc had replaced his leather waistcoat, still heavy with more than enough silver coins to get them safely to their destination in Portugal. For the pilgrims, this marked the end of a long and arduous journey, often filled with danger and grief. The fact that, for most of them, the whole exhausting route would restart in a few days' time, as they turned back and headed for home, was ignored for the moment. Now there was only joy and expectation.

From the top of the Monte del Gozo they could just make out the towers of the cathedral. He did his best to describe the scene to her.

'The cathedral's immense. The towers rise up far, far into the sky.' She gripped his arm tightly, infected by the enthusiasm of those around them. 'There are spires and towers all over the city. I've never seen anywhere like it. Jerusalem and Rome have many, many churches and monuments, but you don't get so many in such a small space as you do here.'

In spite of the increasingly heavy rain, Santiago de Compostela still looked welcoming. Luc held Aimée to one side as the people around them started to charge down the hill. Some took off their boots, so as to do homage to the Apostle by arriving barefoot. Others undertook this final leg of their journey on their hands and knees, as a further sign of adoration and reverence. Once the bulk of the crowd had gone, Luc took Aimée's arm and they started to walk down together. They kept their hoods pulled over their heads. This was partly for shelter from the incessant downpour, and partly to minimise the risk of discovery, if their enemies were lying in wait.

'You know, Aimée, it's actually a good thing it's raining. The chances of being spotted are pretty slim. First, it's unlikely anybody will be out looking for us on a day like this. Second, with our heads covered, we should be anonymous.' He hoped he was right. They had seen no trace of the archbishop's men for a long time now. Maybe they really had given up.

As they drew nearer, the city of Saint James was revealed in all its glory as a succession of spectacular buildings emerged from the gloom. Nobody could fail to be impressed. Like all the others, Luc and Aimée headed straight for the cathedral itself. They found themselves in the midst of a sea of humanity and he had to fight his way through a mass of vendors, offering all manner of souvenirs. Finally they entered the city.

Inside the city gates it was, if anything, even more crowded. As well as innkeepers and their touts, there were moneychangers and more vendors. There were people selling everything from fresh fish to pieces of the true cross. There were jugglers, minstrels, dancers and even prostitutes plying for trade, although it was barely lunchtime. Certainly a pilgrim with money would want for nothing here in Santiago. Luc helped Aimée through the noisy throng, his wallet safely tucked into the waistband of his breeches. He was delighted at the obvious chaos and confusion. All the better to help them avoid detection.

Finally they emerged from the narrow streets into a wide square, paved with huge slabs of marble. The crowd thinned as the pilgrims spread out across the broad expanse, all eyes in one direction: the cathedral. Walls of golden stone, towers reaching up to the sky, a mass of sculpture and, in the middle of the base, the most wonderful of all, the Pórtico de la Gloria. Luc led her across towards it, threading his way through the clusters of awestruck pilgrims. There were crowds just standing in solemn contemplation of more beauty than any of them had ever seen in all their lives. The columns and capitals of the entrance porch were lavishly carved. Struggling through the crowds, he led her first to the central column.

'Here we are. We've done it.' She could hear the animation in his voice. 'We're here at the Pórtico de la Gloria. This is the Tree of Jesse. Do you know what you've got to do?'

She reached out confidently. Her hands landed on the sculpted marble depicting Christ's family tree and felt gently up from Jesse at the base, across David and Solomon and up towards Christ himself. The Apostle James smiled down benignly at every pilgrim who entered. Back down again she found the spot and pressed her right hand against the column, each finger slipping into a depression made by the millions of hands that had pressed upon this selfsame spot in gratitude for having been allowed to complete their pilgrimage.

She turned back towards Luc and breathed. 'Now you.'

Solemnly, he placed his hand against the smooth stone and closed his eyes, mouthing a silent prayer of thanks. The sudden arrival of a noisy group of Germans interrupted him and pushed them on through the doorway into the cathedral itself. This was another awe-inspiring sight. The central aisle stretched out before them, the roof so very high above them, seemingly floating on majestic golden pillars of stone. Just below the roof, a gallery led round the whole building, a few tiny figures visible high above them. Far down at the end of the aisle stood the altar and the sepulchre of Saint James. These were almost invisible behind the mass of pilgrims packing the cathedral.

The noise made by the crowds of people in the cathedral was deafening, especially for somebody who had grown used to the silence of the monastery and the quiet of the open road. There were voices of men, women and children of all ages, and from all parts of the world. All of them were exclaiming and shouting as they admired the magnificence of the interior.

Aimée reached out and let her free hand run across the smooth rounded stone of a pillar. Its size and strength, reaching up to the heavens, took her breath away. She tightened her grip on Luc's arm and asked, 'Where's the Apostle's tomb?'

He turned her head slightly to the right and spoke directly into her ear. 'Down there.'

'Can we go?' She was keen, as he was, to reach the true end of the pilgrimage. He looked down at her and marvelled at her strength and determination, as well as her beauty. She was truly a woman among women. He loved her dearly. He knew that now, without a shadow of a doubt. He bent his head down so that his mouth was touching her ear and kissed her softly before speaking.

'I love you, Aimée. I love you and I'll never leave you.'

Her face jerked up towards his, a soft smile on her lips as she heard the words for which she had been hoping for so long. 'Never?'

'Never.' He knew he meant it.

The crowd from behind caught up with them. They were pushed slowly, but inexorably, down the length of the cathedral to the altar. Beneath this lay the sepulchre of the saint. As they approached, Luc described the imposing stone statue of Saint James above the altar. He was dressed as a pilgrim, complete with cloak and hat, and the right forefinger of the statue pointed downwards towards the site of his tomb, below the altar. Luc found himself thinking once again of the magic of the cloak he had worn on his back all the way from the Pyrenees. As he did so, he mouthed a prayer that the protection of the Almighty would extend from here all the way to the safety of Portugal.

The crowds of pilgrims around the altar were about twenty or thirty deep. The remains of the saint lay down a narrow staircase and everybody wanted to see for themselves. After waiting an eternity, without getting any closer to it, Luc took Aimée by the shoulders. He struggled out of the throng towards one of the side chapels, where they could catch their breath.

'Too many people?' She had to shout in his ear to make herself heard. 'Why don't we just stay here for a moment? Then I would really like to go to confession.'

He shouted agreement. They knelt side by side, backs against the side wall of the aisle, heads bowed, both praying to the saint. She prayed for Luc, for his safety and happiness, and he prayed for her. As he prayed, Luc could feel the never-ending stream of pilgrims passing by in front of them. Somehow, this didn't disturb him. They were, after all, on holy ground. He felt sure they would be shielded from their enemies, as long as they stayed inside the cathedral. He abandoned himself to his prayers. When he finally stood up again he felt purged, restored by his communion with the Almighty. She reached out to him and stood up in her turn.

'Can we go to confession now?'

He shouted agreement. They followed the crowd in the direction of the chapel of San Salvador, where another crowd of pilgrims waited. Inside the chapel, a dozen priests were hearing the confessions of the pilgrims. This had to be done, prior to issuing the all-important Compostela certificate. This document would be conclusive proof that each had indeed successfully undertaken the pilgrimage. Obtaining this vital confirmation could have dramatic consequences. For some, it meant the papal pardon, which would relieve them of time they could expect to spend in Purgatory. For others, it was the extinguishing of a debt, forgiveness of sins, or the completion of a sentence imposed by a court for some misdoing.

At least there was more order to this part of the cathedral. Rope lines had been set up, six or seven abreast, attached to heavy wooden posts. The

pilgrims were shepherded into lines by bored-looking novices, in an attempt
to streamline this most vital part of the pilgrimage procedure. Luc and
Aimée let themselves be guided into the line nearest the wall and settled
down to wait their turn. He counted about twenty people before them in the
queue. Lowering his head towards Aimée, he spoke softly into her ear, no
longer needing to shout, as the chaos around the altar was a good way
behind them.

'Twenty people in front of us so it's going to take a while. Mind you,
though, I've never seen confessions as quick as these. Either the pilgrims
have led blameless lives, or the priests are in a hurry. Are you all right to wait
for a while?'

She gripped his forearm and smiled. 'As long as is necessary. It's the one
thing every pilgrim has to do, isn't it? Bound to be a queue here.'

Yes, he agreed mentally, it was indeed the one thing they all had to do.
So, the thought rushed urgently into his head, this chapel would be the
perfect place for anybody lying in wait for a particular pilgrim. All they had
to do was be patient, and their prey would come straight to them. Nervous
tension flooded through his body. Aimée sensed it.

'What is it, Luc?' Her question went unanswered.

He swung round, eyes searching every face in the crowd. He looked
beyond the sea of cheery, healthy faces, waiting eagerly for this culminating
act of their journey. He scanned the chapels and niches on the opposite side
of the aisle. Then he turned his attention once more to the chapel of San
Salvador. The procession of pilgrims into the lines continued steadily,
without a break. He saw nobody suspicious, no face he recognised, but the
warning bells were ringing in his head. He bent towards her and whispered
urgently.

'We'll look for somewhere else to have our confessions heard. I'm
worried they may have this chapel under observation. Come on, let's get out
of here.' Her face instantly showed concern.

He took her arm and, murmuring apologies to the people behind him,
started to push back through the line. All the time, his eyes searched
anxiously all around them. A few people looked surprised that they should
have chosen to drop out of the line when so close to their goal. But they all
moved good-naturedly out of the way.

Luc and Aimée emerged from the end of the rope lines. He stopped, unsure whether to turn right and make for the exit, or to try for the anonymity of the crowds around the main altar once more. As he was weighing up the possibilities, a noisy altercation broke out behind them. It was caused by a group trying to push into the queues. Luc suddenly noticed that the handful of novices who had been directing the pilgrims had disappeared. Casting around over the heads of the passers-by, he caught a glimpse of black robes scampering off along the aisle. He turned back in the opposite direction, desperately searching for signs of danger.

Then he saw them.

32

SANTIAGO DE COMPOSTELA, MAY 2016

'Hold on tight. We're going to have to make a run for it.' Luke had to shout to make his voice heard over the wind. He caught Amy around the waist and they set off.

Their exit from the sanctuary of the cathedral took them from the sublime into the teeth of an Atlantic gale. The wind collapsed their umbrella, and the horizontal rain set about soaking them in a very short space of time. His intention of viewing the intricate south façade, the Puerta de las Platerías, was hastily replaced by the search for somewhere dry, and quick. They ran for the shelter of the maze of narrow streets radiating out from the cathedral and soon found a restaurant that looked welcoming. They dived inside and were shown to a table near the back of the long, low, stone-vaulted room. Down there it was peaceful, dry and warm.

The waiter came with the menus and to enquire if they desired an aperitif. Hearing no response from Luke, Amy made a quick decision. 'Two glasses of Cava, please.' As the waiter went off to get the sparkling wine, she reached across the table and found his hand.

'I thought we'd better celebrate our arrival here.'

There was only a grunt in reply.

'What's up, Luke?' There was a long pause before he replied.

'Yes, celebrate, of course.' He sounded very hesitant. She gave his hand a squeeze.

'What is it?' Even without seeing his face, she could tell there was something wrong. 'Aren't you feeling well?'

'No, no. I'm fine.' He had to wait while the waiter returned with their drinks. He pushed her glass across the table to her. He watched as she raised it and held it out in his direction.

'Cheers.'

He clinked his glass against hers and studied her over his drink. There was a smile on her face, tempered with slight concern that he was perhaps not his usual self. While he was trying to find the words to explain what he was feeling, she did it for him.

'Are you feeling a bit let down, now that it's finished?' In spite of herself, in spite of all that had passed between them and in spite of the long talks they had had over the past few days, she began to feel apprehensive. 'Are you thinking of doing the pilgrimage again with another girl?' She did her best to keep her tone light.

His reply, this time, was immediate. She heard him place his glass on the table. There was a movement. Then his hands caught the sides of her face and he pulled her towards him. He kissed her on the lips. 'No, my darling, that is definitely not what I am thinking.'

A discreet cough indicated the return of the waiter. Luke sat back as the man took their order. They decided on the tourist menu. The waiter gave them a smile and moved away.

Amy reached across the table and found his hand again. 'So, what is it, then?'

'I suppose what I'm thinking is that, just like our medieval friends, our arrival here is very different from that of all the other pilgrims. For pilgrims, this was their goal, the lode star, the one fixed point in their firmament for weeks, months. Now, they've done it. It's over.'

'Apart from the minor detail of having to do the whole thing in reverse to get home.'

'Of course. But, you see, that's it. They've done what they wanted to do and now they're going home. It's the end of their adventure. For you and me, this is only the beginning.'

She was smiling again. 'You're not still thinking of going to Graceland, are you?'

His voice was still serious. 'I don't care where I go, as long as it's with you.' He raised his eyes towards her. 'As long as you'll still have me. I'm a complicated character.'

She squeezed his hands harder. 'We're both complicated characters, Luke. We've both had a pasting. But the healing's started for us both. I know that and you must feel it too. We're no longer chasing shadows, struggling with memories from our past. We've got a future now. A real future, together.' She heard him grunt again. But it was a happy grunt this time. 'Of course it isn't always going to be easy. There'll be hurdles to overcome, but we'll manage.' She listened anxiously for his reply.

'I know we will, Amy. I know we will.'

She was relieved to hear him sounding more relaxed now. She gave it a few minutes and then decided to return to their medieval story.

'So, do we think they made it here in one piece? Did they fulfil their mysterious mission?'

'No doubt about it. They accomplished their mission all right. Who knows? Maybe it really was the Holy Shroud. Maybe it's lying safe in the vaults of an abbey or castle to this day. Probably Portugal, I would think. No, they made it. At least as far as here.' He picked up his glass again and clinked it against hers.

'To them.'

'To them. And to us.' He took a sip of wine, his mind now back in the Middle Ages. 'Of course, I suppose their enemies might have followed them this far. Assuming they knew that they were carrying something as immensely valuable as the Holy Shroud.' Grudgingly, he felt he had to admit the possibility that things might not have gone perfectly.

The waiter returned with local ham and lovely fresh bread. He placed a bottle of red wine and a jug of water on the table in front of them. Amy hardly listened to Luke's description of the food on her plate. She was turning over possibilities in her mind.

'I suppose it would have been easy for the bad guys to catch them by keeping an eye on that very same confessional area in the cathedral that we've just seen. Every pilgrim in those days would've had to go there in order to fully complete the pilgrimage.' She was thinking hard.

He was already well into his food. He finished his glass of Cava and poured some red wine. 'Mind you, they were only really coincidentally pilgrims, weren't they?' He looked across at her to check, but she was managing to deal with the ham very well. 'I don't suppose they would have been getting their pilgrim passports stamped along the way. Surely there would have been too much risk of being recognised.'

'Absolutely,' she agreed. 'But just think. This is the man who believes he's carried the true Shroud that wrapped the crucified Christ to safety. Assuming that he was aware of what he was carrying, he would have had to be on a massive religious high at the end of such a trip. I wouldn't be surprised if he didn't try to go to confession.'

'I'm sure you're right. But what sort of trap might they find themselves in?'

Not surprisingly, he finished his starter before she did. He was happy to sit and watch her. Her mind was clearly not on the food, much more on their couple of characters. She looked pensive, enthralled and lovely. He took a mouthful of wine and felt his face assume a contented smile.

The waiter came to remove the plates and Luke pushed a glass of red wine towards her. 'Here, some red wine, and there's water in the other glass.' Then he tried to finish off the story as best he could. 'Theoretically they would have been safe in the cathedral. That was, after all, holy ground.' He started off cautiously.

'Try telling that to Thomas à Becket.' Amy's tone was cynical.

'Point taken.' While he was thinking, the waiter returned. The next course was placed before them. After a moment's hesitation, Luke described it to her as best he could. 'It looks like we've just been served clear soup with bits of chicken skin floating in it. Not necessarily my first choice, if I had a choice, but I'll try it anyway.'

'Probably a local speciality.' She picked up her spoon, tried a mouthful, pronounced herself quite happy to eat it and carried on where he had left off. 'Just supposing the archbishop's men were prepared to try to take our man in the cathedral, what chance of escape would he have had? It's the shape of a Latin cross, a crucifix, right?'

Luke grunted agreement through a mouthful of the delicious soup, chicken skin or no chicken skin.

'There would have to be a minimum of four doors, right?' Amy continued with the soup, frowning as she tried to think of the way out for their two characters. 'So, supposing they put guards on all the doors, how would they have got out?'

'Minimum four doors.' He was thinking hard too. 'I would imagine there would have been others. After all, the cathedral in Santiago de Compostela is hardly a fortified church like you would find in Albi or Béziers. There must be other doors. In fact, come to think of it, there was a door set in the wall directly opposite the chapel of San Salvador. Maybe...' He stopped, realising the significance of the door. 'No, that's no good. That door probably leads up to the gallery that runs around the inside of the cathedral. And a long way up it looked, too.'

She had finished her soup by this time. 'That's it. He sees his enemies moving in, so they dash up the stair.'

'The spiral stone stair,' he added for the sake of accuracy.

'Up the spiral stone stair.' She accepted the embellishment gracefully. 'They reach the top and run desperately halfway round the cathedral before he spots another door.'

'A low doorway leading out onto the roof.' He was enjoying his artistic input.

She nodded at his intervention and continued. 'They run out onto the roof...' She corrected herself before he could chip in. 'Onto the gently sloping lead-covered roof of the cathedral. After wedging the door shut behind them, he leads her along to the far end of the west façade, directly above the Pórtico de la Gloria. In front of them is a drop of a hundred feet or more onto the cobbles below, while above them on both sides the towers rise up, offering no hope of escape.'

The waiter reappeared, bearing a tray with hot terracotta dishes still steaming from the oven, and set them down on the table. He collected the empty soup plates and left.

'Very, very hot. Brown gravy and what looks like chunks of potatoes and chicken bubbling in it. Smells wonderful.'

She nodded, keen to continue her story. 'Suddenly he sees a builders' block and tackle on the far edge of the cathedral, where repairs to the roof are being carried out. Helping her across the uneven roof to it, he looks over the edge. He spots a few little figures scurrying about on the rain-swept square below and reaches for the rope.'

'Always assuming that he's not as afraid of heights as I am,' he added mildly.

She reached for her fork and prodded the steaming plate in front of her. As she tried to spear a piece of meat, he made a suggestion.

'Alternatively, how about this as a version?' He had already tried the chicken and was nursing a burnt tongue in consequence. 'And mind out for the chicken, it's absolutely boiling. They spot the enemy closing in on them and make a break for it, up the spiral stone stair to the gallery. They start running along the gallery, perched high up above the crowds below—'

'Vertiginously high.' She was keen to put in her own contribution.

'They start running along the gallery, perched vertiginously high above the crowds below. Suddenly, he sees a cluster of enemy soldiers emerge onto the gallery from another stair, just a short way in front of them. He stops dead and spins round. He and the girl start off again in the opposite direction, but their way is blocked by another group of soldiers. These men come charging out of the next stairway along, less than a stone's throw ahead. He stops, looking back over his shoulder at the heavily armed platoon behind him, and then forward to the soldiers advancing towards him. He feels for a weapon but has nothing more than a dagger up his sleeve.'

He picked up another piece of chicken and immediately had to take a big gulp of wine to avoid getting burnt again. He swallowed and gave her another warning, before taking up the story once more. 'Chicken's still boiling. Take it easy. Anyway, he looks desperately downwards into the main aisle of the cathedral, packed with crowds of pilgrims, blissfully unaware of the drama being played out high above their heads. Even worse, he sees that the soldiers are armed with crossbows.'

She had taken his advice and was sensibly waiting for the chicken dish to cool down. 'But what about my scenario of the pair of them on the roof? Couldn't he stick the girl in the bucket on the hoist and then leap on after her and lower them hand-over-hand to the ground? Once safely on the square, they'd be able to elude their pursuers and make good their escape through the narrow streets. How about that?'

He thought about it for a moment, eager to see a happy ending to their story. The chicken casserole was gradually cooling and he risked another mouthful. It really was excellent. He took his time while considering the various options. Finally he decided.

'Yes, I reckon that's the way it happened. After all, he was strong enough to lower the two of them safely to the ground. Why not? And once they were clear of the cathedral they could head for sanctuary in Portugal.' He took a mouthful of red wine.

'Just imagine.' She was still waiting for the chicken to cool. 'Trapped up there on the gallery. They both knew what awaited them at the hands of the Inquisition. She, in particular, would have been terrified at the thought of torture. Can you imagine being tortured at all? But when you're blind...?'

Luke shivered at the thought, having seen enough medieval instruments of torture in museums to turn anybody's stomach. He knew, with a sinking feeling, that there was only one way it could end. He chose to say it before she had to.

'There would have been only one way out. He would have taken her in his arms. I can't imagine that they would have been able to travel all that way together without getting emotionally involved. He would have taken her in his arms and then, as the archers took aim, he would have turned to her and whispered that he loved her. And then the two of them would have fallen from the gallery a hundred feet to the stone floor below and certain death.' He took another mouthful of wine, feeling saddened by this version of events.

Amy made a start on the casserole, but it wasn't long before she declared herself full. She pushed the plate away, wiped her mouth with her napkin and sat back, lost in thought. Somehow their story couldn't finish like that. Their medieval counterparts deserved to find the happiness they both had found.

Luke looked across the table at her as the waiter cleared away the plates. He saw the pain on her face as she considered the fate of their characters. He caught the waiter's eye and ordered two coffees, keen to get out into the open again and away from this morbid topic of conversation.

She came to a decision. 'No.' Her mind was made up and her voice was firm. 'It's unthinkable that they should have come so far, against the odds, only to find themselves beaten at the last hurdle. They made it. I know they did. Here.' She lifted her glass. 'Let's drink to them and their happiness. We did it, why not them?'

He reached out with his glass and touched hers. It was only right that their companions for the last thousand kilometres should be as lucky and as happy as they were.

'To them and their happiness.' Luke took a mouthful, then added, 'And to ours, Amy. And to ours.'

They clinked their glasses together and Amy had a sudden thought. 'That's funny, we never knew their names, did we?'

33

SANTIAGO DE COMPOSTELA, JUNE 1314

Luc and Aimée found refuge in a small farmhouse on the outskirts of town. By the time they got there, it was almost dark. The weather, if anything, was getting worse. Aimée was exhausted and Luc was little better, the blisters and tears on his palms still bleeding from where the rope had cut into his skin as they made their perilous descent from the roof of the cathedral. He knew they needed shelter, warmth, food and rest. The farmer's wife was only too glad to accept a silver coin in exchange for providing them with bed and board.

'You're very welcome. We don't get a lot of pilgrims coming past. The Pilgrims' Way is a bit south of us, you see. Are you just arriving or just leaving?'

Ruefully, Luc reflected that they qualified on both counts, but he replied cautiously. 'We're on our way to Portugal.'

The cheery lady showed them into a fine, large room and busied herself lighting the fire. 'I'll get my husband to show you the best way to get there.' As the fire caught, and the flames began to lick up through the pile of kindling, she replaced the candle on the mantelpiece and withdrew.

'I'll have some nice hot food for you just as quickly as I can.'

They stood silently by the fire for some minutes, mentally and physically drained. Finally, wearily, Aimée managed a smile. 'The warmth of a fire has never felt so good.'

'Here, give me your cloak.' He removed her cloak and his and hung them up to dry in front of the fire before turning back towards her. She looked so vulnerable, but so beautiful. He reached out his hand and ran it up the side of her face. She raised her hand and caught his, pressing his fingers tightly against her cheek. He moved closer, unable to stop himself. As the flames flickered and the firewood crackled, he leant towards her and they kissed. As they did so, he lost track of their surroundings. The events of that day might as well never have happened. The Shroud, their mission, everything disappeared from his head. All that counted was the two of them.

After a while he pulled back, looked into her face and saw that she was crying.

'Aimée, what is it?' He was suddenly concerned.

'It's nothing, Luc. It's happiness, it's joy, it's all those things I thought I would never ever feel again.' She wiped her tears against his chest. 'When I was in that cold, lonely abbey, I thought the world had come to an end. Today, in the cathedral, it so nearly did. But now, here in this room, I couldn't ask for more. Life has meaning again. I love you, Luc.'

He pressed his lips against her forehead and hugged her to his chest. 'I love you, Aimée, and I'll never leave you.'

And he never did.

EPILOGUE

If you visit the Romanesque gem that is the Church of Santa Maria do Olival in Tómar in Portugal today and have very good eyesight, you may be able to find a grey stone slab, worn smooth by the passage of feet over the centuries. Some of the inscription is now illegible, but the remaining letters that can be distinguished read as follows:

MC...CLVIII
HI... REQUIE.......NT
LU... ....CH...RN...
ET A..M.....
CO.....UNX S...I

Latin scholars are generally agreed that the inscription translates as:

1358
HERE LIE
LU... ...CH...RN...
AND A...M......
HIS WIFE

It would appear that, forty-four years after the events of this story, Luc and Aimée were still together. And they're still together now.

* * *

MORE FROM T. A. WILLIAMS

Murder on an Italian Island, a cosy murder mystery from T. A. Williams is available to order now here:

https://mybook.to/MurderItalianBackAd

ACKNOWLEDGEMENTS

Warmest thanks to Emily Ruston, my wonderful editor at the equally wonderful Boldwood Books, for making this publication possible. Thanks also to the ever-diligent Sue Smith for picking up the typos and inaccuracies I have missed. Thanks, as always, to my wife, Mariangela, for her patience and support while I spent so many long hours buried in books, researching the Pilgrims' Way to Compostela. I am very grateful to her for accompanying me along the Camino (by car). Thanks also to my good friend Ian Muirhead for cycling along with me all the way from the north of France to Santiago de Compostela itself, getting our pilgrims' passports stamped along the way. Without his interpreting skills and determination, it would have been a whole lot harder than it was. And a final shout out to all the hundreds of millions of people over the centuries whose tracks we followed through some of the most beautiful countryside in the world. If any of you decide to do the same, I give you the traditional pilgrims' salute:

Buen Camino.

ABOUT THE AUTHOR

T. A. Williams is the author of The Armstrong and Oscar Cosy Mystery Series, cosy crime stories set in his beloved Italy, featuring the adventures of DCI Armstrong and his labrador Oscar. Trevor lives in Devon with his Italian wife.

Sign up to T. A. Williams' newsletter to read an EXCLUSIVE short story!

Visit T. A. Williams' website: www.tawilliamsbooks.com

Follow T. A. Williams on social media:

f facebook.com/TrevorWilliamsBooks
X x.com/TAWilliamsBooks
🦋 bsky.app/profile/tawilliamsbooks.bsky.social

ALSO BY T. A. WILLIAMS

Standalone Novels

Under a Spanish Sky

The Armstrong and Oscar Cozy Mystery Series

Murder in Tuscany

Murder in Chianti

Murder in Florence

Murder in Siena

Murder at the Matterhorn

Murder at the Leaning Tower

Murder on the Italian Riviera

Murder in Portofino

Murder in Verona

Murder in the Tuscan Hills

Murder at the Ponte Vecchio

Murder on an Italian Island

Boldwood

Boldwood Books is an award-winning fiction publishing company seeking out the best stories from around the world.

Find out more at www.boldwoodbooks.com

Join our reader community for brilliant books, competitions and offers!

Follow us
@BoldwoodBooks
@TheBoldBookClub

Sign up to our weekly deals newsletter

https://bit.ly/BoldwoodBNewsletter